PRAISE FOR M. L. BUCHMAN

One of our favorite authors.

— RT BOOK REVIEWS

Buchman has catapulted his way to the top tier of my favorite authors.

— FRESH FICTION

A favorite author of mine. I'll read anything that carries his name, no questions asked. Meet your new favorite author!

— THE SASSY BOOKSTER, FLASH OF FIRE

M.L. Buchman is guaranteed to get me lost in a good story.

— THE READING CAFE, WAY OF THE WARRIOR: NSDQ

I love Buchman's writing. His vivid descriptions bring everything to life in an unforgettable way.

— PURE JONEL, HOT POINT

PATH OF LOVE: CINQUE TERRE, ITALY

A LOVE ABROAD B&B ROMANCE

M. L. BUCHMAN

Buchman Bookworks

Other works by M. L. Buchman:

The Night Stalkers

MAIN FLIGHT
The Night Is Mine
I Own the Dawn
Wait Until Dark
Take Over at Midnight
Light Up the Night
Bring On the Dusk
By Break of Day

WHITE HOUSE HOLIDAY
Daniel's Christmas
Frank's Independence Day
Peter's Christmas
Zachary's Christmas
Roy's Independence Day
Damien's Christmas

AND THE NAVY
Christmas at Steel Beach
Christmas at Peleliu Cove

5E
Target of the Heart
Target Lock on Love
Target of Mine

Firehawks

MAIN FLIGHT
Pure Heat
Full Blaze
Hot Point
Flash of Fire
Wild Fire

SMOKEJUMPERS
Wildfire at Dawn
Wildfire at Larch Creek
Wildfire on the Skagit

Delta Force

Target Engaged
Heart Strike
Wild Justice

White House Protection Force

Off the Leash
On Your Mark
In the Weeds

Where Dreams

Where Dreams are Born
Where Dreams Reside
Where Dreams Are of Christmas
Where Dreams Unfold
Where Dreams Are Written

Eagle Cove

Return to Eagle Cove
Recipe for Eagle Cove
Longing for Eagle Cove
Keepsake for Eagle Cove

Henderson's Ranch

Nathan's Big Sky
Big Sky, Loyal Heart

Love Abroad

Heart of the Cotswolds: England
Path of Love: Cinque Terre, Italy

Dead Chef Thrillers

Swap Out!
One Chef!
Two Chef!

Deities Anonymous

Cookbook from Hell: Reheated
Saviors 101

SF/F Titles

The Nara Reaction
Monk's Maze
the Me and Elsie Chronicles

Strategies for Success (NF)

Managing Your Inner Artist/Writer
Estate Planning for Authors

CHAPTER 1

*E*rica Barnett was so done with being done with Dwayne. She was even done with being done with being…

Yep! There was the crazy loop that her head had been stuck in for—she did her best not to sigh at herself—far too long. Enough was enough, as her best friend was nice enough *not* to say. Her merely close friends? She'd chased most of them away altogether.

She'd decided to spare those few who remained from suffering through her current lunacy. Which had led to this trip she'd always dreamed of. The Ligurian coast of Italy had fascinated her since forever. And now that she was here…

Well, if there was a cliff handy, she just might be tempted to jump off it, provided it wasn't a very high one. She'd certainly just come too close to driving off one.

Erica sat on the grassy verge of the road, hugged her knees up against her chest, and tried not to look out at the idyllic Italian olive orchard perched on the steep hillside, backed by the vast Mediterranean and the cobalt blue sky. It all looked so perfect that it was easy to imagine the Roman gods still lived here.

She could smell the rich soil and the dry grass. And she could smell the Mediterranean Sea so close. It wasn't like the Pacific, where she could smell the freshness of the air that had traveled ten thousand wild miles since brushing by the last person. Or the Atlantic that seemed to smell of the warm tropics it had flowed by on the way up the coast.

The Mediterranean smelled as if it knew things. It had been here before Greeks, Romans, or Egyptians. It predated the Iron and Bronze Ages. It had been here when primitive man had crossed over from Africa to paint images of their hands on the caves of Lascaux, France. She just hoped that the Mediterranean didn't know so much about her because it would be mortally embarrassing. Pathetic, more like it.

She had come to the land of love—alone! And since she no longer believed in love, Erica decided that this trip could be the dumbest decision she'd made in a long line of them.

For her, it had never been the famous Amalfi stretch featured in every film since Hollywood directors had first discovered it in the 1950s. No, it was the small coastal towns to the north that she'd always imagined visiting. Ones where the bare bones of history lay upon the hillsides in thousand-year-old churches. Bridges and towers that had inspired Monet. Especially the little piazzas where she could sit and watch the world walk by in its elegant, Italian fashion while sipping an espresso with—

But, she'd come here alone.

Which didn't really matter as that *wasn't* the Italy she'd found anyway.

She crouched at the edge of an impossibly twisted switchback—as tight as the snake Ouroboros eating its own tail. From here, she stared over the scrub-brush edge. A crazy path had been carved down the steep, grassy hillside—carved by the tires of her rental car as she'd tried desperately not to die on her first day in Italy.

She'd missed the curve and had plunged a hundred feet down the slope through the orchard. The car had caromed off two aged olive trees, which had slowed her descent from starkly terrifying to alarmingly dramatic. Its final resting place, deep in the land of Really Annoying, lay against the granddaddy of the orchard smelling of hot metal and brutally sharp adrenal panic.

Good riddance. Stomped-on brakes and good fortune had lessened the impact, though she could still feel the harsh line of the seatbelt across her chest.

She'd left the car there and climbed back up to the roadside, but there was no one to flag for help on the remote cliffside road. Her cell phone was still down there in the car, even if she knew who to call. So she sat and glared at the car for lack of anything better to do.

Italian drivers were crazy, but she'd watched enough television travel shows to be ready for that. Tailgaters? No prob. She'd learned to drive in Oakland, the least rational of San Francisco Bay drivers. Manic passing on a curve? Nothing a Boston pro wouldn't try—as she'd learned when life had led her there for the last decade.

It was the Italian roads themselves she wasn't ready for. Narrow two-lanes the size of a US backcountry road were the major thoroughfares of the country. Only the massive *autostrada* toll roads had multiple lanes, which were still painfully narrow. As she'd come here to see the countryside not the highways, she'd taken to the secondary highways at the first opportunity.

Along with every massive truck in the entire country.

The driving was narrow, fast, and terrifying.

Had been. She definitely wasn't getting back behind the wheel for as long as she was in Italy. The car could *rot* right where it was for all she cared. Parked in the olive orchard.

Except weren't olive trees in groves rather than orchards?

And in Italy it would be some other mellifluous word that she'd never remember for three seconds past hearing it. It would end in an "a" or an "i" and sound charming coming from anyone other than her.

And…

Let's face it. She was probably in shock from having just survived her descent into the olive *grochard.*

Better than *orchove.* Maybe *orchova.* Short "a" or long? Either way: *clunky!*

Could you tell when you were in shock or not, or did someone else have to tell you? By being able to ask the question, did that mean she wasn't in shock? Or that she was?

Or that she was losing her mind? Which wasn't really in doubt at the moment—she *definitely* was.

The gray-green leaves, from where the orchard continued across the road up above her, filtered the hot Mediterranean sun of May into dappled laser beams among refreshing washes of shade. Below, leaves no bigger than her pinkie clustered and overlapped so tightly that she could barely see the white car down the cliff-like slope. Beneath the trees, grass thick with dandelions sought the sunny gaps. They smelled of spring newness. Filled with hope, so unlike herself.

Maybe she should sit. Except she already was.

She rested her forehead on her knees.

Ironically, it wasn't the two-lane "highway" with its massive trucks and speeding cars that had defeated her. Instead it had been this isolated one-lane road that wouldn't have been considered a decent driveway back home. According to her map, this narrow, switchbacked, and paved *goat trail* was the main road into her randomly chosen destination, the tiny cliffside town of Corniglia perched high above the Ligurian coast. It lay in the heart of Cinque Terre—the "five earths"—that made up her idea of heaven on earth.

Or it used to. At the moment? Not so much.

One blink of inattention for her first ever glimpse of the Mediterranean Sea. Looking back to the road in time to see a tour bus larger than the Starship *Enterprise* zipping up the hill as she'd descended. Overreaction, a tire out onto the shoulder—except there was no shoulder. And she'd plunged off the edge. The bus had continued obliviously on its way.

"Perfect metaphor for your life, Erica." And it really was. The moments of inattention had always caused her the worst problems.

So she squatted on the verge and stared at the impossibly blue sky over the miraculously blue sea—and its far-too-knowing smugness—visible through a gap where the road passed through the *grovocharda*. Erica wondered how hard it would be to get back to the nearest airport and just go home.

Except that was gone too. Right now her belongings (those not down the slope) were filling a corner of her best friend Becky's garage—a very small corner of it. Her job had imploded due to the worst bit of inattention in history. When her car was stolen, just to emphasize the total and complete failure of the worst week of her life, she'd given up the apartment and come to Italy. She had to be the lamest excuse for a twenty-eight-year-old ever born.

But she couldn't go home yet even if she still had one. There was the rental car. She should at least let someone know it was there before it disappeared under blackberries or kudzu or whatever it was that plagued Italian *ocharovino*.

—*ovino*? A plague of grapevines? Maybe she needed wine...a lot of wine. Like a plague's worth. How much wine did it take to kill a plague of inattention? It was like she'd caught the disease and couldn't rid herself of it. What if it was an illness that compounded with age? As a little girl she'd always been told that she focused *so* well. She'd taken the praise to heart and honed it into a fine business career. Too bad that her personal life seemed to get all of the inattention parts. Maybe there was a fixed amount of inattention in a person and because she'd shut it out of the business part it was…

She was looping almost as badly as she'd done about Dwayne—the guy she'd sworn to never think of again.

Maybe she could find someone who could just change everything back as if it had never happened. The car. The flight to Italy. Leaving Boston. Sleeping with her boss—her *married* boss, so full of promises and lies.

How had she been so naive? So…desperate? No illusions, she'd *let* herself be handled and maneuvered by the preying bastard for almost two years. The saddest part of it all was that she still missed him. He'd been the most considerate lover of her life, and the lowest toad in the forest.

Erica double-checked that her little reflective traffic triangle was perched on the road's edge behind her. "All Italian car," the rental agent had told her as if it was the most important secret to driving in Italy, "has reflective triangle. Must use if is, ah, *incidente*."

It was the only remaining bit of control in her life, placing that foot-high red-plastic triangle beside her on the edge of the road.

Danger! Here sits a disaster of a woman. Approach at your own risk.

Better yet: *For your own safety, stay clear of this woman!*

Since her car was off the road, its nose crumpled against an ancient tree, she figured it counted as an *incidente* as well as the worst start *ever* to a trip. Her pack was still down there somewhere with her cell phone. But, by god, her little red reflective triangle was on the road where it should be.

A smoothly dangerous sound had her turning in time to see a hot pink Ferrari convertible slide to a stop close behind her. A cheery brunette, whose dark brown hair spilled down over her shoulders in lazy waves, leaned out of the car. Their hair was similar in color, but that's where all similarity ended. Her own was a straight fall to her collar as if it had just collapsed from its own anxiety and desperately needed a Xanax before it could even whimper.

"Are you all right, *mia amica?*"

"*Amica?*"

"My friend. Let's face it, luv, you don't look happy." The brunette offered Erica a small frown of sympathy that made her look even more lovely. Though the broad English accent was a jarring surprise, Erica wanted to hug her for it.

"I've had better days," she pointed down-slope at her car. An elderly gentleman had come from somewhere in the trees and was inspecting the disaster.

The woman half rose out of her seat to peer over the edge of the drop-off.

And giggled.

"Your car?"

Erica couldn't believe that the first real conversation she'd been able to have with someone in Italy was with an Englishwoman. She'd naively thought much of Italy, at least the parts situated to deal with tourists, would have a little English. England English. She wasn't so ethnocentric as to expect American English. And why was she clarifying her thoughts in her own head where no one else was listening? At least she hoped to god no one was or they'd all back quietly away.

"Rental," Erica peeked down the slope to see if it had maybe been stolen by an evil Italian fairy—*fairiovino?* Drunken Italian fairy?—and would no longer bother her. But there it sat, shining mockingly in the dappled sunlight.

"And you are not hurt?"

Other than her pride, her hopes, the shredded remnants of her soul… Erica shook her head no.

"Oh. Everything is okay then."

"How do you figure that?"

The brunette climbed out of the blazingly pink Ferrari. She was tall and generously built. She wore simple Italian chic: a silk blouse with the same warmth as her deep brown eyes, tight jeans, and stylish black suede boots with the little zipper on the side that Erica always wanted but could never seem to find. The light leather jacket looked to be for style rather than warmth on the fine spring day. It worked. She radiated a woman in her prime.

Much of Italy struck Erica that way, which made her want to stamp "Warning: Dowdy American" on her forehead—maybe with a little red reflective triangle logo.

A rotund brown-and-white Cavalier King Charles spaniel lumbered down from the low door sill of the Ferrari and came over to sniff at Erica's hand. It appeared immune to the triangular warning sign blazing brightly on her countenance, so she pet it. The dog sighed happily, so she pet it some more. The first thing to make her feel good all day.

"I'm Bridget. He's Snoop. And I am guessing that you need a place to stay."

"Well, I'm thinking that I shouldn't leave town until that is dealt with."

"Oh pfft!" Bridget waved a hand at the car as if it was of no consequence. Maybe not in the land of buxom brunette Englishwomen wearing Italian elegance like a birthright, but it definitely was in dowdy American land.

"Shouldn't I contact the police or something?"

"Conrad can take care of that for us. Can't you, darling?"

Erica turned to see that the man who had been inspecting her car had now climbed the hill carrying her pack. He handed over both it and her cell phone very solemnly. He was an older gentleman who looked to be far above such menial tasks.

"Is that your tree?"

"They all are. You have parked your conveyance in my olive grove." His smile was unexpectedly easy and made his blue-gray eyes brighten. His English was as high brow as Bridget's was common. Again, England English. Again she wondered why she was always explaining things to herself. Especially since the one thing she couldn't explain satisfactorily to herself was…herself.

Grove. It *was* a grove of olive trees. A new fact learned and filed. Perhaps a second ray of hope other than the surprisingly solid little dog leaning happily against her thigh as she continued to rub his ears.

She turned back to the grove's owner. "I'm terribly sorry. Let me know if there is any damage. I'll repay it…" *somehow.* She was an unanchored craft in the storm that was her life. She had savings—some scraps of it dating back to a near continuous stream of babysitting jobs that had defined her teen years—but it wasn't as if she had some deep bankroll to survive whatever was happening to her. What did a tree cost anyway?

"These trees have been standing since long before the Medici first rose to power in the 1400s."

It sounded as if they cost a lot. Maybe that's what hope looked like—somehow to remain standing through the ages. Even when people were busy running cars into you.

"They have seen far worse than your *piccola macchina.* I shall call Marceto and see that it is returned where it must go. Would you perhaps desire a replacement?"

"Not on your life," Erica blushed. Conrad did not seem like a man who should be addressed so casually. As a matter of fact, he didn't seem to her the sort of man who should be addressed while sitting at his feet. She rose to face him, much to Snoop's disappointment. "Sorry, but no thank you. I'm quite done with driving in Italy."

"*É finito!*" He snapped his fingers as if he could work magic.

She peeked. Nope, the car was still parked very solidly against the olive tree below.

"Hal, my love?" Bridget was talking into a cell phone. "Do we have a room open? *Sì? Perfetto!* I will be home soon and bringing a guest."

The woman stepped up and kissed Conrad on both cheeks.

Was Erica supposed to do the same? Unsure of herself, she held out a hand. Rather than shaking it, he bent over it and placed a kiss on the back of her hand like a gentleman of old.

"Conrad, Conte di Evenston, at your service." *Conte* was a count or earl. His English fit that—pure upper crust. And she'd wager that his Italian would sound equally sophisticated to any ear more discerning than hers.

"Erica Barnett at yours." She felt as if she should curtsy but knew it would look even clumsier than her twenty words of guidebook Italian sounded.

"Oh, Connie, you old hound," Bridget teased him, but Erica felt touched.

And no way could she imagine ever addressing the sophisticated Count of Evenston as Connie.

"We must find another woman for you. Your wife is long gone now, rest her soul."

"She will have to be a very special one," his smile teased that Erica was the model for any future candidates. *As if.*

Besides, he was at least twice her age, maybe closer to three times. He was handsome, polite, and at least wealthy enough to own an olive grove, but there were limits. Besides, she had an image in her head, had it since she was a little girl. The image had looked almost *exactly* like Dwayne who—she was so done with the older-but-wiser-man scenario. Fantasy. Thing.

"Come!" Bridget called as she popped open the trunk. "We have a most charming B&B. You must see it. You will never want to leave."

With a little squooshing of the corners, Erica's pack filled the Ferrari's tiny trunk. She'd filled the big hiking pack, which she'd purchased used years before with the best of intentions, with the things she wanted to keep no matter what. If Becky's garage was robbed or a temporal wormhole opened and sucked up her small stack of boxes, delivering them to a bewildered Queen of the Faeries, she wouldn't care. Not really.

If one sucked *her* up, would she care? Erica looked at the beautiful woman buckling into the spaceship-like Ferrari, then rested a hand on the luxurious leather of the seat. Perhaps that's *exactly* what was happening to her. Alien dog who only looked like a Cavalier King Charles spaniel but was actually the secret ringleader of the *Rocky Horror Picture Show: Revisited.* She, the hapless Susan Sarandon, sucked into the wormhole of...downright foolishness. Though she liked the idea of waking up and being Susan Sarandon. Susan wasn't Italian-elegant, but there was no questioning that she had her act totally together.

Erica slid into the car's passenger seat, which felt even better than first class looked after a twelve-hour flight in economy. It even smelled like she'd always imagined fine, Italian leather would smell—like a Gucci store only better. She pulled on her seatbelt, barely in time. Snoop climbed up to sit on her lap and rest his chin on the door's edge over the lowered window.

The engine roared to life—like the quiet, throaty sound of a mountain lion moments before it jumped down and snapped your neck before dragging you away as dinner. Bridget flashed a wave to Conrad who waved a solemn hand in reply from the verge above his olive trees. The Ferrari leapt forward, slamming Erica back into the seat as they raced down the narrow, twisting road she'd barely been able to creep along. Snoop leaned his side into her chest and she wrapped an arm around him as his ears flapped out in the wind.

"Snoop for Snoopy?" Erica asked the dog, who turned to roll his eyes at her as if he'd heard that far too many times.

"Snoop," Bridget slalomed through the descending twists of the road as if it was built into her DNA. "As in Snoop Doggy Dogg."

"You rap much?" she asked him softly. He just put his head back out into the wind and let his ears flap to some secret canine rhythm.

She was in the hands of strangers and had no idea what came next.

~

Ridley Claremont III slowed to a stop and looked at the sign.

Chiuso.

It wasn't much of a sign, but then it wasn't much of a road —so that, at least, fit. The meaning was clear enough though—even if he didn't know Italian.

Behind the knee-high steel tripod with its one-word sign, someone had dumped a load of boulders across the one lane of pavement. Cliff above, steep fields below, and not a single gap big enough to slide his Indian Chieftain Classic motorcycle through. Even if he did, the prospects weren't good.

Closed.

The sign was weathered by more than a week or month. Several seasons' detritus had gathered around the base of the boulders. Beyond must lay a washout that they'd fix…someday. When they got around to it. As if. This was Italy. He was no longer in France. Or Switzerland. Or Germany. Time moved very differently here and he still had no handle on it.

He wondered how many signs on his way here had warned him, in Italian, that this route was closed. On the map it had looked fine. The high coastal road wandering above the seaside cliffs had seemed like the route to follow rather than the *autostrada.* He was in no rush. The scenic route suited him just fine.

He'd picked it up at the French border and spent the last couple weeks following its wandering way south as it climbed up inland to Apricale and back down to Portofino. This time, not far past Monterosso (and the lovely Magdalena—a Polish housewife seeking an adventurous holiday—whom he'd been only too happy to accommodate) and Vernazza (with a harbor so lovely that he hadn't minded exploring it alone), the coastal road had finally let him down.

To backtrack fifty or more kilometers inland across the winding hills to pick up the *autostrada* was more than he could face. At least for today. Maybe tomorrow too. It wasn't as if he had anywhere he had to be…or anywhere to be at all, for that matter.

There had been another road just five or so twisting kilometers back. No bigger than this one, but he'd decided to give it a pass. It was just another tiny path down to another tiny cliff town he'd never heard of—Cornflakes? No, that couldn't be right. He'd been able to see it down the coast and a thousand feet below, perched atop a cliff-wrapped prominence. Just like a hundred other scenic little Italian towns, clinging to the rocks for dear life. It wouldn't be any different than the others he'd rolled through since entering the country.

He shrugged his shoulders inside his black leather. It had been too hot rolling slowly along the twisting road. Now, stopped in the sun and staring at the blasted *chiuso* sign, it was cooking him alive. He'd never liked the damned thing anyway, preferred his old denim jacket. But women could somehow tell that he was wearing a couple thousand bucks of Fendi and it seemed to work for them. Besides, it was one of the last gifts his mom had given him. Bibi had been the best mom in history. Four months wasn't near long enough to accept her loss. He still turned to her without thinking, multiple times a day, but she was no longer there.

Resigned, he kicked the Indian Chieftain back to life and backtracked. It turned out to be only three kilometers but it was so slow and twisty that it felt like twenty. Twenty that he'd never intended to retrace. His goal had been to always keep moving forward until he'd seen what Europe had to offer. The place was no bigger than the continental US, shouldn't take that long to catch the highlights. Maybe he'd hit Australia next, rolling the big bike across the vast Outback and see what the deal was.

"All part of the adventure, Ridley," he told himself without much enthusiasm. That had been lacking lately. "Some grand adventure." Barely three months on the bike and he'd already covered whole chunks of Europe. Nothing seemed to hold him for long—not even the women. Of course, they never had.

He stopped at the turn and looked back over his shoulder: no hint that the road was closed ahead. At least nothing that said *chiuso* or anything similar. Maybe you were supposed to just know. Yeah, that had worked just so well for him up to now. He "just knew" jack shit!

Taking the turn, he rolled down the cliff road. It followed torturous switchbacks too tight to really unleash the bike's 1800cc engine and have any fun. Napa Route 121 and 128. Now that was the place for a midnight ride on a big bike with a long-legged blonde just hanging onto him for dear life. Winding through the scrublands and vineyards, wrapped in the warm smell of dry grass and laurel, climbing over the ridge to run along the shores of Lake Berryessa. If he got lucky—and he was skilled at getting lucky—a little moonlit skinny-dipping and even closer contact with said long legs.

The French Alps. Oh yeah. Once he'd figured out that he just needed to suggest a motorcycle ride along a section of the Tour de France bicycle race route, he'd been set. The French loved their bicycles and he'd certainly enjoyed the French women. Worked better than a dinner date at the Celadon or The French Laundry in Napa. Cheaper too.

This tiny bit of nowhere Italian cliffside town was so obscure that only lost souls like himself would ever come here.

Shit!

He kicked down a gear and let the engine take the load of trying to move slowly enough on the steep downgrade.

Not *lost* soul. *Wandering* soul. That sounded better. Even if it was less accurate.

Third son of a top Sonoma vineyard family. Two shithead older brothers who had always hated his guts, which was only fair, he supposed, as he'd always hated theirs. Was it his fault that he was the son of the trophy wife? Bibi had been a fun mom. As an added bonus, being young—especially compared with Father's friends—and beautiful, she'd attracted young and beautiful friends. And their equally comely daughters.

It had been a sweet setup—until Father's old ticker gave out at the wheel and ran the Maserati off the edge of Big Sur, taking both of his parents out of the game. So much for having the sexiest mom in all of Sonoma.

Clarence and Evangene—no wonder they were such shits with names like those—had wanted him off the property the next day. To prove the point, they'd torched Grandfather's old Indian Chief Blackhawk that he'd spent two summers restoring himself. Then they offered—without quite being stupid enough to say it aloud, which was too bad because he'd had a recorder running—to do the same to him.

He'd liberated a couple cases of Clarence's Private Reserve Merlot, sold them for forty grand (about a tenth of what they were worth, just to rub it in), and bought himself an Indian Chieftain Classic. He could have paid cash himself, but where was the fun in that? Compared to the old Blackhawk, the new bike had newer gear, a bigger engine, and the plus of having a double seat for the ladies to ride. (He'd had a monster Ducati crotch rocket for picking up the local ladies, but it would suck for touring.)

If it wouldn't have gone back to them, he'd have shoved the rest of the inheritance down his brothers' ungrateful throats. Of course, what he'd do without money was an issue he'd have thought of later rather than sooner, but choking them with it still sounded attractive.

They'd tried to cash him out, but Bibi had survived Father by a full day. Because of language in the will and his brothers' overeager attorney, they'd filed with the court before she died. That meant that Bibi was entitled to receive a quarter share along with the three sons. (His brothers' mom got three million to shut up and go away.) When Bibi finally succumbed, with only Ridley in attendance, her own will gave her quarter share solely to him. Half owner of the stunningly successful Claremont Family Wines. Not too shabby. *Thanks, Mom.*

And he'd trade it all in to sit and crack another bottle of their Signature Pinot together. How many beautiful evenings had they spent like that? She never held back in telling him how he was messing up with the girls and how to treat them better. Bibi didn't have a coy bone in her, even if Ridley was the only one in the family to appreciate her brain as well as her looks.

His brothers wanted him gone, fine. But they'd have to pay him a half of everything for life and he'd hired a total shark of a lawyer and auditor to make sure they couldn't hide a penny. He considered giving his half of the stock to a drug dealer or a street gang just to screw them. For now, though, he was keeping his options open.

He was getting the feel for Italian roads. They weren't about speed—not real speed like Route 128, which was more suited to his Ducati Multistrada superbike. These had a certain flow to their winding paths. Sharp twists, hairpins so tight they practically undercut each other, though there was always an olive tree or a cluster of grapevines somehow squeezed into the gaps. No land wasted here.

Getting the feel for it, he was about to pop up a gear and let it really roll. Then he spotted a small red triangle in the road. Two weeks in the country and he'd already seen enough of those to be slamming on the brakes by instinct alone.

Good thing that it was there. Just around the next blind corner, the road was completely blocked by a tow truck. No sign of a car, just a cable disappearing downslope into the trees. Since no one was going anywhere until he was done, Ridley parked his Chieftain in the middle of the road, dropped the stand, and climbed off to go enjoy the show. The dry grass reminded him of Sonoma, but the sea was close enough here to fill the air with its saltiness. Baked by the sun, it had an unexpected richness.

An elderly man in khaki pants and a white button-down shirt stood at the edge of the road looking down the slope.

"Hey, buddy. *Parlez vous anglais?*"

"*Je parle* English," the man replied. "In Italy you may wish to enquire: *Parli inglese.* It would be somewhat more appropriate."

"Right. Sorry. Just came out of France," not that he spoke more than a couple of French phrases—most having to do with, *Want a ride on my American classic motorcycle?*

They both looked down the slope as the tow truck operator climbed laboriously up the steep grade. Once he arrived, rather than starting the tow, he joined them in staring down at the small white car far below among the trees. Someone else who'd been driving on this road also parked and came over to join them in looking down at the car.

He and the old chap rattled some Italian back and forth, but neither seemed in any real hurry; just watching the day go by. The other local started another topic: soccer maybe. That went on for a while before petering out.

The car in the orchard was like that moment in James Bond's *For Your Eyes Only.* The lovely Melina Havelock's— undeniably the hottest Bond girl ever except maybe the original Honey Rider—tiny Citroen C2V plunging down through the olive grove, dodging all the bad guys in their vicious black Mercedes.

"Yours?" Ridley asked after they'd gone quiet for a bit.

"A friend's."

"They okay?"

The old man turned to inspect him carefully from his boots to his untrimmed hair.

Ridley knew women liked hair long enough to toy with. Bibi had given him that and other tips on cultivating the "bad boy" look when he'd gotten old enough for his interests to turn to girls. "Bad boy with money." It took him a while, but he'd eventually gotten it down and it had worked like a magic charm. She'd also attempted to cultivate "bad boy with heart of gold" but that had never really taken. It made him sad to remember how often she'd teased him about that failure. Maybe he'd try again someday for her sake.

"Are *you* quite all right?" The guy narrowed his eyes as if seeing inside him.

"What do you mean? I wasn't the one who crashed my car down into an olive grove."

The man studied him again with those eyes of blue steel. He might be a slender man who stood a few inches shorter than his own six feet and much older, but the look suggested that he wasn't a man to be messed with.

"Just asking if your friend was hurt." Was it bad here to be polite and ask about a stranger?

"She is unharmed by *this* experience. Merely shaken."

"Shaken, not stirred?" The guy could be an elderly James Bond like David Niven in the original *Casino Royale*.

The man's baleful gaze was certainly up to Niven's standard of making a man feel small and inconsequential.

The tow truck driver finally lost interest in a conversation he probably couldn't understand, revved up the truck's engine, and engaged the winch. With a loud groan, it began hauling the car up the slope.

"Do you know anything about this town?" Ridley had to shout to be heard.

Again with that Niven look.

"Got any suggestions on where I could shack up for the night?"

"Shack up?"

"Sleep. Hotel, whatever."

"Where are you from?" The man led him aside, out of the

tow driver's way and distant enough from the truck to speak without shouting.

"Sonoma. It's in California."

"Some nice wines there," the man said in the same tone one might use to say there are clouds in the sky.

Ridley was…had been…*was* proud of Father's wines. He and Father had each spent more time with Marissa, the chief vintner, than his two brothers combined. Maybe he should have taken over the winery and thrown *them* out. Little late to think of that. But hell, even Bibi had taken an interest in the process once Ridley had started really telling her about it. *Some nice wines? Shit, man! Better than a lot of your overpriced Italian ones, buddy.*

"What is your name, young man?"

"Ridley Claremont III. Folks call me…Ridley." It sounded dumb, but *no one* was allowed to call him Lee anymore. Not since Bibi had died, because that had been her nickname for him and it still hurt too much to hear it coming from someone else's mouth. It was as if was suddenly someone else. Something about that amused Conrad, or at least made him thoughtful.

"Conrad Evenston." The guy had a grip of steel even tougher than the one in his blue eyes.

The guy studied him for several long moments before answering.

"There's a nice café, *Il Cane.* The Dog. You may make inquiries there. You may find it at the base of the main *carruggio.*"

"*Carruggio?* Don't know that one."

"It is a local Ligurian word. I believe Americans unimaginatively call it a pedestrian zone. Much of Corniglia is *carruggio,* not open to vehicles. Not even your conveyance."

"Corniglia. *Il Cane.* The Dog. At the base of the main *carruggio.* How do you say 'thanks' in Italian?"

"*Grazie.*"

"*Grazie* then. Appreciate the tip."

A final deafening groan from the aged tow truck and the crumpled little car heaved into view over the grassy shoulder. Like most cars on the Italian roads, it wasn't much bigger than his bike. Right side fender and door bashed in. The front metal was a mess as well. No head-punch mark on the inside of the windshield and the airbags hadn't been unleashed; still... Ridley glanced down the long slope.

"Rough ride."

"Eh?" The tow truck driver asked him.

Ridley turned to Conrad to translate for him, but the man was gone. He caught just a glimpse of Conrad's silver hair as he disappeared beneath the olive trees.

CHAPTER 2

*P*erhaps Italy wasn't a total disaster.

Erica was feeling much better about the day—now that it was evening. She leaned against the railing of her tiny balcony. Her stance practically plunged her face into the wild array of flowers planted in boxes along the wrought iron rail. Geraniums in purples, pinks, and whites that looked so happy it was impossible not to grin at them. She'd had a hot shower, changed into fresh clothes, and cradled a stoneware mug of tea that smelled of lemon and honey. Not honey-honey, but Italian honey. Like it had been made by little beret-wearing bees. No, that would be France. Happy bees anyway, singing little Italian bee songs as they sought pollen from among the flowers.

The room was so Italian that it would have been a cliché if she wasn't standing in it.

The B&B was in a stone building that probably dated back to the Medici just like Conrad's olive trees. The ground floor was a café that Bridget promised her she'd like when she was ready to come down.

"The first floor flat, that one is ours," Bridget had explained, then added in a conspiratorial whisper, "Snoop is so fat that we don't have the heart to make him climb higher even if it would be good for him." The building was only big enough to have one tiny suite per floor.

She'd offered Erica the second floor, but she'd opted for the third—which would be the fourth in America. A three-flight walk-up however it was counted.

The instant she saw it she was in love. The narrow stone stairs had twisted as darkly upward as any medieval turret. An incongruously cheery bright green door had promised a surprise within and had delivered.

The small living room was awash with the golden glow of the settling sun—not quite plunging into the Mediterranean yet—streaming its last light in through the gauzy curtains fluttering in the breeze. The walls were painted in a pale blue with a rich red edging that made the room feel much larger than expected. The space was just sufficient to fit two chairs, a tiny writing desk, and the small couch meant for curling up on with a trashy novel. The only way they got the king-sized bed in the separate bedroom was so obviously an act of black magic that she'd decided it was better not to ask. Perhaps the massive four-poster had been built in place, after the trees had been grown there for a few hundred years before being felled and carved where they stood.

After the shower, the black-and-white diamond-patterned tile floor was cool under her feet. The balcony, just large enough for a clothesline and two plastic chairs (if their occupants rubbed shoulders), was the ultimate treat. Her own personal fairy-tale tower. Because the building was perched at the edge of the *carruggio,* she could look down and watch the couples walking together looking for a restaurant. Stone buildings rose up from the other side of the walkway. A group of boys—the age that would just be figuring out tricycles at home—were indeed playing a game of soccer across the slanting cobbles of the narrow street. Each stray kick sending a tiny boy scrambling down into the one lower open area where any cars that had survived to make it this far had to turn around and go back.

Doorways were marked by carved wooden signs that looked as old as the town. Small planter boxes abounded with great sweeps of more geraniums—each flower bigger than her whole hand. The stone might be gray and the buildings done in stucco painted in pastels, but flowers abounded everywhere. Great curving arbors of roses. Pots of petunias. Everywhere there were flowers.

Laughter echoed up the rock walls. A third floor (or fourth in America—still explaining things to herself when no one was listening, bad sign) neighbor across the street, no more than twenty feet away, called out a friendly *Buonasera*—"Good evening." That one she knew, now that she'd heard it. She happily returned the same.

Looking in the other direction, vineyards and olive trees covered the vertiginous hillside. What would have been terrifyingly steep, if it was rock, had been softened by hundreds of sinuous, built-up terraces, each planted with dozens of grapevines. Tier upon tier of them covered the hillside. Like a green topographic map.

And beyond. Beyond it all lay the vast sweep of the Mediterranean Sea. The blue really was as unique as all of the movies made it out to be. She knew the dark, turbulent waters of the Pacific and the smooth dark blue of the Atlantic. The Med was part turquoise and it shone as if there was gold hidden just below the surface. The sun, now gone into the sea while she'd watched the children below, cast a deeply orange glow upon the distant liquid horizon, giving it more colors and variations. It was an Italian water mosaic.

Somehow, through all the challenges, she had arrived. Past cars wrecked in olive trees (a grove). Through leg cramps on the interminable flight—so bad she'd have screamed if she hadn't feared being labeled as an in-flight nuisance.

"Today's movie selection is listed in the backs of your magazines. Beverage service will start in a few minutes. And the woman screaming her head off in seat 37F has been officially labeled as an in-flight nuisance. Please observe the little red warning triangles posted along that section of the aisle."

She giggled at her own joke. Erica decided that was a good sign. After the day she'd had, it was a freaking miracle that she could laugh.

"Call the Pope!"

Then she slapped a hand over her mouth. This was Italy, they probably *could* call the Pope. There was certainly a large church easily visible on the other edge of the narrow town. The big square clock tower rose upward, holding aloft its pinnacled steeple, which swept up even further.

"Close enough for God to be listening." And though she didn't really believe, there was a serenity that seemed to emanate from the church and spread over the town.

Her sanity at least partially restored, though she could still feel the goofy smile on her face, she slid on a pair of lovely sandals. Not Italian-level lovely, but she liked them. Thankfully, her better judgment had won out and she'd bought the ones with flat heels back in Boston rather than the spiked monsters Dwayne had wanted her to purchase.

They do great things for your ass. And you've got such a great ass, honey.

She certainly should from all the stress she worked out on the stair stepper at the gym.

That those sky-high sandals would also have broken her feet—and perhaps her neck—had been of no consequence in his opinion. It had all been about *his* pleasure in viewing *her* ass.

Going down the B&B's stone steps would be a challenge under most conditions. The iron handrails were frail and intermittent on the steep steps. In heels it would take a suicidal runway model to navigate them.

She made it down the twisting, steep stairs in one piece in her flats.

Oddly enough, it was these sandals and Dwayne's comment that had been the first ripple in a still pond. When she'd surfaced, it had been with the speed of a breaching whale. Or maybe the reaction to getting whacked by a fairy godmother's wand—really sharply on the nose. One week she'd been all safe and cozy in her dream of a splendid future. And the next she'd been single, unemployed, and had her car stolen. Maybe Dwayne had arranged that too. He hadn't seemed the vengeful type, but then he'd also seemed to be the honorable type. Apparently she was a pathetic judge of men.

At the bottom of the stairs she stepped onto the *carruggio* with all the ease she could manage and entered the café through the wide door, open to the warm evening.

It was like being wrapped in the arms of garlic, basil, an oregano red sauce, and fresh baked bread. Pesto originally came from Liguria. Focaccia as well. It smelled like heaven.

As Bridget had promised, the café was lovely.

It was also full.

Vibrant Italian poured out through the doors—some of it soft-spoken, some with laughter, and some with no real way to tell if it was a horrible fight or simply a good story well told. For now, she'd assume the latter.

Done in dark reds, terracotta, and beiges, it felt warm and safe. Here the stone walls were left exposed in most areas, adding to the rustic feel. A large mosaic of a rumpled, dreadlocked Bergamasco dog graced one wall. He looked very Italian in his tiny gray and black tiles.

The tables of dark wood appeared well used but were in good enough condition to also say they were well cared for. They were scattered about on the concrete floor. Simple, durable, but not unsightly concrete gray. It had thousands of small stones embedded in the surface. Some glittered with the promise of crystals, other with the warm colors and smooth surfaces of beach-washed gravel. All of it laid out in some intricate pattern that invited the eye to follow wherever it led —which didn't appear to be anywhere.

The bar wasn't some long, forbidding oak or steel thing like in the US: a hard bastion for dozens, maybe hundreds of people to crowd close and demand a drink. It was a low affair, kitchen-counter high, made of dark wood, and scuffed with more centuries of service than the US had been a country.

Next to the cash register stood a ceramic statuette of Snoop, so close to life-sized that for half a second she thought it was the real one. But it wasn't quite fat enough. Then she spotted Snoop curled up in a dog bed near the end of the bar.

The requisite espresso machine wasn't a multi-throated monster like the Starbucks one she'd learned to work as a college-age barista going through hell and poverty. It was for making one drink at a time. Even now a big man with a graying ponytail and a tie the color of the sunset was working its controls with an easy confidence.

Bridget was carrying a large calzone and a stack of plates to one of the tables off to the side where a couple and two children were chattering away in Italian. Bridget's responses were fluent and Erica could feel the warmth of them despite the language barrier.

Bridget came up to her as the bartender finished making the espresso…then began to drink it himself.

"Better?" Bridget asked her.

Erica could only smile. "Whole new person. I can't thank you enough. The room is perfect."

"*Molto bene!* Now, what can I get you?"

"Um," Erica looked around. All of the tables were full. "Where?" She didn't want to go looking for somewhere else to eat.

"Hmm… Ah!" Bridget snagged her arm. Not a mere grip, but looping her arm through Erica's like they were old friends. Bridget turned her about and guided her back out the front door to one of the tiny round tables facing the *carruggio* just as it vacated.

"Perfect!" Erica couldn't believe her luck.

"*Perfetto!*" Bridget filled in.

"*Perfetto!*" she agreed and took a seat. The last brilliance of the multi-colored sunset lit the golden stone walls of the buildings across the street with warm red.

Bridget was waiting. Oh, for her to order. And the place was very busy. Yet she didn't act hurried.

"Could I have something local? Authentic?"

Bridget just glowed. "I will have Hal make you an espresso and then I'll make you a dish to welcome you to Liguria." She whisked away, pausing to admire a child, tease a man, and admire a new scarf of airy silk that was amazingly Italian-elegant. She looked down at her good blouse and jeans and then searched for something else to look at.

The cobbled narrow street lay before her.

Carruggio!

It was the word that had always made her dream of Italy. Towns that knew being a pedestrian was a good thing. Interactions, impossible while zipping to suburban malls in traffic-jammed lines of cars, suddenly happened on quiet, shadowed streets. (Not shadowed like dark and dangerous. Shadowed like cool spots tucked away from the hot sun so that warmth was always just a step away, her internal voice clarified.) Even as a little girl she'd dreamed of the slow pace and easy friendliness. Perhaps she'd watched too many movies, but she wanted all that. That and more.

It was all so peaceful. So Italian. So—

A big American motorcycle came thudding up, close beside the building. With an arrogance that proved the rider was also American, he barely pulled it to one side before parking. Another six inches and he'd be *on* the *carruggio*. It was a monster of a machine, like the kind that rode on big American highways.

She knew nothing about motorcycles, but this one looked old in style yet brand new. It had a little Indian-head lamp mounted on its curved front fender that appeared to be searching for a tomahawk to scalp her with—if it only had arms. The metal was a glossy burgundy accented with white pinstriping. The fenders covered the top half of each wheel in a manly swoop. Large saddlebags hung at the rear, but the bike was all about the massive, bright-chromed engine that dominated the machine.

When the man pulled off his helmet, he revealed a dark tan. His near-black hair fell to the collar of his Fendi jacket, which emphasized his broad shoulders. Entirely too handsome for his own good, just like the fair-haired Dwayne. He didn't remove his sunglasses despite the descending evening, giving him a dangerous look as he climbed off the machine and stood there as if he owned the world in his faded jeans and black boots.

What would that feel like? That easy surety? She couldn't imagine.

Erica felt that the motorcycle needed little-girl streamers off the ends of the handlebars to complete the picture. The thought made her smile.

~

Ridley now knew exactly why he'd come to Italy. He was even willing to bless the stupid *chiuso* sign that had turned him back.

She wasn't his type: he had a major weakness for tall, leggy brunette models with hair down to their ass and a chest that never stopped giving. The woman at the small table couldn't top five-six or a hundred and ten pounds. Her neatly collar-long hair had a deep auburn red that the sunset only accentuated. Her face was nearly elfin in its fineness, with just a sprinkle of freckles across her nose. Her wide brown eyes should be too big for her face, but they weren't.

She sat at a small table aiming a smile at him that could put the Italian sun to shame.

Then she turned that same electric smile to a woman, who was much more his type, as she set an espresso on the tiny table before disappearing back inside.

The smile didn't diminish, but neither did it turn again in his direction. Instead she was looking up at the wall of stone buildings and offering them her radiant attention. He looked up, but saw nothing special that could so hold her attention—towering stone that nearly touched from either side of a slit of dark sky.

When he looked back down, she was inspecting him, but

the radiance had gone away leaving behind a pretty woman with freckles across her nose. He'd moved several steps closer without realizing.

"*Parle...*" No. "*Parli...*" What had the old guy said? Shit! He really had to learn some of the language. If this one slipped away because he had no Italian, he was gonna be pissed.

She watched him steadily with those big browns.

He'd settle for pidgin to keep her engaged. "Corniglia?" Ridley waved a hand at the town.

"*Sì*," she nodded.

"*Il Cane?*"

She shrugged. She wore a shining walnut-brown blouse that would have put lesser eyes to shame. It flowed over her trim figure in gentle waves. Nice shoulders accented by the light blue shawl that had slipped down around her upper arms.

Stumped, he looked around. The only other directions he had was *carruggio* and it was obvious that part he'd already achieved.

A sharp snarl drew his attention to somewhere around his feet. A knee-high brown-and-white spaniel with bulging eyes glared at him. Not quite to bared teeth yet, but definitely not welcome.

"Snoop, shhh," the woman reached out a hand and the dog shifted to her side for a scratch.

"Hell of a guardian."

~

"*Sì.*" Erica was going to find out where to buy doggie biscuits and make sure that Snoop was set up for life. However, there was only so long she could keep the motorcyclist at bay with that one word of Italian.

Then it registered—past her inattention—the man had spoken English: *"Hell of a guardian."* She even knew the accent. It was American English, not England English. More, it was Northern Californian…and she was doing the justifying things in her head again. But it was like hearing a voice from home, even if it was a decade in her past. Still, staying safe behind her one word of Italian seemed like a good idea. Actually she had more than that: *buonasera,* and Bridget had given her *perfetto* and *mia amica.* That had been her first real Italian word: "my friend." How portentous. It boded well for her vacation. Or trip. Or last hope. Or whatever this was.

"Mia amica," she told Snoop as she pet his head. Or, since Snoop was male, was there supposed to be some other ending: *Mio amico? Mio-myo ami-mayo?* She needed to learn the phrase for "my hero."

Quite why she didn't want to reveal herself to the motorcyclist—definitely ignoring any unintended innuendo of that wording—was baffling. He was just your typical, full-of-himself male and she'd had more than enough of that with the man she'd never think of again.

Then he pointed at Snoop, *"Il cane."* Ca-nay.

She had no idea.

"The dog." He twisted to look at the café and nearly flattened Bridget along with Erica's dinner. "Excuse me. Is this The Dog Café? *Ist es—* No, that's German. Crap!" He finally just pointed at the café. *"Il Cane?"*

Erica couldn't help herself and laughed aloud. "Yes, Snoop is a dog."

"You speak English. Thank god!" The fervency of his relief had her laughing again. He shoved up his sunglasses and dropped into the seat across from her without even asking.

It would have knocked their knees together if he hadn't

sprawled in the chair and stuck his legs out to the side, perhaps hoping to trip any unsuspecting passersby thinking it was safe to walk the *carruggio*.

His dark hair and deep tan only accented his blue-grey eyes. They were so unexpected that it gave her a jolt. What else was unexpected about him?

"Is this place *Il Cane*? The dog? Or is only the dog the dog? Wow, that didn't make much sense."

Bridget set a bowl and a monstrous glass of white wine on the table. The wine captured the reds of the fading evening and the golds of the café lights. But that wasn't what riveted Erica's attention. It was a large white bowl filled with an enormous portion of cheese tortellini, liberally mixed with shrimp and mussels, all drowned in a pesto so deeply green that she wanted to dive in like it was a magic sea. A chunk of focaccia big enough to use as a life raft in case of emergency water landings was tucked at the side.

"Oh my. Bridget, there's no way I can eat all this."

"Trust me. You will walk it off. Tourists in Cinque Terre burn many, many calories on our steep hills." Then she turned to the motorcyclist. Erica could feel the sudden temperature drop and looked back up in surprise.

Snoop hadn't liked the stranger either.

"Yes, this is *Il Cane*." No effusive welcome. No *mia amica*.

"Great!" The guy appeared to be too oblivious to notice the lack of welcome. "This guy, name of Conrad, said you might have a room. I hit that stupid road-closed sign a couple hours back. At least it seems like a couple hours. I need a room for the night. I can't imagine riding back out of here; I could barely follow that twisting excuse for a road in broad daylight. I'm Ridley, by the way. Ridley Claremont." He said it all in one breathless American rush.

In just one day Erica herself had already slowed down so much that it seemed crass and uncouth, even to her.

"Conrad sent you?" Bridget narrowed her eyes at him as she looked him up and down.

"Slender guy. Posh accent. A glare that could melt steel."

Erica suspected that if even Conrad had disliked him, it boded very poorly for the stranger to find any accommodation.

Bridget had shifted from disbelief to curiosity. Through Erica's own hand on Snoop's head, she could feel the subvocal growl was still in place.

"I might have a room," Bridget conceded reluctantly.

Erica tried to warn her off with narrowed eyes, but Bridget offered a tiny *"we'll see"* shrug. "Why don't you eat something first and I'll see what I can find for you."

"Awesome! Really appreciate it. I'll have whatever. I'm not a real picky sort of guy." He reached out and picked up Erica's wine glass. "May I?"

He barely waited for her astonished nod before tasting it.

His face went quiet. Suddenly it was possible to see a different man sitting at the table. He sniffed the wine again, swirled the glass and held it up to the café lights as he inspected it with narrowed eyes. Another sniff.

"Don't know it, must be local. Good body," he said mostly to himself. He swirled the glass and peered at it intently, "Great legs. Nice nose for a dry white." Another sip, and a long moment where he closed his eyes as he tasted it. He set her glass back down and turned to Bridget, "Another glass of that would be awesome."

Then he turned to face her for the first time since he'd sat at her table uninvited. "Mind if I join you? Be nice to talk to a fellow Yank for a change."

"You've already had my wine." But she said it too *nicely*. Erica really had to do something about her kneejerk politeness. Kneejerk politeness? Oh, that was far too accurate...politeness that always drew the jerks. She needed to toughen up and give them the knee right, well, there. But—she sighed to herself—that wasn't any more likely to happen this week than last week.

~

The lady at the table wasn't responding the way he was used to. Fancy bike, good looks, obvious money—they always drew a response. Until now it had always been a more enthusiastic one.

Maybe she'd been waiting for someone? But she hadn't used that excuse to shoo him off. Wanted to eat alone? Maybe. He tipped his chair back far enough to see inside the café...no open seats. A couple of men stood at a low counter, chatting with the bartender as he served them up espressos, despite the hour, and a bottle of beer. They all appeared happy to stand and chat. He dropped the iron chair back to the cobbles with a clank.

"Popular place."

"Um," it was a happy sound, but she wasn't looking at him. She was eating the first bite of her dinner and that radiant smile was fast reappearing.

"That good?"

"Um-hmm."

"I'm from California."

"Um-hmm." Apparently she already knew that, but was less enthusiastic this time.

"How about you?"

She shrugged as she sipped her wine.

"Just a traveler?" He guessed that's all he was now. Bibi

gone. The house closed to him. Oh, he could go back and fight for his rights—he owned half, not forty-nine percent—but who wanted that hassle. He was a big fan of the easy road.

Again the shrug of those fine shoulders.

"Not exactly thrilled with my intrusion?" Damn it! There were some thoughts he really should keep to himself.

"No, it's not that..." she leapt to the apology too quickly, then couldn't seem to complete it.

"Exactly that," he sighed. "Sorry. Mind if I stay anyway? No other table open. Oh man. That's a trap too. Seriously, not trying to do that either. Crap!" What was it about this woman that was screwing up his smooth? He never fumbled around women.

Her smile didn't go radiant, but at least it opened up enough to acknowledge his discomfiture.

"Bibi always said I was too pushy." But usually when he pushed, women fell over easily enough.

"Our first dinner together and you're already telling me about your ex?"

"Worse, my mom." Though he liked the sound of "first dinner" as if there might be more.

"You call your mom by her first name?"

"She didn't like Mom, said it made her feel too old. She had me when she was nineteen."

"What mother names her daughter Bibi?"

"She named herself. Picked her name out of a James Bond movie somewhere in her teens after running away from an abusive home. She looked a lot like Bibi, the blonde bombshell skater in *For Your Eyes Only*. Father met her when she was working on one of the later Bond movies—minor role, sexy hostess at the Napa Valley resort in *A View to a Kill*. Dumped his first wife and kept her."

~

And the glorious pesto turned to dry carboard in her mouth. A sip of the dry white wine threatened to shrivel her throat so badly that she had to gasp for breath.

"You okay?"

Erica tried to nod. Couldn't. Tried shaking her head. Nothing.

"I'm not going to apologize for being the son of a trophy wife. Bibi's awesome. Father's first wife was an avaricious, spoiled shrew." His voice turned angry, defensive.

She shook her head. That wasn't the point at all.

"Dwayne—" was all she managed to choke out. He'd promised he was leaving his wife, but never did. Not for her. Not for poor little Erica. It had been a trap. A tease. A weapon in his arsenal of control. She had loved him, or thought she had—though it had never felt like what she'd always thought love was supposed to feel like—and he had used that.

Not this man's mother. Bibi too had run away from home, and she'd found her love. But she'd found the man who loved her enough to keep his promises.

Unable to sit still, she jolted to her feet and turned away.

The man—she'd forgotten his name—stumbled to his feet.

"Don't!"

The last thing she needed was a stranger's sympathy to emphasize the depths of her failures.

"Just...don't."

She hurried off into the night, shivering beneath the thin shawl she'd tossed over her shoulders for a bit of style. Too thin to hide her shame.

~

"What did you do to her?"

Ridley turned to face Bridget. She had shifted over to some darkly elemental state of fierce. She held his dinner and a glass of wine in such a way that they might be weapons. Not hard to picture her as some kind of shield maiden—tall, built, and lethal.

"I don't know." He tried to see the woman down the shadowed street, but she was already gone from view. "I honestly don't. We were just talking. I told her about my mom. She muttered someone's name and bolted."

He turned back to Bridget.

"Am I going to eat that?" he nodded down at the dinner plate of steaming seafood over pasta. "Or wear it?"

Bridget inspected him for a long moment, "The jury remains out."

"The way it smells, I'd prefer the former. But if it's the latter, I guess I'd understand. Though I swear that I don't know what I said to upset your friend."

At length, Bridget set his plate and wineglass on the table, and cleared away...he hadn't even gotten her name. Bibi had taught him to never forget a woman's name, but he'd never even heard it.

"I think I will believe you, Ridley." Like a good hostess, Bridget hadn't forgotten his. "As to what upset Erica, perhaps we need to find that out." Then she reached into a pocket and dropped something on the table before turning to her other customers.

Ridley looked one last time up the street, but saw only couples moving along, momentarily lit by the occasional glow from windows. He sat back in the chair and sipped the wine. It was different, richer, with a citrusy depth and a slightly mineral-salty finish. By the dim lighting it was more golden than Erica's half-finished glass. It should be a nice match for the meal.

Erica. Erica Schroeder wrote the theme song for *Goldfinger* —so easy enough to remember the woman's first name.

He set down the glass and looked at his dinner. Close beside the plate lay a room key with a dangle on it that said "2."

CHAPTER 3

The warm glow of the sunrise woke her despite her late night. Erica had gotten miserably lost in the dark, twisting streets. She was fairly sure that the whole town only had three or four of them, but they seemed to curve the wrong way every time she thought she was close. It had taken forever to stumble once more upon the B&B. She must have walked every street of the entire town multiple times before finding her way home. *Il Cane* had been dark and shuttered and she might have passed it by in the thin moonlight if not for the monstrous motorcycle parked at the corner.

By the time she was ready to return, even the wonderful scents of the café weren't there to help her. Italy had smelled so…Italian in the evening: the air thick with cooking scents and laughter. She'd been able to smell the lemons hanging thick on their trees and the early roses that had perfumed the air. At night, all that had faded away and all she'd been able to smell was the all-knowing Mediterranean. All she'd been able to hear was the sea's laughter of waves crashing on rocks.

She hated—hated, hated, hated (repeating herself didn't

seem to help)—that Dwayne was able to gut her so thoroughly from five thousand miles away.

Maybe, if the Roman gods were with her, (Please, Athena... or was Athena Greek? Either way: please, please, please. She was repeating herself a lot this morning), they'd let whatever his name and his motorcycle be gone this morning. Then she could start all over on her project of forgetting the man she was never going to think about again.

The warm, brilliant morning gave her hope that maybe it would work today. Or at least be better today than it had yesterday. Which wouldn't be hard.

She was down less than a flight of the stone steps when the door on the next landing opened.

The motorcyclist from last night looked up at her in some surprise. "The sunlight here is really something. Punches down like a monster headlamp on high beam."

"I suppose." She had reveled in the cleansing wash of light emerging over the mountains to the east. It had painted the Mediterranean in its glorious color. It was hopeful somehow, especially after such a dark night. She had woken up in Italy after all. How many years had she dreamt of doing that? The air had smelled fresh from the sea, and of pastries from below —which is what had finally drawn her out.

He frowned at her for a long moment. Enough that she considered going back up to her room, as the landing was too small to brush by him.

"Look, I don't know what I said to upset you last night. But I just wanted to say I'm sorry for ruining your dinner. I'll steer clear."

"It's not that. You don't need too. I'm not feeling—" She didn't know what she was feeling other than that she was babbling. She was a skilled business manager. Managing anything was easy, except her own life.

Really suck at that, Erica. She sighed. She did.

"Here," she held out her hand. "We're about to meet for the first time and pretend that last night—" and her entire life before this moment "—never happened. Hi, I'm Erica Barnett."

"Hey, Erica. Barnett, that's easy to remember. Melina Havelock uses two different Barnett crossbows to kill…" His smile bloomed. "You don't by any chance have a crossbow in your kit, do you?"

"I have no idea what you're talking about."

"*For Your Eyes Only.* James Bond. Never mind. Hi, I'm Ridley Claremont III," he offered her a big smile and a warm handshake. "Pleased to meet you." He had big hands, strong ones that made her own feel cool and fine. "Want to have breakfast together?"

Erica hadn't thought ahead about that obvious consequence of starting over. Trapped by her own words, she nodded her inevitable acceptance. At least he'd been nice enough to make the unavoidable into a question.

Ridley was a surprisingly pleasant breakfast companion. At this hour, *Il Cane* was quiet. Just the occasional pastry and cappuccino to go—apparently espresso was for evenings. They'd taken a table inside as the morning was still cool along the shadowed *carruggio*. They ate apricot brioche, a hardboiled egg with the shell already cracked all over, and deep cups of hot chocolate so lush that you could paint walls with it.

She'd asked about his motorcycle, expecting that to occupy him throughout the meal; he was a guy after all. But he moved on from it quickly. Atypically for a guy, he asked about her—a topic she had no interest in pursuing. That seemed to confuse him enough to dip his brioche into a glass of fruit juice.

"My travels are only in Day Two, so I have nothing to tell. How about yours?" She congratulated herself on dodging that bullet, or crossbow bolt, fairly neatly.

He harrumphed, "I'm around the end of *Month* Three. Sort of touring Europe."

"No job?" And she winced. The constant measure of someone back in America. What do you do? Who do you know? Where did you go to school? Yammer, yammer, yammer. "Ignore that, please."

"No, it's all right. Guess I've never really had a job."

Erica could only blink at him in surprise. "I scrabbled for everything from the moment I was born, or at least it seems that way."

He waved his soggy croissant in an inviting way and she surprised herself by continuing.

"Kind of Cinderella. Mom's second husband had a pair of daughters already. Then, when Mom bailed on him for Husband Number Three—who didn't want someone else's kid interfering with his new life—he somehow ended up stuck with me."

"Evil stepsisters, huh? Could introduce them to my evil half brothers."

"They weren't bad, really. Just enough older that they had no real interest in a kid stepsister tagging along. Stephen tried, but he was a single-dad longshoreman with three daughters. Long hours, and money was always tight. Earned my own way from the time I could babysit. Made college at sixteen—*so* not ready for that social scene despite having older sisters."

"I'm in the presence of genius."

"Don't say that!" Dway— *He* had always said that.

"You're clearly smarter than the av-er-age bear," he said it just like Yogi Bear in the cartoons.

And she was, "About some things." And she was never going to talk about the others. "Tell me about your evil half brothers and how you never had a job."

He chose the former topic, even though she was more

curious about the latter. The rest of the meal passed with funny stories of the rivalry between himself and "the boys" older than Ridley's mother.

"You really don't have a problem with my mom being a younger wife?" Ridley seemed genuinely puzzled.

Dwayne had been older as well—not May-December, but older. He'd been so worldly, so smoothly sophisticated. She'd initially been charmed that someone like him had even noticed her. So naive as to think that made her special rather than malleable.

"Had to defend her a lot?"

"Maybe," Ridley shrugged, but she could see the tension under that. "Against my brothers. My friends at school. Everyone on the planet except for her friends, and even some of them because she was a runaway turned actress who married so well."

Which finally answered why he'd never had a job. And that's when she connected the disparate pieces.

Last night, she'd liked the wine. He had relished and analyzed it in minute detail, obviously possessing a highly-trained palate.

San Francisco accent.

Ridley Claremont III.

Claremont Family Wines of Sonoma Valley. Down in Oakland they called them "lucky spermers"—the kids born into true winery wealth. And Claremont was near the very pinnacle of the vines. Lucky spermers were almost always trouble: wild, conceited, thinking that women answered the merest snap of their fingers. Worse, they were usually right.

Not her! She knew better now. A pleasant breakfast companion, but that's all Ridley Claremont was going to ever be. Lucky spermers had no depth to them. No commitment. They didn't hit college at sixteen—she done it with brutally hard work, not genius. Every single babysitting gig she'd ever had, she'd actually *done* her schoolwork from the moment the kids were asleep rather than watch TV. Which was why they never got to stay up a minute late. Full scholarship at sixteen was how she had escaped home and stopped being a burden to Stephen, her stepfather, to their mutual relief.

Yet Ridley Claremont III had never had a job.

Until this week, she'd never had a *vacation*. In the past, a week off from work was a week to revise a business plan, build a presentation, catch some online training, get her project management certification, or other ways to focus on anything but herself. Her time away with Dwayne had always been on business trips, which had saved him—she now realized—from ever explaining anything to his wife.

"All work and no play makes Erica a dull girl."

"What's that?" Ridley was actually listening to her. Strange. Not typical of guys, not even Dwayne, who'd only appeared to be interested. Instead, he'd taught her to be interested in him. Another pit she'd apparently crawled into without noticing, during yet another massive moment of inattention. Maybe it was the times she actually *paid* attention that were the exception. All it had taken was a the total train wreck of her life to snap her world into focus.

"I've never had a vacation before. I'm not really sure what to do next. Yesterday all I did was crash a car into an olive grove. I don't think that counts."

"That was you?" he pointed up into the hills and snorted out a laugh.

∽

Erica's glare answered that question.

"Okay, not my most tactful. But you've got to admit that it's pretty funny."

"Bridget thought so as well. Personally, I'm having difficulty finding the humor in the whole mess." Ridley supposed he could see why.

"Glad you're okay."

"Why?"

She was the strangest woman he'd ever met. Even such a simple pleasantry was taken apart and investigated. She'd practically run a Spanish Inquisition—and not in some comedic Monty Python sense of the word—about his relationship with Clarence and Evangene. He'd never told anyone so much about them. The hurt at them shutting him out when he was little. Which had grown into anger at how they'd dismissed Bibi no matter how hard she tried to be nice to them. And finally active hatred—though he hadn't even realized that was there inside him until he told Erica about them burning his grandfather's motorcycle.

"I'm just glad you aren't hurt. Shaken, not stirred." Again with the dumb line. That Conrad guy had gotten under his skin, poking him about why he cared. Though it no longer felt like an idle question. Picturing Erica wracked up and alone in an Italian hospital was a foul image. Especially when compared to the lovely woman who ate so neatly that he felt like a pig in his wallow, getting so self-conscious that he'd ended up with a pomegranate-soaked pastry-thing—which hadn't been a good combo.

It made him think of Bibi, or rather her shattered remnant, lying in the hospital bed and wired to the myriad machines that had sustained her for so little time. When the doctors had deemed her case hopeless, he had insisted on pulling the plugs himself.

No one, absolutely no one—especially not his brothers—were ever going to touch Bibi's life or death in any way ever again. He'd buried her beside Father and made it clear to his brothers that if they ever tried to change that, he'd first burn the winery to the ground and *then* he'd hunt them down personally. With good reason, they'd believed him and left her to lie beside the man she loved. To be sure, he had his lawyer check the graveyard once a month and leave flowers—perhaps the most expensive flower delivery service ever and worth every penny.

Bibi and Erica had both gone over cliffs and it was suddenly very important that Erica hadn't been injured or worse by her descent. Protective was not a verb he'd ever applied to himself about women, at least other than his mom. He was fast growing attached to the idea.

"I'm an expert at vacationing," he announced. "Let's go." They'd talked. She'd kept him talking until the sun was well up and the *carruggio* was lively with the first tourists.

She followed him reluctantly to her feet. "I was thinking I would go—" He could hear the word "alone" coming to the fore.

"None of that," Ridley cut her off. "First rule of vacations: no thinking." He held out an arm.

She eyed him like he was a lunatic.

"It's Italy. Even friends often walk arm-in-arm."

"And we're friends now?" Her tone was amused rather than acerbic. *Progress!*

"Sure. You know all about my evil half brothers. Now you can tell me about your evil stepsisters."

After another hesitation, she slipped her fingers around his elbow, and he barely resisted the urge to lay his free hand over them. He liked the way her light touch made him feel. Again that word "protective" wandered by uninvited.

He stopped them at the threshold. "Which way?"

"I thought you were the expert on vacationing."

"Sure, done it my whole life, I guess. On vacation, the direction doesn't matter. There's an adventure waiting along every path. It's just a matter of choosing one."

"But how do you know which…" She trailed off before completing the question. Then she looked up at him.

She barely reached his shoulder. Yet when that smile went bright and lit her eyes, she made him feel ten feet tall.

"That way," Erica pointed to the right along the *carruggio*. "I went off that way last night, but I didn't see much. What with it being dark…and all."

"And all," he acknowledged her softening tone. In the state she'd left their table, she probably could have walked square into a wall and not seen it. But asking why? Even *he* knew that would be a bad move at the moment. Instead he prompted her with, "Evil stepsisters."

"Cindy, Cin for short, is the oldest and the only one to remember her real mother before the cancer took her. Her nickname is like a stupid joke, but she could never shed it. She's the straightest-laced girl you can imagine. She has the sense of humor of a rock."

Ridley hadn't seen much of that in Erica either, but kept his mouth shut. At the first storefront, he guided her toward the door.

"What?" Erica ground to a halt.

"Store. Shopping." He knew women liked shopping.

"Where?"

He had to laugh. "See the purses?" Three leather purses and a nice sandal had been looped over a wire that had been tacked into the mortar of the stonework. The low door was cracked open against the cool morning. In the shadowed interior, he could see a narrow display counter. He swung the door open and tugged her along.

"Buongiorno," a blonde who looked more Californian hippie artist than Italian merchant greeted them. Then continued with, "Welcome into Italia." Her accent and halting English said that she was authentic despite first impressions. Also that she was sharp-eyed enough to see that Erica was newly arrived and out of her depth.

Along the stone walls were vertical racks of scarves, pretty tablecloths, and other girly things. *Jackpot.*

"All Corniglia *artisti,*" the woman waved a hand over the jewelry in the display case.

A little gaudy for Ridley's taste, but there were one or two pieces that would look good on Erica.

But she had drifted away and was inspecting a tiny purse of well-tooled leather that dangled from a long thin strap. Big enough for a wallet and a small tube of sunscreen. He kept half an eye on her as she hung it over her shoulder, twisted to look down at where it hung by her hip, then—after peeking at the price tag—hung it back up. He made a note of which one it was. Maybe he'd come by later and get it for her.

He spotted a wallet clearly done by the same artisan. He tapped the display case, *"S'il vous plaît."*

The woman giggled at him, then corrected him with, *"Per favore."*

He still had France on the brain, if no longer French women. As a matter of fact, under other circumstances, the blonde shopkeeper could be interesting. She had an easy smile and began telling him about the leatherworker in a relaxed manner far more effective than any sales tactics.

He also noticed how she slid her name, Claire, in very smoothly. Clair Dowar was an MP in *Skyfall,* but she'd kind of been a bitch, so he wouldn't use that. Claire Danes had been serious eye candy, and not half bad in *The Family Stone* that some Silicon Valley tech heiress had dragged him into. They looked enough alike for that to be a memory jog.

"Is *molto belle.*"

He'd assume Claire was talking about the wallet being very good, despite her tone. It *was* well made, with a nice feel.

"Need a new wallet?" Erica had slid up to his elbow without him noticing. There was a quietness about her that was intriguing. No flaunting, no begging for attention that was so easy to give. One moment she wasn't there, the next she simply was.

"Not really. But maybe something to remember Italy by."

"You only just arrived and you're already leaving? Let's see your old one."

He pulled it out. It looked brand new. It practically was. Belgian Cordovan leather, designer label, it reeked of money— like the Fendi jacket he'd left hanging in his room.

She didn't touch either one, just raised an eyebrow at him. Just one. Damn she was cute. She was also right.

He handed the Italian one back to Claire, who put on a very Italian pout that she clearly knew looked good on her.

"Moving along?" he asked Erica.

She nodded, and they stepped back out onto the street. He peeked through the unlit windows of a small restaurant. Seven...eight tables packed the narrow space from one stone wall to the other beneath an arched ceiling. Wine bottles lined every ledge. He couldn't quite read the chalkboard, but it looked as if the upper half was wines and the lower half food. Definitely his kind of place.

"What is it with you and wine?"

Ridley changed when he talked about wine. The casual

charmer slid away as if he'd never existed. Without naming his family's winery—which earned him points for not playing the obvious wealth card—he talked about growing up with the wine.

"I was worse than a stray dog, following Father and Marissa from the moment I could walk."

"Let me guess. Marissa is beautiful."

"A gorgeous Latina. Having a serious crush on her may be one of my first memories."

And he appeared wholly unabashed by the admission. Erica felt she should be repulsed, but there was something genuine about Ridley admitting it so freely.

"The first vines I pruned," he went right back to the important topic, the wine, and looked a little dreamy about it. "I couldn't even reach the upper branches—probably not the middle ones either. But I knew what to keep and what to drop before I hit grade school. By junior high I could tell most of our wines apart blindfolded right down to the year. Our merlot I could even tell you which field the grapes had grown in."

As he talked about things she'd never heard of from soil acidity to tensiometers (which had something to do with soil moisture and nothing to do with tension in any way she understood) to sling psychrometers versus capacitive hygrometers (whatever either of those were), Erica could see that there was structure to all of the elements. She'd never given any real thought to what went on behind a wine, but with each passing moment the complexity increased. She started to understand why they were twenty dollars or more per bottle whereas a six pack of decent beer was half that.

They ambled past a cantina, little bigger than her bedroom at the B&B but lined with three television screens all showing different soccer games. Even at this hour, several men were crowded about the tiny tables, their cappuccinos forgotten at their fingertips as they watched the screens intently.

"Isn't it a little early for soccer?"

Ridley looked around until he spotted the screens. "Season's well started I'd think. The World Cup is June, July. Something like that." So, he wasn't one of those sports guys, which was a relief. With Dwayne she'd found it useful to learn all of the Boston teams, their lineups, and records. And their primary adversaries.

"They seem awfully intent."

"It's Italy." Which was actually an interesting statement. It answered a number of questions. Why were Italian fathers pushing baby strollers at least as often as the women? It's Italy. How did they both manage to look so elegant despite the baby and a toddler running loose? It's Italy. She'd have to remember that.

For a while, Ridley even joined in a game of what else was true, just because it was Italy. It passed the time as they wandered through a kitschy souvenir shop, past a café setting up tables around a small war memorial in a tiny square dominated by two olive trees, and a gelato shop that wasn't open but would be soon. She couldn't wait to have her first Italian gelato.

The surface of the street was made up of thousands, perhaps millions of rounded beach stones all set on edge in cement. It might have been done a thousand years ago. Every stone, regardless of size, had been set so that the tops were level. The lines of stones struck patterns of light and dark, of angles and swirls. The incredible patience to do this was another thing she'd never really thought about.

For the last twelve years she'd been deep in the hustle of business. More than that if she counted the summer internships during her undergrad work at Boston College's Carroll School of Management.

And yet someone long ago had taken the time to painstakingly set every stone along the entire *carruggio*. It twisted back and forth as it narrowed toward the end. Another B&B, another shop. It was all starting to blur as the ancient stone buildings seemed to squeeze in, threatening to crush her for her presumption of coming to Italy. Or thinking she could have a life in the first place. These buildings had spanned so many centuries that her visit was less than the flap of a butterfly's wings to them. So what purpose *did* her presence serve? Here? In her life?

Up broad stone steps of slate, Ridley was still expounding on sugar content and refractometers. Was he even aware of how much he knew for someone who had never "had a job"?

Or of how little she knew of how to be a woman? How to be human? She was a walking, breathing, business machine. That's what she'd honed herself into. What possible purpose could she have here?

Ridley's hand rested easily over her frozen fingers, trapping them to his elbow. It was all that kept her from flight. Back to the B&B, back to Boston, all the way back to San Francisco. Where she would serve even less purpose than a single stone worked into this Italian street.

She needed to be gone. To get away from everyone. Everything. Herself. She could just—

"Now that's seriously awesome!" Ridley came to a halt.

Her trapped hand stopped her as well.

She blinked away the darkness and saw that they had emerged from the narrow shadows of the *carruggio*. At the very end of the street there was a small patio. It had a stout stone wall barely waist-high—all that separated them from a fifty-story plunge down into the Mediterranean.

She'd been here last night. In the dark. Sat on the wall unaware of the vast fall mere inches away. Oh, she'd seen the ocean, but she'd missed the drama. Edging up to the balustrade, she peeked over the edge. It was a sheer plunge down to the rocks and the pounding waves below. One slouch the wrong way…she shivered at the close call.

"Look, there are the other towns," Ridley was pointing down the coast. "You forget how close they are. Monterosso, Vernazza." Then he turned the other way. "Hard to see Manarola, but I think that's Riomaggiore peeking out down there."

She forced herself to look where he indicated. Slowly, so slowly, the dark spell cast on her by some evil wizard abated. The need to run back to America faded. Her desperation to lock herself in her cloistered tower eased. It took her some time, but finally she was standing in the Mediterranean sun, admiring the view, with her hand caught around a surprisingly handsome man's arm.

Erica finally managed a breath that didn't sound as if it was trying to become a whimper. If she could just hang on to…

"This gives me an idea. Stay here, I'll be right back." And Ridley was gone.

Erica could feel herself wavering unsteadily, as if she was indeed perched atop Dwayne's ass-enhancing stilt sandals.

She could do this. Piece by piece she pulled herself together. She didn't need a man. Not even one as unexpectedly pleasant as Ridley. She could look at the scenery and not think about how much of her life was on hold. Enjoying Italy didn't mean that she wasn't herself.

But there was a dark canyon there that was hard to skirt around the edges…who was *herself*? She didn't even know anymore. It was—

"Chocolate or vanilla? They had so many flavors that I

figured we better start simple and pace ourselves." Ridley held out two small cones of gelato. "I'm thinking chocolate, it matches your eyes. They're great eyes by the way."

She took the vanilla. He shrugged easily, bit into his chocolate, and made a loud yummy sound.

"So much better, don't you think?"

Erica tasted the vanilla. It *was* good. And she wasn't going to see it as a metaphor for the choices she'd made in her past. Plain vanilla.

No!

Instead, that was who she had been.

Maybe she'd find a flavor of gelato to tell her who she'd be next.

~

Ridley sat on his tiny balcony long after sunset and cradled a half-finished glass of the Cantina Cinque Terre DOC. Banana and a touch of mint on the nose. A rich lemon on the palate with a mint and salt finish. Young, fresh, full of life.

It reminded him of Bibi. Even when he was being a total shit of a male teenager, she'd never lost that gift—always finding the joy in everything. She'd laugh at his moods. Tease Father when he grew too grumpy about business problems or poor rainfall. Where had she found that endless supply?

Only once, after they'd both had too much wine, had she told him about her past. She never told him her real name, her name before Bibi, so he couldn't hunt down her bastard father and torture him to death for the abuse he'd heaped on a young girl. But he'd certainly thought about hiring a PI and doing it anyway. Except he knew it would make Bibi unhappy if he did.

"I was born that day I snuck into the theater, a half-starved street urchin, to lose myself for a few hours in a James Bond movie. I chose my name and my future and I've gotten it beyond my wildest dreams. Tell me why I would waste a minute on the past."

And now he'd met another. How could a woman look so happy about *vanilla* gelato? And yet Erica had. Who would have thought that two euros of gelato could light up a woman that much.

Yet despite spending the day together, earning him a handshake of thanks—of all ridiculous things—he still knew almost nothing about her. She was like a bottle of 1934 Private Reserve—too expensive to open and risk finding out what hid beneath the cork. Forever sealed. Traded in the blind from one collector to another but never opened.

"Never had a job." That one rankled. He hadn't been able to shed it all day. The tiny scraps that Erica let out all pointed to a deeply committed workaholic. Had he ever dated one? Not that he could think of. He'd certainly never been one.

Purpose? Drive? A dream?

What was he lacking that he had none of those?

He stared out into the night and pondered the dark hillside. Just beyond the edge of town, cliffs so steep that they'd be hard to walk soared up from the ocean. Yet every ten feet or so, a dry-laid stone wall with no cement or mortar made a little terrace. Each terrace had twenty or so vines in a tiny patch of dirt. Above it, another, then another. Stretching across the face of the hill as well. Hundreds of them were cultivated. A damn hard way to make wine.

The rolling hills of Sonoma were child's play by comparison.

He squinted at the night, but could see no answers.

Shit! He couldn't even see the questions.

CHAPTER 4

" Let's go exploring!"

She'd managed to tiptoe past Ridley's room, only to find him waiting in the café wearing a foam smile from his cappuccino. Resigned to her fate, though it didn't seem a particularly evil one, Erica joined him at the table close by Snoop's dog bed and a window overlooking the vertically-stepped vineyards.

Snoop gave an excited whimper, so she scratched his head and he thumped his fluffy tail against the bed.

Ridley gave an excited whimper and leaned his head forward.

She considered dumping his hot coffee in his lap. Her smile must have given her away because he desisted, then answered her grin.

Yesterday they had run the gamut of Corniglia, which wasn't saying much as it was a tiny hamlet with five streets. But it was geared for tourists and, with Ridley's prodding, they'd investigated it all, with far less timidity than she would have. He blustered into shops, chatted with the postman in pidgin English and Italian even lamer than her own. She wouldn't have spoken until she was sure she had the vocabulary and pronunciation at least somewhat accurate. He plunged in and was greeted with warm welcomes everywhere he went—and not only by the women.

His charm was about more than sexual attraction. There was an openness, an innate kindness that Ridley Claremont III wore as easily as his tight t-shirt—which fit him very well. Others sensed that openness (and the women surely paid attention to the chest revealed by that clingy black covering) and everyone responded. What did those same people think of her? Perhaps she didn't want to know.

They'd poked their noses into the combined city hall-school-post office, and found quiet trails leading into the vineyards that surrounded the town in every direction not bounded by a cliff.

"Well…" she hesitated a little to torture him and was touched by his pained expression. "I suppose you can come along with me, if you really want to."

He went from pained to eager faster than the gods' messenger Mercury, though he tried to hide it.

"If her ladyship doesn't feel that I'll be in the way…" he drawled out.

"Oh," she waited until he had taken a big bite of his flaky brioche. "Every princess' court needs a fool." She'd thought to say jester, but changed it at the last second, surprising herself. Fool was funnier.

He sputtered out a laugh, inhaled a mouthful of flaky pastry, and spent the next several minutes coughing and trying quick sips of his coffee, which appeared to also be burning his mouth. She did her best to behave as daintily as a princess just descended from her tower and ignore the antics of her fool, but it was very hard not to laugh in his face.

Hal served her hot chocolate and a chocolate cornetto. His tie was bright blue, covered with the black outlines of different types of train cars and engines. He winked at her, then whisked off to other tasks.

"So, Fool," she could feel the blush, but couldn't do anything to stop it. "Where are we off to today?"

~

Ridley knew that was his cue, but was having trouble answering it.

Saying "Fool" would have been funny. Saying it with the blush said just how sweet a woman Erica Barnett really was. He'd never dated sweet. If he'd ever even *met* a sweet girl, he probably hadn't noticed her.

Yet he couldn't stop noticing Erica. She never smiled without it reaching her eyes. Her laugh was as rare as it was musical. And his fingertips itched to brush at the freckles across the bridge of her nose.

Even so, there was a brittle untouchability to her that befit a princess—at least he supposed so, not that he'd met more than a couple. Bibi's parties had attracted all sorts; invitations to her Claremont Manor events had become one of the hot "gets" of the valley's social whirl. She'd been smart: mixing celebrities, chefs, and restaurateurs in a way that had also enhanced Claremont Family Wines' profile nicely.

He could almost picture Erica at one of those parties, off by herself in the library that had consumed Bibi and held so little interest for him. His mom would have liked Erica, he was sure of it.

"Where are we off to?" He repeated the question aloud to remind himself of what was actually going on here. Tossing an imaginary coin in the air, he watched it flip and spin, then snatched it and whacked it onto his wrist.

A quick peek.

A thoughtful "Hmmm" sound.

She answered with a single arched eyebrow closely followed by that killer smile.

Before he lost all ability to think, he peeked under his palm again.

"Vernazza."

"*Perché?*"

"Perch? Like the fish?" It was one of the words they'd both learned yesterday but he couldn't resist playing a little stupid.

"*Perché?* Like *why.*" Not even a glimmer that he'd been joking. It was pronounced "per-kay" but spelled like the fish with an extra e.

Then her eyes went even wider than normal as she figured out he was teasing.

"Gudgeon here," she admitted.

"Okay, that one I don't know."

"Gudgeon is a type of fish, a particularly gullible fish. It will apparently bite a dry hook as happily as a baited one. Second evil stepsister Sally joined the Navy. I guess it's a Navy saying and apparently my photo is in the US Naval Academy dictionary as the prime known example. I always fall for the straight line."

"I'll have to remember that." Actually instead of his usual, remembering that to tease her with it, he realized he needed to remember not to do it too much.

The grimace told him that it *had* been used on her far too much. He'd really have to be vigilant.

"So, perch Vernazza?" Of course, he couldn't *totally* resist.

"*Sì. Perché* Vernazza?"

"Next town that away," he pointed straight out to sea.

"That would be Gibraltar, but I get the idea."

"So, you're not a total gudgeon?"

"Not anymore. I think that finally got beaten out of me."

He wasn't aware of the rage that washed over him until she rested a hand on his clenched fist.

"Not that way. He never hit me. Just about everything else, I suppose, but not that."

And the sadness in her eyes was as deep and pure as the joy when she smiled. He hated seeing it there, as if it was a spot of Powdery Mildew or Grey Mold on the grapes that needed intensive treatment to be eradicated before it infected half the vineyard.

"Good. It saves me having to kill him. Is it okay if I just despise him?"

"I suppose someone should. The memories just make me sad."

Ridley tried to think of what to do with that. And maybe he understood Bibi's attitude toward her past just a little better. Maybe it really was best left in the past.

He held out a hand palm up as he rose from the table. She accepted the assistance to gain her feet. He hadn't appreciated how she looked earlier. Slender jeans that revealed slim legs and stopped short of ankles as fine as her hands. Today's blouse was short-sleeved and the shawl had been replaced with a brightly colored scarf of fabric too thin to do more than look nice.

Ridley tucked her hand about his elbow, suspecting that her hand wouldn't stay in his long no matter how nice it felt, and led her out the door.

"I knew a very wise woman once. She had a thing or two to say about the past."

"What was that?" Erica voice remained soft and sad.

"She said 'Who gives a shit?'"

"I suppose I do," she answered it matter-of-factly rather than laughing as he'd intended. They stepped out of the *carruggio* and onto the busy street—busy in relative terms. A small bus waited in the tiny square. He was fairly sure that it was the shuttle to the train station at the foot of the cliff. Even as he approached to ask, an equally small garbage truck backed up, square into its back end. There was a crunch of glass as a taillight and a back window shattered.

They were almost to the windshield at that point and could plainly see the driver. He'd been lounging in his seat reading the sports section of a newspaper, but was nearly jolted out of his seat. He tossed the paper down on the dashboard, slammed open the door, and descended to confront the garbage truck driver, who had also climbed down to see the damage.

The bus driver gave a "You-idiot!" shrug, holding both hands aloft, gripping the air, then they started yelling at each other. Clearly the garbage driver thought the bus should be parked ten feet over, closer to the tourist street. The bus driver was holding two fingers in front of his own eyes asking if the garbage driver was blind. With the broad gesticulations all Italians used, it was fairly easy to follow the argument.

"I don't think the bus is leaving any time soon." He couldn't tell if Erica was being dryly humorous or simply realistic. Knowing her, probably the latter.

"That leaves the stairs for us," he turned her about. They'd discovered them yesterday.

When he'd remarked on there being 382 steps down from the town to the station, Erica, of course, had more information.

"One guide book said 388 and another states 365, one for each day of the year. It makes me feel sad for leap years. Why is it that the outliers always get left out? I'll have to count them for myself one of these days. Though if it turns out to be 365, it will always make me feel a little sad, so maybe I shouldn't."

She'd said it all as if such trains of thought were perfectly normal. Maybe they were for her. There was a fascinating mixture of the concrete and the fanciful. Ridley had merely thought, "Wow! That's a lot of steps," and been content with that.

"A year of steps it is," she waved him to lead the way. Others were making the same decision. They headed up the road in a loose band that gave the day a slightly festive feel. As they walked up the road to the head of the steps, her silence let him think back to her earlier remark.

"So, you *suppose* that you give a shit about the past?" If she was going to open up, even a sliver, he wasn't going to let the opportunity drop.

"I seem to." She didn't sound happy about it.

"Perch."

"Perch? Oh, *Perché?* See, I warned you I was a gudgeon."

"Just answer the question, Erica."

"Why?" She murmured it more to herself than to him.

They reached the long stairway of red brick. It was wide, well-built, clearly meant for tourists. It wound its way down the face of the cliff in switchbacks rarely more than fifteen or twenty steps along. Unlike the *carruggio* with its uneven stone surface, the brick was laid flat and solid without a single wiggle. Nice, modern craftsmanship. And he took a bet with himself that the *carruggio* would still be standing five hundred years after these steps had slid into the sea.

But a man felt safe escorting a lady down such steps, as if he was helping her descend from her throne. He wanted to laugh and share the image with her, but when he glanced over. She appeared deep in thought, so he kept his silence.

The "Fool" escorting the princess? How many times had he

been the fool, escorting some woman around because they looked good together or because she was fun. Never thinking one bit deeper. A quick review suggested that he walked as thoughtlessly out of relationships as he walked into them. He never failed to deliver on his promises...by never promising.

So he wasn't deep. *Sue me!*

But Erica was deep; deep like an unplumbed well. So deep that he half wondered what would happen to him if he fell in?

❧

Why *did* she give a darn about the past?

No, that wasn't the question.

Why did she give a *shit* about the past?

Not a harsh bone in your pretty, little body, Dwayne used to tease her.

Well, maybe with his help, she was finally developing some.

So why *did* she give a shit? Dwayne had been all about himself. It was always about him. She'd learned to ask about his day, his worries. He'd complimented her ideas on how to run the business, but always proposed them as his own. That had been fine—she was just the business manager; he was the boss. It's the way it was supposed to be.

Wasn't it?

That niggling sensation that she'd long since learned to deeply respect poked at her for the first time since...since she couldn't recall. All the way back to her babysitting days—when a client's husband tried to take her for more of a ride than a trip home—that voice had been with her. Thankfully so had the can of mace that Stephen had purchased and insisted that she carry.

She'd learned to listen to those tiny warnings. She'd taken to calling it the quiet voice of her inner brain.

So where were you during the Dwayne years? Huh?

No answer. Not that there'd ever been one when she asked something directly.

But now it was telling her that her role in Dwayne's business was yet another thing she'd misread. He'd taken her ideas as his own because it was just the kind of manipulative— she took a breath—*bastard!* that he was.

So why did she give a *shit* about Dwayne? Why did she care one little…

"I need a better swear word."

"What's the context?"

"Huh?" She looked up at Ridley in surprise. They were standing among a loose crowd on a long train platform. He held a pair of passes that she hadn't noticed him purchasing. She'd been in plenty of train stations, and not a one of them had been like this. Corniglia perched atop the cliff high above them. To the right and left, train tunnels punched into the cliffs like black fists. The tracks themselves lay out in the open air mere feet above the crashing sea.

"Wow!" was all she could unimaginatively manage. Apparently exclamations today were as elusive as appropriate curses. Maybe she should take a course on swearing and exemplary exclamations of wonder and surprise. Perhaps there was an online course.

"You need a context for a good swear word. Swearing with the standard seven really doesn't cut it."

"The standard seven?"

"Old George Carlin routine. He actually updated it to eleven. You gotta watch the video. He was hilarious."

"Okay, I need something besides the standard seven or eleven or whatever to describe how little I care about what someone in my past thinks."

"Scatological version: squat—with all the implications of what you do while squatting over a toilet. Direct version: shit."

"Already used that one."

"Lower life form: rat's ass. Complex:—"

"No. No. Stop! That's perfect! I don't give a *rat's ass* about Dwayne. Talk about a lower life form. No, let's not talk about him. Whoever told you not to give a *rat's ass* about the past at all was a very wise woman."

"My mom."

"Wish I could have met her."

She stretched up on her toes and kissed his check as the train roared into the station. It blew her hair into his face, burying him in Erica's warm scent. His mind tried to label, categorize, and evaluate. No hint of lemon or lime so indicative of the Cinque Terre wines he'd had so far. No earthy tones. Not nut or fruit. Neither woody nor mineral. He couldn't pin it down. It was like a whole new array of scents he'd never encountered before in all his years.

It only lasted an instant, then she was back on her heels with the top of her head barely reaching his chin.

As the last of the clatter of the wheels rattled down the track, the sorrows of the past had moved from her to him. If only Bibi *was* still alive to meet Erica.

CHAPTER 5

*V*ernazza unfolded like a miracle.

The train shot in and out of tunnels. The Mediterranean flashed into being and disappeared again like a strobe light. Inside, the car echoed with rattles, metallic wheezes, and dozens of conversations. Most were Italian, adding layers upon Cinque Terre layers. But there was a cosmopolitan air that somehow even San Francisco and Boston lacked. German ground past French and wound around something that she guessed was middle European. For a few, the ride was mundane; for most, it was adventure.

It wasn't rebirth. She definitely wasn't there. The Fairy Godmother's wand-bop on the nose was still totally MIA. But there was a…lightness. Yes, a lightness that hadn't been with her in a long time. Perhaps even lighter than when she'd believed herself safely in love with Dwa— Yes, with him.

They ascended from the Vernazza train station on the Via Roma and she dragged Ridley into the first gelato shop. She could see two more further down the street, but this one was first and somehow that, too, mattered.

Yesterday she'd opted for chocolate for her afternoon gelato, feeling a little guilty at indulging twice in one day. Ridley had laughed at her lack of adventure, but she'd wanted to build slowly, layering on the experience.

"What's the flavor to start the day?"

Ridley missed her joke about planning to have gelato twice in one day again. Surely that was the very essence of being on vacation?

"Ridley? Erica to Ridley?"

"Um," he blinked in surprise as if he didn't know where he was.

"Gelato. Flavor. Important decisions here."

"You go first." It was like he'd been out of focus and was only partway back.

She turned to the long glassed-in display. Despite it only being midmorning, they were already doing a brisk business. She had to peek in between and among other patrons to see the flavors. It took some doing. A good gelato shop in Boston, where they were few and far between, boasted perhaps a dozen flavors. There must be thirty or more here and each a different color just begging to be tried. Every one raked into elegant swirls making each look more sumptuous than the one before.

She saw some of the patrons asking for a taste of this and a taste of that. Each time they were handed a tiny plastic tasting spoon with a little gelato on it.

Not for her. If she was on vacation, she was going to take the plunge.

But where to begin? There wasn't just *Limone* with its bright yellow color and—hint, hint—slices of lemon tucked in the corners of the tray. There was also *Limone e Basilico* and a pair of basil leaves atop the lemon slices told her that it wasn't lemon with balsamic vinegar. There was pineapple, mango, and many fruits she recognized. Then there were ones for the wildly adventurous: "Pine Tree" and "Indian Cinnamon."

There was a whole category of *sorbettos* but she hadn't come all the way to Italy to have a sorbet when the siren call of gelato echoed through the shop.

"Pistachio," she called out when a server looked her way.

The server held up a tasting spoon and she shook her head. "Cone," she tried to make a pointed shape.

"*Cono,*" he responded as he pulled one out. "*Uno, due, tre?*"

Three! No way could she eat three scoops. She held up a single finger.

The man teased her back holding up two fingers.

"*No! Uno.*" She answered with one.

"*Sì, due,*" he had a nice smile. "*Pistachio, sì?*"

"Wow, pistachio," Ridley whispered close beside her ear. "Such adventure."

"Pistachio with Nutella," she told the server.

When Ridley started to laugh, she managed to elbow him sharply enough to make him grunt. "Be silent, Fool. Or take your jokes to another court."

"As my lady commands," he whispered before turning to the server. "*Cono. Due. Sorbetto Di Fra-go-lay?*" He stumbled over the last.

"It's strawberry to you, buddy," the Italian server offered in perfect English and scooped him a double ball stacked atop the tiny cone. Erica noticed that her single scoop was only a tiny bit smaller. She paid while Ridley continued stumbling about the word until the server finally put him out of his misery. "*Frag-o-la.*"

"*Fragola,*" Ridley muttered to himself a few times as they wandered back onto the street. She was doing the same, but she kept it inside.

The first taste of her gelato exploded with cool flavor. First the heavy chocolate of the hazelnut Nutella. But close behind it ran the cheery zing of pistachio calling out, "Here I am. Here I am." As if a mythical brownie had gotten brief control of her tongue. It was a merry flavor that made her want to laugh.

Far more than the cliff-top eyrie of Corniglia, Vernazza showed that this seaside resort knew the origin of the bulk of its income. Every storefront was open and filled. No three purses and a tied-up sandal here. The signs weren't obtrusive like American shops, but they were there. The large windows showed a much greater stock. Attractive racks just outside the door made any signs irrelevant. Beach gear, postcards and knick-knacks, a cluster of umbrellaed tables to mark a restaurant and a chalkboard of what they actually served. The small tables outside made it easy to interpret the price without a menu: Small tables of well-painted wire mesh and tiny folding chairs—affordable. Similar tables but preset with napkins and silverware—moderately priced. Tablecloth—whoops! No need to look at those price tags. Only the largest enterprises took up two storefronts. Most would have tucked into her old apartment living room at Newbury and Exeter in Boston's Back Bay.

Like Corniglia, Vernazza's buildings were three to four stories of stone—most built separately by their stonework, but standing solidly against each other to create a unified front. There was less stone and more stucco, all done in classic Tuscan colors that seemed to soothe her eyes after so many years of dreaming about them. Soft golds abounded. Gentle blue blended. And everywhere were variations of terracotta red that just made her want to curl up here and never leave.

The unknown yet large number of steps to Corniglia did indeed keep the tourists at bay. They were ten times thicker here. They came in by ferry boats (which didn't stop at Corniglia) and by tour buses (of which only the most suicidal attempted the town—as she'd discovered to her dismay among the olive trees). They didn't jostle yet, apparently that came with the summer, but there were certainly bustling crowds of them everywhere she turned.

Yet she and Ridley, walking arm-in-arm, didn't cause problems or logjams as they would have on any American sidewalk. Perhaps it was because they were being so Italian in their *passeggiata*—their leisurely walk. Tourists certainly hustled by them, not wishing to miss a thing. And though the Italian couples moved even slower the she and Ridley, they were more in tune with the Italians than the foreigners.

"I think we're doing pretty good for our second day." And she was glad Ridley was along. Partly for kicking her butt about the past, but partly because it was more fun to explore with two than one.

"Depends. How's your gelato?"

"Luscious. How's yours?"

Instead of answering, he held it out for her to taste. Such a simple gesture, but it took her a moment to figure out what to do with it. It was one of what Dwayne had called her "crazy buttons" though he'd learned to respect it. If he reached out to taste her meal at a restaurant, she'd just shove the whole plate over and be done with it, her stomach winding in knots. She'd never starved or even been unable to afford a meal, so that wasn't it. But she remembered the first time she'd bought her own meal in a diner at thirteen with her own money—she'd earned it and it was hers, by god.

Yet Ridley was simply offering her a taste, with no agenda that she could see. Steeling herself (against what she had no idea) she leaned over and took a tiny taste. The sorbet was icier than her gelato, grainier. But the strawberry bloomed to life in her mouth.

"It's like bottled springtime."

His laugh was easy, "Guess it is. May I?" He nodded toward her own pistachio-Nutella.

It would be rude to not reciprocate. Another breath, and she held it out.

He took a bite and considered, almost as if he was tasting a wine. "The chocolate is a little far forward for my taste. It sort of overwhelms the pistachio. No. No…the nut is there in the finish. Maybe the hazelnut is conflicting with the pistachio. I'll have to try a pure pistachio one next and compare."

He continued leading them forward among the shops.

Erica looked down at her cone and the neat divot that his teeth had cut into the gelato.

No big deal. The world hadn't ended. And he did ask first. She wondered what he would have said if she'd told him no. He'd probably have given one of his easy laughs and asked, "Perch?"

Maybe she'd simply disliked sharing with Dwayne.

"And what does that tell you, girl?"

"Hmm?" Ridley looked over at her.

In answer she took a big bite right on top of his. Within seconds she had to clap a hand over the right side of her face while making "Ow!" noises with a full mouth.

"Brain freeze! Brain freeze!" Ridley couldn't help laughing as Erica alternated between scowling at him with one eye squinched up, then again slapping a hand across half her face and going "Oo! Oo! Oo!"

He'd nearly done it to himself on his first bite, only narrowly dodging the bullet.

"Oh my god!" She gasped out and he looked at where she was pointing, her pain apparently forgotten. "I'm here."

"We certainly are."

The street had ended with a bend and an abruptness as sudden as a train tunnel. They stood on the threshold of a broad piazza. Up to the right, the town climbed a narrow ravine in tightly packed buildings painted in a myriad of soft tones. Across the way, a tall church with an even taller steeple dominated the scene. To the left, their side of the town trailed along the side of a promontory. And before them, down a wide ramp, lay one of the prettiest little harbors he'd ever scene.

The piazza might be covered with groups of Crayola-brilliant umbrellas but it was clear that, during the hard winters, it was where the fishing boats had been pulled up the ramp to keep them out of harm's way. A great fleet of small boats must have once fished from this port. Now a dozen craft —perhaps fifteen feet long and most painted a cheery blue— bobbed on the gentle waves. The harbor itself was broad but didn't have any of the larger craft. The massive tourist yachts that completely overshadowed nearby Portofino's wooded harbor were nowhere to be seen. Only smaller craft for Vernazza.

"Never been a boat guy myself, but this place makes it easy to imagine becoming one." No sailboats. Skiffs with oars and motors. Working craft. It was like the actual guts of the winery, not the long rows of aging barrels and posh tasting rooms that were shown to the tourists. Instead, it was the vintner's cluttered desk, the log book, and a tasting glass. That was the true core of a winery. That was the bones. The bones of the town here might be old, but they were laid bare for all to see.

During his moment of inattention, Erica was gone from his side.

He caught sight of her easily—she stood out in any crowd despite being short. She was hurrying down along the wharf. Practically bouncing off other tourists as she kept looking over her shoulder like all the demons of hell were after her.

It reminded him of the first night...*Christ! The one before last, was that all?* When she'd sprinted into the night. Well, this time he was going to follow her and find out what the hell was wrong.

He gulped down the last of the gelato and rather than detouring for the broad ramp, jumped down over the low balustrade almost landing in some poor sucker's impromptu picnic.

He tried to mutter out an apology, but that's when the brain freeze hit him square in the eye.

Screw it!

He blundered ahead, not even bothering to mutter apologies. Made it to the edge of the ramp. Squinted his wincing eye open long enough to estimate the height, and jumped again. Thankfully that got him to the bottom level, only a few feet above the harbor. It was wide and he broke into a lopsided run, still barely closing the distance.

Damn she was fast.

She finally slowed, which was good as she was almost out of pier.

A few hesitant steps. Hanging her head forward over her hands as he rushed up behind her.

"There!" Erica spun back toward him, raising her hand as she did so, smacking him hard enough in the nose to make him cry out in pain.

"Are you all right?" They shouted in unison as he now held one hand over his frozen eye (which was thankfully easing off) and the other testing his nose (which he suspected had only just begun to throb).

"Ridley? Are you okay? I'm so sorry."

"Forged aboud be!" Okay, no blood. Maybe his nose wasn't so bad. "Whad aboud doo?" Or maybe it was. It hurt to even talk.

"What about me?"

He nodded and wished he hadn't.

"I found it."

"Whad?"

"This," she held her phone up in front of his face.

He had to struggle to focus his one functioning eye. It was a photo. A photo of… He turned and looked over his shoulder. And he recognized it as exactly the same gesture Erica had been doing—looking back over her shoulder at the town of Vernazza.

It was the same perspective, but there hadn't been time for her to take the photo. Then he saw that while the photo had a single little blue boat anchored in the foreground, there was now a pair of them.

"I donn ged id." He wiggled his nose again. It was definitely still attached, but *ow!*

"Years ago I told my stepdad that I wanted to go to Italy someday. He was broke, but I was too little to know that and I asked him to take us all there. For Christmas he bought me a little poster, this poster," she held the photo on her phone up to his face again. "And now…." She aimed the phone carefully and he heard the bright snick of the shutter. And another.

Her hands fell to her side and he plucked the phone from her nerveless fingers so that she didn't drop it overboard into the harbor. He waved her a step or two into the picture and tried to line it up the same way.

"No. I—"

"You can always delete it later, but you shouldn't. You get to be in the picture." But she didn't look happy about it.

"I thought somebody had tried to knife you or something."

It earned him a hint of a smile.

"You know you gave me a total brain freeze when I panicked and raced after you."

"Ate your sorbet before coming to the rescue of a damsel in distress? Doesn't sound very knightly."

"I'm not a knight. I'm the court fool per your ladyship's command. Besides, for something as important as sorbet, I can multitask."

He caught the edge of her laugh. It wasn't a big one, but it was enough to light her up as brightly as the town wrapped around behind her.

~

Erica flicked through the photos to make sure she'd captured the place, the moment. There it was.

Vernazza. Brightly painted little boats bobbing on the quiet water—except at long last it was *her* photo, not some nameless photographer's. Then the startling image of her standing there. Standing there and laughing.

She had never pictured herself in the image.

But she looked up. There was the real town. She looked down at herself. And here she was. It was so weird that it was almost surreal.

It was as if she had finally come into focus. She could see the twists and turns like the *carruggio* of her life. The youngster's dreams. The teen's hopes. And the mixture of everything since. She loved business and had become damn good at it. Even during the personal-life aberration of the last two years, she was proud of what she'd achieved.

And who she'd become. By whatever convoluted path, that dreamer of a little girl was now standing square in the piazza of her life. Maybe the past had included trolls, even dragons. And the future might include more. And while she wasn't exactly a white-knight-on-a-charger sort of gal, she could see that she wasn't the lonely handmaiden either. Others had made her feel that way.

No, take responsibility, Erica.

She'd *let* others make her feel that way.

So done with that. So completely, absolutely—she'd have to solicit another appropriate curse word from Ridley—done with that!

Then she flicked to the last pair of photos.

A passing tourist had offered to take their picture together and Ridley had handed him her phone before stepping over beside her.

He'd silently raised his arm in question.

She had, of course, never hugged Dwayne anywhere in public...which was another stupid, stupid clue. It wasn't that he didn't like to hug; it was that he didn't want to get caught with his mistress. She got it now... *Little bit late, Erica.*

She had slid under Ridley's arm and clasped him around the waist—hard. The tourist had snapped two photos, the first with her looking fierce and him looking shocked.

The second one though... In that one they'd both been smiling. She could still see the fierceness—and his surprise—but it didn't make the truth of the moment—the joy of it—any less real.

It had felt good. Really good. And she wasn't ready for that. Maybe she wasn't a knight-errant, but she was done with being cowed.

She held up her phone to Ridley, who looked at the photo for a long moment.

"It's a good photo," his voice was carefully neutral.

"It is." She blanked her phone and tucked it in her pocket.

But that wasn't the problem. She dropped onto a stone bench.

"You've got to get away from me, Ridley."

"Why's that?" And he sat right next to her as if he couldn't see the red warning triangles springing to life all around her. "Other than you punching me in the nose?"

"I didn't— I wasn't— Never mind."

"Not getting off that easy, lady. So, Perch?"

"Perch? Oh, *perché.* See? I'm so bad I can't even remember a joke for ten minutes. Why? Because I'm a total mess. I'm such a mess that I don't even know which parts of me are me."

"Well we know one thing, you're an incredibly lovely mess."

"Don't!" And then she buried her face in her hands.

"Don't what?"

"See? I can't even let you pay me a compliment because I don't know if it's me or—" she was *not* going to say his name "—some rat's ass trying to manipulate me. You need to just go. Look, Ridley. You're a nice man."

"No I'm not." He said it as enough of a growl that she almost looked up at him.

"You just need to get away from me while you still can."

"Before what? Before you turn me into a *not* nice man? Good luck with that. Already did that myself."

Maybe if she never looked up again, he'd retreat while he still could.

The silence stretched. Unable to hold her hands to her face any longer—when did hands become so impossibly heavy?—she let them drop into her lap. By her view of his boots, she could see that Ridley was still there.

"I just..." But she didn't know what.

"Erica—"

She could only shake her head to silence him.

Again it stretched thin. They were in their own little sonic bubble. Tourists' feet passed by, but made no sound. A nearby fisherman started his boat engine and motored slowly away, but she couldn't hear a thing.

She was in the place she'd always dreamed of coming and it was as if she'd come full circle…on nothing.

"In a goddamn pig's eye!" Ridley sounded furious.

He grabbed her shoulders hard enough to make her yelp in surprise. His hands were big, powerful. They clamped on and she was helpless to resist as he forced her to turn to him.

"I'm *not* a nice guy, Erica. Trust me on that. You make me want to be, and that's giving me some major issues. But to hell with that for the moment. I'm *not* nice. I'm the guy who comes along, woos you blind, beds you but good, buys you some goddamn trinkets to remember him by, and rides off well before sunrise. I'm the total shit they always warned you about. By the way, the phone number I'd leave on your dresser? It connects to a Chinese take-out place in Sausalito. I'm just a rich asshole of a guy with a few manners plastered over the surface for me to get what I want."

"No…" That wasn't right. He was the man who'd made her laugh over cornetti and try new flavors of gelato. He was her expert on vacationing and—

"Trust me. Meeting someone like you only throws it into sharp relief. I've never had any problem with that, I know what I am."

His brief grimace told her he was less content with that than he liked.

"But whatever degenerate asshole made you think you're less than amazing, he's the one who's pissing me off. You *are* beautiful. You! The woman right here in front of me. Funny even when you don't mean to be. You have an honesty that runs so deep that every feeling shines out of those gorgeous eyes of yours. And I'd wager there's a sharp brain hiding in there was well. That I can't pay you a simple compliment without you flinching away, that's making me beyond pissed off. I—"

A polished wooden staff came between them, making them both jolt back to the limits of his hands still clenched around her shoulders.

"Are you okay, *signorina?*" An Italian policeman asked her softly in rough English as his police baton lay across Ridley's forearms.

"No, but it isn't his fault. He's trying to help."

"*Signore* will drop his hands, *per favore.*" He tapped his wooden baton lightly on Ridley's forearms. A small crowd had gathered to observe the goings on.

Ridley made a show of opening his hands slowly and then dropping them to his lap.

The break of connection was too abrupt. Too much was whirling in her brain that she still didn't understand. She wished she had a recording of what he'd just said to her. The words had blurred beneath the weight of his fury on her behalf.

On *her* behalf.

When was the last time someone had defended her? When was the last time she had?

Erica reached out and took his hand in hers, despite the looming police officer. The guy was slender, but his shoulders and his sidearm said not to underestimate him. Nor his far grimmer looking partner standing a few feet farther back—his palm casually on a taser.

But despite the way Ridley had just handled her and yelled at her, Erica took his hand. First eyeing him, then the officer with those big browns of hers.

"It's okay, officer. He's a friend. He *is* trying to help."

Is that what he'd been doing? He didn't even know. He felt

like a poker player who'd dropped his cards face up on the table and now was supposed to play.

But that someone could make a woman like her feel so small just made him want to—

"Ow!" Her squeak of pain as he crushed her fingers in his hand had the policeman's baton catching him sharply enough under the chin to force Ridley to look up at him.

"Sorry," he managed, barely able to swallow past the baton. Ridley attempted to withdraw his hand. But still, Erica held onto it.

The policeman turned to his partner and they traded some fast Italian back and forth. He hoped he was wrong about hearing *arrestiamo* in there somewhere. It sounded like a question. Not good.

"Maybe you should let go of my hand, Erica. They think I'm trapping you."

Instead she laced her fingers more deeply in his. Then, with her free hand she tapped the officer on the arm.

He looked down at her as they were both still seated.

"Watch," was all she said.

Ridley watched her and could only wonder. It was as if a different woman sat beside him. She had great posture, but now it was exquisite.

"Eh?"

With a surety that he'd never seen in her before, Erica leaned over and kissed Ridley on the lips. And not just a little kiss. She kissed him like she'd meant to anyway and wasn't merely demonstrating his innocence.

The smell of her hair had been nothing compared to the taste of her. The richness of a Barolo, with the sweetness of a Glacière, and the aged depth of a Burgundy Grand Cru. And the heat! Her lips were warmer than sunbaked grapes near bursting on the vine.

The baton slid away from the bottom of his chin and the officer might have said, "*Ah, amore.*" But Ridley couldn't be sure because his senses were on complete overload. He touched her only at their interlaced fingers and their lips, but it was more than enough to trigger a synergistic circulation of energy greater than any vintner's peristaltic wine-transfer pump running at full bore.

"Whoa," he managed to mumble. "Just…whoa!" He placed his free hand on her shoulder and eased her back. It took him a moment to recover enough to gasp out, "What the hell was that?"

"It worked, didn't it?"

"What worked? What are you talking about? Making my blood boil from overheating?"

"The police, silly."

He looked around and they had indeed moved along. The crowd had dispersed as well, though several passersby were giving them knowing smiles.

"That was your whole plan? To kiss me until they went away?" Then why were Ridley's ears still ringing?

She offered a very Italian shrug that said "of course." He didn't buy it. He didn't want to buy it. Not after a kiss like that. But he'd already learned that her emotions always showed and they weren't, except…

"Your ears are bright red."

She shook her hair forward to cover them, but he reached up to brush one into the clear, enjoying the soft feel of her cheek.

"You blush ears first?" As if she wasn't cute enough already.

Erica sighed. "I do," as the warm glow extended, finally, to her cheeks.

"Good to know," and he knew what came next:

awkwardness, hesitancy, maybe even regret. "So, what do I have to do to get another one of those? *Beat up* a cop?"

She glanced after where they'd gone. "I don't know. They look pretty tough."

"You're right, they do. Maybe if I find an old Italian woman..."

"I wouldn't try it," she glanced at him, then away, but not soon enough to hide her smile. "Have you seen these old Italian women? I wouldn't dare take one on."

"I think my manliness has just been insulted."

Erica finally turned to face him. "No, if that kiss was any indication at all, your manliness has nothing whatsoever to fear."

"What in the world am I supposed to do with you?"

She narrowed her eyes at him, but he wasn't willing to explain.

She'd said it as if it was simple fact. Not a tease. Not a joke. Simply a statement. Goddamn woman confounded the crap out of him.

"I think you're supposed to be teaching me about vacationing," she went for the nearest subject change.

His own thoughts didn't follow. Instead he should be finding the nearest hotel room to drag her into and to hell with waiting for the train back to Corniglia.

"Come on," Erica rose to her feet and their still-clasped hands had him rising to his own. "Look, there's a tower."

Look, there's a tower? Was that the lamest line ever in the history of womanhood? Definitely in the slender volume *Erica: Womanhood of - a study.* Very thin. And very lame.

His kiss...his *amazing* kiss...had snapped her back to her

senses. She supposed that maybe Ridley was right about being the bad boy—but he was *so good* at it. If Ridley could deliver on even a tenth of that kiss' promise, maybe she'd sign up for a course entitled: *Bad Boys: How to Find and Never Tame Them.*

She could feel a wildness in her. She had no reference for that. Barely knew what it was, but it had her thinking crazy thoughts that didn't seem very Erica-like. Good thing or bad thing?

Unknown.

So instead, she'd fallen back on the lamest line in the book: *Look, there's a tower.*

Of course there was a tower. This was Vernazza, Italy. The ancient fort loomed over the harbor entrance, carved into the cliff face that soared upward from the inner edge of the modern breakwater.

Ridley fell in beside her without remarking on her record-worthy lame-i-tude. Maybe, just maybe, he needed a moment after that kiss as well. Again, good thing or bad thing? She couldn't tell. He'd seemed to enjoy it, hadn't he? Her mind was blurring again.

The fort. Somewhere around here was the fort. Right! Directly in front of them. She clung to the idea of the fort like an anchor in a storm. An apt metaphor in a harbor town. Did she get a bonus for that? No, because she hadn't connected that beforehand. She really needed to stop talking to herself.

The far side of the harbor was a near vertical wall—so steep that it barely had the terraced grape vineyards. The town spilled from the head of the ravine down to the water, reaching a last thin trailer of buildings along the inside of the cliff that curled protectively around the harbor. Beyond the end of the cliff, the broad, overly geometric, modern breakwater narrowed the harbor mouth even further, creating a place to stroll and watch sunsets over waves.

But historically the town had ended with the great fort built against pirate raids of half a millennium before.

Here, at the point closest to the ocean, were the fanciest restaurants and shops. The white linen tablecloths were preset with silverware and both thin and round wine glasses. A greeter stood casually nearby and waved them toward a table.

"Welcome to Italy," he called in happy English (England English, but thick with charming Italian). "Come. Come. We have a wonderful sea bass caught just this morning," he wave toward the sea. Then he continued, pointing to the mountains, "I have also imported from Lake Como very fresh perch. Come. Come."

Erica couldn't help herself and laughed in his face. "*Scusi. Scusi,*" was all she managed as she scurried by. Ridley's belly laugh wasn't helping matters.

"He said 'perch.' I couldn't help myself," she whispered as soon as they were clear.

"Tell me about it," Ridley was still chuckling.

"He said 'per—' Oh. You're agreeing, not asking me to tell you about it."

And that friendly laugh of his rolled out again and included her. By their joined hands, he tugged her in and kissed her on the nose. It was a happy gesture, rather than a meaningful one. It was just that he was happy to be with her for the moment, so why was she busy overthinking it?

Because rat's-ass ex-boss would have used it to kiss her whenever *he* wanted as a demonstration of control. Ridley was merely glad to be with her.

Stop thinking, Erica. Good advice? Or was that what had trapped her in the first place? And here she was, thinking again.

Fort. Follow the fort.

The entrance to the stairs was easy enough to find and she

plunged into the narrow passage with the relief of entering a swimming pool on a hot day.

It rose in short, steep flights carved into the stone, making it impossible to still hold hands. Maybe that too was a relief.

A little sign said "Just 9 to Go" in Italian and English. A couple squeezed by them on their way down—it was all there was room for.

The next turn said "8."

At "5 More" she realized that with the steepness of the stairs, her behind was right at Ridley's eye level. The Erica Barnett she knew would have been horrified by the thought. The Erica Barnett who had just kissed a man on the Vernazza waterfront for the police and everyone else to see hoped he enjoyed the view.

That thought almost made her stumble. She really did hope that he enjoyed it. She'd had a taste and was slowly realizing that she wanted more. More what, she wasn't exactly sure. But more Ridley Claremont III was definitely a part of that.

"Just 2 More Turns."

She looked up, but the carved stone ceiling showed no signs of ending. The stairway itself twisted and turned as it snaked its way upward. She could imagine ancient Italian fighters defending each turn to the death. Swords ringing against iron shields. No room for a bow. It was a hand-to-hand sort of corridor. Her intellect knew it must have been a bloody and awful affair, but there was a fanciful air to a battle so long gone.

"Last 1!"

Erica hurried up the last flight toward a bright wash of light.

At the top of the flight, the stairway twisted left and continued upward. But straight ahead was a tiny open patio carved into the cliff.

"Oh, this is lovely." Ridley came up beside her.

And it was. They'd progressed high up the cliff and their efforts were rewarded with a peekaboo view out over the harbor and the piazza. But that wasn't what had captured her attention.

"Look," she pointed behind them.

Ridley turned, then shrugged his confusion. Nice shoulders. He had such nice shoulders. Erica forced her attention away.

She tapped the sign. "Gallery Zero." It was posted beside a wide open door that led into what had probably been the old guard room. A few nice art prints propped on easels invited them in.

"Huh," was Ridley's brilliant comment and made her want to giggle. He was *so* male. Rat's-ass boss was practically effeminate by comparison. Perhaps effete was a better word. Always so careful about how he presented himself and how he was perceived. Ridley was simply...Ridley.

"The marketing of it. The countdown. They upped our anticipation with such simple little signs. Made us eager to reach zero. And now that we have, how could we resist going in?"

"I didn't even notice that, but you're right. They totally nailed me." Then he smiled down at her. "Told you there was brain in the beauty."

Erica could feel her ears starting to heat up and stepped into the gallery.

～

Ridley watched her go and admired the view.

Everything about Erica was neat. Her hair, her gestures, that fine behind of hers, which had so distracted him during the ascent—those were the least of it. He too had seen the signs, but she had cataloged, categorized, and instantly understood the full implications of their purpose. Even the strategy behind it.

Bringing a picture of a childhood poster on her phone so that she could find the exact spot.

She'd even found the perfect solution for the policeman. A single gesture that an hour of protesting his innocence could never have achieved.

Erica's mention that she'd been a business manager had been an offhand, castaway comment. His guess was that she'd been a damn good one. He hoped that whoever the rat's ass was, he was missing Erica's skills badly.

He ducked to clear the low doorway and followed her into the gallery.

It was a small space of low stone, just high enough for him to stand without flinching at every step. Rather than feeling cramped, they had again been smart in their marketing. He tried to see it through Erica's eyes. The display cases were stocked without being tight-packed, which might have felt cramped, and were brightly lit. Other lights highlighted the pale-painted stone as if it too was of interest. A flip rack of prints to one side. A postcard spinner to another, letting you see all of the art twice—simple reinforcement. A low display of leather work—it was more commercial than the work of the Corniglia artist, but even a glance revealed the obvious quality. And three open shelves of jewelry. A lone woman in her fifties sat off to one side.

"Welcome!" She called with a brightly American accent.

Ridley blinked at her in surprise.

"Yes, I'm American. Two girlfriends and I always wanted to go to Italy. Clara, the painter, made it first. She made us come visit her. Our art was portable, our ex-husbands were not, so we came." She held up a half-made bracelet of intricate beading to demonstrate that the jewelry was hers.

"Living the dream?"

"Twenty years now. We take turns working here in the gallery. It is not a burden," and her smile confirmed that. He could hear the Italian inflections that had worked into her language. Her flowing blouse and bright summer skirt said that she'd gone Italian in more ways than one.

He also recognized the smile of interest, or at least curiosity. It was a look he knew well. In answer, he took a step toward Erica. The shopkeeper was good—her smile didn't diminish, it just shifted to a simple welcome.

Erica was flipping through the prints. Watercolors mostly. He spotted the harbor, Corniglia, and what he presumed were the other three towns of Cinque Terre. A painting of Portofino showed it with just a few boats and revealed the uncluttered beauty that a tourist would wish to remember rather than the over-crowded "place to be seen" that it was.

"She's good."

Erica nodded and kept flipping.

"But your picture captures it better."

She did one of her quizzical looks and left him wondering just what she was thinking. She turned back to the posters and he realized that even not underestimating her, he'd been underestimating her. He'd seen a cute, screwed-over, kind-of-messed-up woman that wasn't his type at all but, hey, a woman was a woman.

Unless the woman was Erica Barnett. He liked more and more as they spent time together rather than his usual less and less.

She was damned smart no matter what she said. Full scholarships weren't given to sixteen-year-old underachievers. He'd loafed through school, enjoying the parties, playing third base (even making the varsity baseball team), and toying with the cheerleaders. She'd earned a full ride at a top undergrad business management school.

"Ha!"

"What?" She asked from where she was inspecting some of the jewelry.

He shook his head. He'd wager she'd gotten an MBA at night school while working, because it was the kind of thing Erica would do. He had aced an oenology masters at UC Davis—growing up in a top winery had been a great prep for that. UC Davis had also placed him well in the field of coed action.

Another couple had come in and were chatting with the artisan in fluid Italian. Dressed too high to be locals—tourists over from Rome or down from Milan.

Something told him there was a whole other world going on inside Erica. A world that he suspected she showed to absolutely no one. Who was she inside that world?

He watched as she held a necklace up to her throat and peeked in a strategically placed mirror. With Erica's insights, he noted the tiny spotlight that was probably aimed just right to make the jewelry glitter when viewed there. It certainly looked good on her.

But she set it back down, smoothing it onto a display pillow in probably the exact form it had been when she picked it up. Was she so careful about everything in her life? It was hard to imagine what that would be like. He certainly hadn't been. And he'd gotten that straight from Bibi, who had seemed to bound through life in great leaps gulping down whatever life brought her way.

Erica picked up a necklace of fine sea glass stones. It was a deceptively simple band of stones on a fine gold chain. But the shapes and colors were not random in any way. The artisan's eye had formed balance and accent. And the colors were so perfect for Erica.

She laid it across her forearm first, and the colored glass seem to come to life. The amber tones picking up her skin. She laid it at her throat and turned for the mirror. There were also dark red stones that caught the natural highlights of her hair. And the pale blue that changed the necklace from formal to fanciful, bringing the colors of the cool Mediterranean.

He stepped forward and took the dangling ends from her fingertips, fastening the clasp behind her neck. She scooped her hair back with one hand and turned to inspect the effect.

Ridley let his hands fall to her shoulders, so delicate in his big hands, yet containing such great strength within that he could feel it vibrating against his palms. He spotted the tiny price tag dangling down the nape of her neck. Not outrageous like fine jewelry, but not cheap either.

"At the risk of paying you a compliment, you have to have this."

Her nod of agreement was slow, but it was agreement.

"Let me buy it for you. Not as some trinket. Just…" he never *just* bought a woman jewelry. There was always some agenda— usually not a very hidden one. Typically "let's have some fun together" or "thanks, babe, it's been fun."

Not in this case.

"Just…because I want to." Her eyes met his in the mirror as he looked over her shoulder. Again, one of her long, unwavering assessments.

"I think you actually mean that."

To his surprise, he did.

"But I need to buy it for myself."

When he flicked the price tag at the nape of her neck, she nodded.

"Despite that."

~

Erica rested her hand on the necklace and felt the cool stones warm against her skin.

This is me. I deserve something that makes me feel like me. The me that can choose to make things happen.

She wasn't believing it, not entirely…yet. But if she bought the necklace, maybe she would come to believe it.

Ridley's hands worked a moment at her neck. Warm hands that made her want to shiver with every touch. Shiver, not from fear, but from anticipation. Rather than undoing the necklace, he'd undone the tag and held it out to her over her shoulder.

No argument. No battle of wills. He'd accepted her statement that she needed to buy it herself at face value and didn't try to shift her to his way of thinking. However much he might think he was the bad boy, he had a kindness that ran through him like a shining light.

She turned back to the jeweler and held out the little tag.

"I thought of that piece the moment you walked in the door. I didn't want to push, but it is so perfect for you." Whether it was real or part of her sales pitch, she made it sound completely genuine, so Erica chose to believe her.

She'd always liked buying from the local artists at street fairs because they were so passionate about what they did. The big stores could barely be bothered to wait on you.

"I really mean it," the woman rested a hand over hers. "But it doesn't mean I'm giving you a discount."

And Erica laughed and paid happily. It was only as she and Ridley stepped out of the gallery onto the small porch with the shocking view of Vernazza, that she glanced at the credit card receipt before she tucked it away. A small note had been scrawled across the bottom: "A 20% discount for the joy of seeing it on the right woman. Anne."

Erica glanced back inside, but Anne was once more working on her elaborate bracelet, perhaps a little too studiously. Erica could feel them sharing the same smile without looking at one another before she turned back to Ridley.

"Up?" He nodded toward the ascending stairs.

"Up," she agreed. Definitely the right direction.

Ridley was not used to being the slow one, but Erica made him feel that way.

Atop the cliff had been a broad platform with a garden offering spots of shade. At the center, a stone watchtower rose another two stories and she had stood atop the ultimate platform with her eyes closed and her face into the gentle breeze. It had fluttered her hair back and made her seem indeed an Italian princess of old—face raised to defy the pirates.

She'd let him buy her lunch at the restaurant built into the face of the cliff. Most of their tables were down on the piazza, but a few were placed on a porch halfway up the cliff. The small balcony was accessed through a massive submarine's hatch bolted right to the rock. The door was salt-crusted on the outside, but the bright condition of the fastenings said that it wasn't just for show, and powerful winter storms must slam against the harbor wall to reach so high. Neither of them had ordered the perch.

Throughout the long afternoon they'd wandered the streets

and back alleys of Vernazza. They'd turned it into a game, who could spot the "perch." It had become their phrase for whatever was most touristy, most kitschy.

She'd found the real prize and he'd insisted on buying it for her.

It was a ceramic refrigerator magnet. It was the unlikely super-fit upper torso of an overly handsome Italian man. The tiny scene behind him was of a beach with sun, sea, and sand. About his waist he wore a kiddie's flotation ring with a large duck's head springing forth from the front. He wore it low enough that it was an obvious statement about how Italian men were built below the waistline. The ring was labeled with "*Benvenuto Vernazza.*"

"I will treasure this and think of you every time I see it," Erica had clasped the two-euro bauble to her chest as if he'd just bought her a diamond necklace.

They'd laughed, eaten gelato, and made a dinner of bread, cheese, and Pellegrinos at the outermost tip of the breakwater.

They watched the sun set over a glass of wine at a small table on the piazza. The church bells had rung out so loudly and clearly in the narrow ravine that speech was impossible. Five, perhaps ten minutes it had carried on, leaving a hushed silence in its wake. They were slow to resume their talk as he taught her how to taste the wine. Erica, no surprise, had turned out to be an apt pupil picking out the pineapple nose and the herbal palate of the exquisite Cheo Cinque Terre. The young apple eluded her, but it was very subtle.

During the train ride home she'd wrapped both arms around one of his, snuggled close, and rested her cheek on his shoulder for the short ride. Thankfully the bus had still been running or they might have had to sleep at the base of the three-hundred-whatever steps (now she had him doing it) back to Corniglia.

At the second floor landing outside his room, she had melted against him. It was only their second kiss, but it proved that the first had not been only in his imagination. His arms fit around her like they'd been made just for her. He had to lean his back against the door to make sure he kept them steady enough to not tumble unexpectedly to the first floor.

She'd ended the kiss too soon...*never* would be too soon... and simply laid her head upon his shoulder. He nuzzled her hair and held her.

But he knew if he kept holding her, he'd be dragging her into his bed. No matter how much he wanted that, it still seemed too soon for Erica.

Her reluctance at being shooed up the last flight to her own room had almost undone him, but he'd been firm and she'd gone.

Now he lay sprawled in his bed and wondered at what kind of an idiot he'd been.

Since when, Ridley, do you turn down a woman who wants to be in your bed?

Since never! He wished he could give Bibi a call and ask her what the hell was going on, because he most certainly didn't know.

Erica might be "good girl" to the core, so why didn't he jump at the chance to corrupt her a little?

Somewhere Bibi was laughing, but he couldn't quite tell where.

A whisper of air washed in from the open window. He'd left the curtains open and a thin slice of moonlight was etched across the darkness. Even as he watched, an apparition moved through the light.

A woman. In a long white gown, gone almost before he could see her. Not tall with Bibi's long fall of bright blonde hair. Short, with dark hair neatly to her shoulders.

Close beside his bed, he could just make out the white outline, but not the figure within. If he spoke, the vision would be over. Gone.

Even as he watched, the cloth parted and fell out of sight at the edge of the bed as if empty. Then the covers lifted and Erica slid in beside him.

～

"Are you ghost or are you flesh?"

The sheer wonder in Ridley's voice told her she'd made the right decision.

Good-girl Erica had gone upstairs to her room alone. She'd gone through her nightly routine, only briefly flummoxed by the clasp on her new necklace. She'd pulled on her flannel nightgown and left the patio doors open to the moonlight before sliding between the cool sheets.

New-girl Erica lay there wide awake and wondered why she had done any of those things. A thousand rationalizations had done nothing to answer those questions. She was a woman grown—she was twenty-eight, for crying out loud. She wanted Ridley…badly. Yet she'd walked away.

Good-girl Erica always did what others expected of her. She'd worked hard to ease her burden on Stephen. She'd studied hard to get the scholarships and get out early. She'd worked hard to prove herself to… She wasn't even sure who.

But was that who had come to Italy? Even *she* hadn't expected herself to do that. Each stage of her journey a surprise: letting go of her apartment, walking down the jetway, passport control and the surprising entry stamp, plunging her car into the olive trees only to arrive in a fairy-tale medieval tower complete with a handsome courtier.

None of that sounded like Good-girl Erica.

But if it was New-girl Erica, she wasn't sure quite why she was lying alone in her bed. A handsome and willing man lay mere feet below. And she *wanted* to be with him.

The Good-girl had considered getting dressed, perhaps even donning the necklace, knocking on his door, and asking if they could talk.

New-girl Erica hadn't even stopped to run a brush through her hair or slip on sandals. Instead she'd eased down the stairs, into his bedroom, and finally naked into his bed.

And except for the one question, "Are you ghost or are you flesh?" (to which she wasn't sure of the true answer), he silently opened his arms in welcome.

She curled against him. No question that he was the sort of man who slept without clothes and she'd been right. But the shock of skin on skin as he'd pulled her against him almost overwhelmed her.

He made her feel so…alive.

Tucked tight against his side, her head on his shoulder, her arm across that broad chest she'd been admiring throughout the afternoon, she wanted to burrow in. She turned her nose into his chest and just breathed him in.

Rich and complex like one of his wines. Male was too small a word for Ridley. Walnut, she decided. Strong like oak, but less mainstream, more unique. The sea salt that pervaded the Ligurian air now lay upon his skin, but was warm and bright. There was a flavor there as well, but it was beyond her to figure it out.

He fanned his fingers through her hair.

He began some question, but she stopped it by laying a finger upon his lips. It would be, "Are you sure?" or some other question that was for Good-girl Erica.

She didn't want to hear those questions. She didn't want to have to answer them. Her entire life had been bounded by asking herself that exact question and she was done with it. Being unsure—at least a little unsure—wasn't necessarily a bad thing.

She scooted up enough to replace her fingers with her mouth, and Ridley's transformation was so instantaneous that there was no chance of keeping up. From calmly holding her against him, he now dragged their bodies together. His hands didn't roam, they consumed. Everywhere they slid over her left a trail of power.

She had caused this.

She had chosen this.

And it was glorious!

When his mouth began to follow the exploration of his hands, all she could do was clench her own hands in his hair and be taken. She might have thought it was an act had she not felt the need shuddering through him just as she could feel it shuddering through her. His merest touch evoked the day, but in snapshots of chaos.

Kissing him under the chin, she could almost taste the cool wood of the policeman's baton. When he buried his nose against her sternum and went suddenly quiet between her breasts, his hands slid up to clasp her shoulders as they had after placing the necklace. When he rolled momentarily away, the cool of the night slid between the sheets with a tease of gelato on the tongue. And when he embraced her once more, it was with all the gentleness of the breeze atop the fort's watchtower, brushing away the past and leaving only the hopes of the future.

His hands, mouth, body asked and hers gave. Gave until her mind blanked. Gave until her body slid out of her control, out of his, and answered instead to its own inner call she'd never heard before.

~

Ridley had heard women call sex "devastating." He'd never understood.

Not until now.

He was a dead man. Sprawled on his back and wondering if he'd live to see the morning.

Erica lay equally limply upon him. Her soft "hmm" of contentment proved that she, at least, still lived.

Unable to wait any longer, he'd scrabbled up some protection, and even as he sheathed himself, she had straddled and taken him. Frantic didn't begin to cover what had passed between them. Their need hadn't soared, it had exploded in one massive, blurred, fantastic, frenzied bout.

Her gasp of surprise as he felt the orgasm slam into her had sent him right off the edge. Somehow, that simple sound, that *he* was the one to cause her that much pleasure, had made him feel all-powerful. His own release had slammed into her and she'd dug her fingers into his chest as they both rode through the aftermath.

No words.

Not a single one.

Women always wanted words...unless it was just plain sex. But there was no mistaking this for anything plain. Hell, the word sex barely applied. Something more had passed between them. Maybe so big that it didn't need words either.

Another happy hum vibrated through the woman lying on him.

"Being bad feels awfully good," she mumbled, and raised her head just long enough to kiss the center his chest before resting her cheek back on the spot.

"There wasn't a thing bad about that." He could actually speak! So, he was still alive.

"Was it…okay for you?"

"Okay?" He tried to raise his head enough to see her, but her head was tucked up under his chin. "That had nothing to do with okay."

"Oh, I'm sorry," and she began pushing herself up. It took him a moment to figure out what was going on and he barely managed to clamp his hands over her butt to keep her in place.

"Erica, it had nothing to do with okay, but it had a whole lot to do with fantastic."

"Really?" Her voice was so small that it barely filled the tiny space she'd managed to open between them.

He ran a hand slowly up her spine, smoothing her back down against him until he'd once more coaxed her head onto his chest.

But the tension remained.

"Tell me again why I'm not killing the bastard who made you feel like you had to perform for my sake?"

"Rat's ass," she corrected. And he had to laugh at her unintentionally funny line.

"Rat's ass."

"Because," and he could feel her sad sigh ripple between them. "Your mother was right about not wasting energy on the past."

"Never said I agreed with her, but I learned young that there was no point arguing with Bibi once she'd made up her mind."

"Fierce, huh?"

"Let's just say that I only tried to blow my school-night curfew once…ever."

He could feel Erica's smile against his skin. "The more you tell me about her, the more I like her."

"She'd have approved of you."

"Me and how many others?"

"Actually, truth is, my mom wasn't a big fan of my tastes in women."

There was another one of Erica's silences that he now theorized was an inner dialogue.

"Just say it, woman."

"I'm just wondering, if you have lousy taste in women, what does that say about me?"

And that was Erica. She might not volunteer her thoughts, but she never hesitated to be honest.

What did it say about his taste in women? That Bibi had been right and him wrong for all these years? That maybe, in a moment of weakness, he'd let a decent woman past his guard? Or maybe having gotten a taste of the right kind of woman, he was gonzo confused and out of his depth? Or…

"Honestly, Erica…"

She offered a softly inquisitive "Hmm?" as she settled once more upon him.

"I'll be damned if I know."

He couldn't tell if she stayed awake long enough to hear his answer.

He was certainly awake enough to catch his non-answer loud and clear.

CHAPTER 7

The guilt wasn't there yet, but Erica could feel it coming. She'd actually bought a one-way ticket to Italy, having no idea when she'd be returning. The first week had spun by so easily that it had barely been an afterthought to ask Bridget if the room was available for a second one.

"*Sì! Sì!* It is yours."

A week. She and Ridley had followed the same pattern with each village: Manarola, Monterosso, and Riomaggiore. They spent a full day exploring each tiny town and the nights in his bed making love. Twice they'd never even left his bed except to grab some takeout. She'd never done anything like that in her life.

Of course she'd never had a lover like Ridley before. Actually, she'd never been with a man she thought of as a lover —it sounded very European. She'd had boyfriends, even affairs, but neither word fit whatever it was they had between them. Her most thoughtful prior lover had spent maybe half an hour in the preludes to actual sex—a few times, but not as a regular thing. Ridley had spent an entire afternoon making such gentle love to her that it had become one long blur of joy.

She wasn't fooling herself, or not much. She wasn't expecting more than a fling with a man like Ridley Claremont III. He was handsome and wealthy and could have any woman he wanted. But at the moment, he wanted her, and she hugged herself tightly at the wonder of that knowledge.

Initially, her plan had been to collect a trinket from each town, something to mark each day. But after the first day they'd spent in his bed together with nothing to show for it but a single pizza crust, she'd let go of that idea. Instead, she'd collected memories where they found them together—and she knew that she would be holding those memories close for a long time to come.

One of her favorite memories would always be the church bells of the tall Corniglia church. Every evening at 7:30 ("Each town has a different time so that they don't overlap," Bridget had explained. "On the quiet evenings, you can hear three or four different ones from your little balcony.") From Ridley's room they could only hear the bells of Corniglia. But each night at 7:30, unless they were very, very involved in something, they would get up and dance to the church bells. It was like a slow children's waltz, rung in a dozen tones of brass so that it echoed over the town. When they *were* otherwise occupied, they incorporated the rhythms in ways that made them both laugh.

"Let's go hiking," she poked Ridley awake. It had fast become clear that he was far more of a night owl than she was. Getting him moving before midmorning was the exception, not the rule. Especially not if she woke him in the middle of the night, or he her, for an extra round of discovery.

Ridley grumbled something unintelligible, snagged an arm around her waist, and drew her back to spoon against him.

She now knew this game. If she settled there, he'd fall back asleep with an arm draped around her waist and the other serving as her pillow. If she pulled free, he'd let her go, though it might earn her a cute whimper of distress. Instead, she lay her hand on the back of his and slid it slowly lower, opening her legs to welcome his touch. A little wiggle as she pressed her behind more tightly against him and he was soon fully awake. Early mornings made no exception to his skills, and his attentions soon sent her soaring and ready to leap from the bed.

"Lazybones," she teased him as she stepped out of his shower and saw him still sprawled in bed.

"Best view in the house," he leered at her.

"Hiking in five minutes." Then she teased him by merely scooping up her nightgown and going naked out the door and up to her room. She wasn't sure why, but she still changed there and came to his room at night. Maybe she needed the boundary knowing it wouldn't last—she could retreat here and lick her wounds when it ended without everything reminding her of what she'd so briefly held. Maybe he needed the boundary but was too polite to say so. Either way, she'd certainly never walked naked out into a B&B hallway, even if no one came up here except Bridget later in the day.

She trotted up the stairs to her private tower. First, she brushed her hair back, not quite long enough for a ponytail, but getting close. So many Italian women wore their hair long, she decided to give it a try. It made the washing and drying horribly inefficient (a decision she'd made as a teen), but it did look nice on the women she saw.

Maybe it was time to live however she wanted to, rather than following only the path of what was most practical.

Jeans, boots, and a blouse of smoke-gray cotton. She accented it with a gold scarf from Riomaggiore and a slather of sunscreen for her non-Mediterranean skin tone. She'd never been one to tan, but maybe if she lived here, she'd—

Erica froze and studied her reflection in the mirror.

Maybe if she lived here?

Where had that thought come from? Even a princess in her tower should be smart enough to know that a fling was a fling and nothing more. Smart princesses didn't build happily-ever-afters on men like Ridley any more than they should have on lying rat's-ass ex-bosses. Ridley was not a man to stay in one place for long.

Just enjoy it while it lasts. And think about whether or not the "living here" thought meant anything after he was gone.

Her hand was halfway to the tiny jewelry box Ridley had bought for five euro from a street vendor in Monterosso—just big enough for her new necklace—when she stopped.

That didn't sound like her.

Good-girl Erica would be sensible. Back away. Set herself up to ease the heartbreak that she knew she would feel when this ended. Ridley might not know how special he was, but she was fast beginning to. Good-girl Erica would buy a ticket for a week from now: set a boundary, draw a line on the calendar.

And go back to what?

She wasn't going to go back to a rat's-ass ex-boss. But neither was she going to find another Ridley Claremont.

Good-girl Erica would know to end it now. Experience had taught her that she could be packed and gone before Ridley was out of his shower—he was a total hedonist about long, hot showers (he'd was also doing a splendid job of converting her to the joy of long, hot showers for two).

Just cut it off before it had a chance to rip out her heart.

But New-girl Erica reached out and opened the small clamshell, so cleverly hinged with a bit of tooled leather and tiny brass hooks, to extract and don her sea glass necklace.

New-girl Erica didn't shy away from pain. Because with the pain came the sweet, and the sweet was so very, very fine.

~

Ridley was trying to figure out what he was doing right.

Amazing wake-up sex. Erica always delivered amazing sex: middle of the night, wake-up, or in the shower. Every woman had some time where it wasn't amazing, where it was just sex —par for the course. Erica rocked his world every single time and, according to her, she wasn't missing out either.

They'd taken the train back to Vernazza. They were still a long way from repeating gelato flavors and today's had been no exception. She'd selected the *Caramello Al Sale*—salted caramel. When he'd asked for a taste, she'd taken a bite and then kissed him deep and long—he could still taste it. It had been intimate, public, and sexy as hell.

Her ears had been bright red by the time she pulled away, but her smile had been nearly blinding.

He'd opted to be brave and try *Pino Mugo*—because she'd teased him about a lack of bravery in not trying something labeled Pine Tree. It was one of the only flavors to be labeled in English as well as Italian to avoid any mistakes. It even had a little pine branch laid over the gelato tray to doubly confirm it. He still felt as if he was inhaling the Pacific Northwest with every breath.

And now, beneath another stunning Italian spring day, he was following an exceptionally fine ass up the trail out of Vernazza. He'd dated models; hell, he'd dated supermodels. But he now understood that some of the shine came off because that's how he saw them—as the supermodel.

Again that weird honesty that Erica embodied so thoroughly. When she'd walked naked out of his room this morning, he'd been utterly mesmerized. *That* was his lover. They were past sex and on to being lovers. And damn, it looked good on her.

There was no shadow over her, no extra layer blurring who she was: model, actress, heir to a Napa fortune, hot townie cheerleader.

Erica was simply Erica. Through and through. Right to the core. And that unthinking honesty and purity of message from the inside all the way out was messing with his head.

He stopped a moment to catch his breath from the sharp ascent. Erica, of course, didn't appear the least bit winded. He could keep up with her, but that had as much to do with his longer legs as it did her stamina—the woman was a hiking machine.

And *this* was apparently her idea of hiking. A trail connected the five towns of Cinque Terre. But the five towns were perched on the edges of cliffs, separated by a sea that might look tame but definitely wasn't. The trail (really no more than a footpath) had connected some of the towns for centuries for commerce, and others for the first time just a century before after being so long apart.

Already they'd climbed high above Vernazza. He shot a bird's-eye photo that captured town, harbor, and fort all in an area he could cover with his hand. The footpath clung to the cliffside much as the towns did. A fall of fifty stories onto wave-thrashed rocks lay on the other side of a railing that would never pass an American inspection. Above the trail, the last of the town's terraced vineyards was petering out. The stone walls were slumping; the vines overgrown and too long untended.

It was his first chance to really inspect them closely as this last terrace was just chest high.

"What are you looking at?" Erica had doubled back and slid

under his arm in a move so natural that it was hard to imagine her ever not having done that.

"The vines, the soil." He reached out and dug a hand into the soil. "Rich enough to hold nutrients and moisture, but rocky enough to turn dry and challenge the grape."

"Grapes like being challenged?"

"They do. Napa and Sonoma have topsoil going down forever, but I sometimes think the vines have it too easy. Up in Oregon they have dry, rocky soil. It doesn't bode well for the big-bodied wines, but Pinot thrives there in a way that we can never reproduce. This place makes Oregon look like Sonoma, but it's still good soil. You can see it in the vines. Stout root stock as big around as your arm."

She held up one of her slender arms. "You mean as big around as yours."

She then stroked a palm down his forearm making him aware of his own strength. No woman had ever made him so aware of himself. But she did it all the time in unthinking ways. Not just how she touched him, but how she looked up at him as well. The way she seemed permanently aware of where he was. They could wander a hundred feet apart in a busy crowd, and he could look up and see her looking at him as if he'd shouted her name across the entire market square.

"Right, as big around as mine," he made it suggestive and lewd. Which backfired when he remembered how amazing it felt to be all the way inside her, but the trail was too busy for a chance to do anything here.

"You're not that big, thank god," she pointed at the vine. The woman he'd first met would never have said such a thing. The woman who'd graced his bed for a week hadn't even blushed. She was changing and he decided it was for the better. Of course if Erica got any better than she already was, he was a dead man.

"You can also see," he forced his attention back to the vine, "how desperately these need tending."

"Water?"

"Pruning. The latest pruning cuts are at least three seasons old—that's years. Viticulture is thought of in growing seasons. And it was a slap-dash job at that. I guess these vines lie too far from town to be profitable anymore. Makes me sad."

She turned and they started up the trail once more. They walked side by side as much as the trail and the occasional passersby allowed them.

Some were walking the trail from the heights of Corniglia to the seaside of Vernazza, the opposite of the direction Erica had chosen. Of course, she wouldn't opt for the easy way. But there were others who didn't as well.

Calls of "Links. Links." announced that Germans were fast overtaking them and asking for clearance to the left. They usually were remarkably fit couples with ski poles for balance and packs big enough that they could set up a base camp on Everest. Well, not that big, but ridiculous for a two-hour day hike. Germans were never unprepared.

Chattering families, coaxing along little kids, were doing the hike as well. Once they were overtaken by a hoard—a hiking group of fifteen to twenty stormed past them on a particularly steep part of the trail as if they did this every day. Even Erica's inner ibex couldn't match that. Then a single old Italian man, who had to be at least sixty, walked by them as if the prior group had been standing still.

"Wow," was all she managed. She had on one of her thoughtful looks.

"Spill it, hotshot."

She shook her head, which was unusual. It made him doubly curious. Not beneath a little subterfuge, he glanced up and down the trail. They were alone for the moment.

He spun her into his arms and pinned her back against the cliff face—the trail was little more than a six-foot wide notch in the cliff at this point. He kissed her until her arms slid up around his neck and she did that gooey thing of melting against him.

"Spill it," he muttered, but covered her mouth again before she could answer.

"Come on," he teased, again not giving her time to respond.

"If you just—Ow!" Ridley pulled back and clamped a hand over his mouth to check for blood. "You bit me!"

"Not that hard," she didn't look regretful at all.

"On the lip!" he pointed and accidentally jammed his finger against the sore spot making him curse again.

"Just what you deserve. Come here. I'll kiss it and make it better." She went up on her toes and kissed him lightly. And it did feel a little better.

"The kiss of the princess is magic."

"The court fool's one isn't bad either." And she started up the next section of trail.

They hiked along for another ten minutes or so and the silence seemed to be stretching thin. Actually, it was becoming pervasive. He looked around. Here they were, on the coast of the sea, high among rocks that should be covered with birds— and he didn't see any.

"No birds," he broke the silence and his voice sounded overloud against the quiet breeze and their footsteps.

"What? Oh. I hadn't noticed."

They reached a wider section of the path. Or it would have been if not for a rock avalanche. A pile of boulders took up most of the width. Above them a massive net of heavy steel wire had been draped over the cliff. Any rock that broke free would slither down between cliff and net and hopefully not land on a tourist's head.

Erica sat on one of the boulders, which wasn't like her. She always seemed to see what was going on around her. He debated moving her along, but didn't know how well that would go over at the moment. She sat there toying with her necklace, rubbing each stone between her fingers as if polishing it. Something she only seemed to do when she was thinking the most deeply.

"I was thinking back there… I guess this morning too…" She stared out at the ocean, her face strangely quiet.

Since silence seemed to have cracked the dam, maybe he would try doing something atypical and try more of it. It wasn't like him, but then he didn't usually care that much about how someone felt past having a good time. Even that was selfish, he supposed. If his date was having a good time, then he was more likely to as well. He'd always thought of it as his "being positive feedback loop." Maybe there was a "being quiet long enough for someone to think loop" as well.

"I wondered what it would be like to be in that kind of shape. For them, in a way, it's easy. Walk out your door here and it's a workout. Steep streets, steep hills, gorgeous trails right out your door."

"You'd have to live here."

"I figured that out myself," Erica kept staring at the sea. Not some trivial thought then.

"And this morning?"

She nodded.

"During or…" No, he didn't want the answer to that, but she reached out and patted his knee.

"Don't worry, Ridley. When you're making love to me, there is absolutely no thinking going on in this girl's head, except *More!*"

"Well, that's a relief." And surprisingly similar to his own response to her. He'd thought that was mostly a guy thing.

"It was after. When I was up in my room getting dressed. I don't know why it bothers me. I realized that I have nothing to go back to."

"Another job?"

"For who? And why? Wrapping all my Good-girl Erica protectiveness around me again? What the hell's the point of that?"

"You swore." There was something way deeper in what she was saying, but it was just making her more and more unhappy. So he latched on to his point. "You just swore."

"I did, didn't I?" And her demeanor brightened.

"You sure as hell did."

"I did," she agreed in some surprise and he had to laugh at her.

"Say, 'I sure as hell did'."

"What's the point? I already said it."

"Swearing isn't a one-time license, Princess." But he pulled her into his arms and kissed her temple before hauling her to her feet. "Come on. Too beautiful a day for moping."

"It is," and once again she led off, slowly picking back up to her usual pace.

As he followed, Ridley wondered if he'd just done the right thing. It had been his usual thing—find the funny. When women started getting all introspective, that was his cue to change the tune or step out of the picture.

But Erica was wrestling with something deep and he'd just made her shove it back into the dark. What would it take for it to surface again? Probably something drastic.

Ridley felt an itch between his shoulders, but a glance back revealed no one behind him.

But the itch hung on. It told him that perhaps that hadn't been his best day's work.

CHAPTER 8

*R*idley had been so gentle last night that Erica almost wanted to cry. Her lovers tended to think about themselves; the good ones making sure she enjoyed herself as well.

He'd made last night all about her. It had started with a massage for a leg cramp—she really had to get out on these trails more. Boston wasn't known for its rough and steep trails any more than Oakland had been. Stair-stepper conditioning was not the same as the real world.

But Ridley hadn't stopped when the cramp finally let go. Slowly, using those powerful hands of his, he turned her into an Erica puddle.

When she'd asked, he'd admitted to dating a masseuse or two. She'd smiled into the pillow she was facedown in. Was there any type of woman Ridley *hadn't* dated?

"They seemed to enjoy my amateur efforts to return the favor. So I took the classes. Never got certified, which ticked off the instructor, but I've since found it useful. Uh…" And that was her Ridley—sometimes thinking just a little too late about what he was saying. "Like for your leg cramps," he'd attempted to recover. She'd been on the verge of teasing him about it, but then he'd progressed to moves he'd never learned in any massage class but she'd like to personally thank the masseuse who'd taught him those. If she ever recovered.

Erica puddle had become happy Erica puddle of joy. When he'd finally let her stop, finally let her come down from the unimagined peaks he sent her to, she was helpless to do more than curl up in his arms and be held.

"Later," she'd promised. She'd try to do the same for him…later.

This morning, she woke to an evil smile.

"Uh-oh." It seemed that later had just caught up with her.

"Do you have a leather jacket?"

She nodded carefully.

"Boots, jeans, leather jacket, and sunglasses. Let's go."

Her head was still spinning too much from last night to do more than agree and hurry from his bed. She'd showered, changed, and met him downstairs while her body seemed to be continuing along just a few steps behind her, still off in some dreamy place.

Bridget served a too bright and too knowing smile along with her cocoa. She kissed Erica atop the head.

"He is so very good for you, *mia amica.* It makes my heart smile," she whispered before moving to the next table.

"What are you up to, Ridley?" Erica didn't want to ponder Bridget's comment too deeply.

"Heard about a place that I thought you might like. It's a bit of a ride."

"A," she swallowed hard, "ride?" Then she turned to face the big motorcycle that had spent the week parked against the side of the B&B. Unmoving until it had become a fixture she no longer noticed. Now it loomed large, its headlight glowering down at her. "I've never…" Her throat went dry despite the hot cocoa she'd been sipping.

"Never been on a motorcycle?" Ridley's evil grin shifted to maniacal delight. "You are in for *such* a treat. Been a while since I've met a motorcycle virgin."

"Can't we take a train?"

"Doesn't go there."

"Maybe you could borrow Bridget's Ferrari."

"Bridget has a Ferrari?"

"I do," Bridget answered as she delivered the morning pastries. "I liberated it from someone who didn't deserve or appreciate it and I'm not giving it back. And no, Mr. Claremont, I'm not entrusting my beautiful car to the likes of you."

"I suppose not…it is bright pink after all." Erica couldn't resist the next line. "We can't have such a smirch on your manliness."

Ridley groaned most satisfyingly. But it still wasn't much payback for getting her on his motorcycle. Had that been why he'd made such love to her last night? No, there'd been no mistaking his intentions. He'd been so "manly" that the sex hadn't needed to be about him. But he had her trapped anyway and she knew it. Giving in to the inevitable after they'd eaten, she listened carefully as he told her the dos and don'ts of motorcycle riding.

"These pipes don't get particularly hot, but it's still a good habit to never touch them. On some bikes, the slightest touch will cook you good. Your feet rest on these. Always lean with me, even if your instincts say not to. You'll get the feel of it fairly quickly." He dug a helmet out of one of the saddlebags and plopped it on her head. "Oh good, a better fit that I expected."

"Do you carry one in all the women's sizes? No, don't

answer that. I don't want to know who else has worn this." Erica shrugged off the shades of prior women. "Thank you, Ridley, for buying this nice, brand-new, never-before-used helmet, just for me."

He was smart enough to say, "You're welcome," and leave well enough alone.

Rather than thundering to life, the engine gave a small squeak and turned over to a soft rumble.

"Indian Chieftains are very well-behaved bikes." He swung a leg over, kicked up the kickstand, then let the bike roll backward a few feet. With an expert twist he aimed it toward the road rather than the *carruggio*. "Your turn." His voice sounded inside her helmet.

"There's a radio?"

"Sure, let's us talk easily while we ride. Bought nothing but the best…just for you." He hesitated a little too long before completing that sentence, which she was going to ignore.

A tiny seat no bigger than her butt was perched on the rear fender. To sit on it, she'd have to wrap her arms around Ridley. That was fine—she expected to be hanging on for dear life the whole way. And by the look of it, her entire field of view would be of his shoulders. How exciting. Actually, since she also planned to bury her face against his back and not look up once, that was fine as well.

She managed to raise a leg high enough to get onto the seat with an awkward sideways slide.

"Next time," Ridley pointed at the tiny footrest, "Step there and swing your other leg over the back."

She managed to get her feet placed and not touch the Chrome Pipes of Death. So that was good. She made sure she had a good fistful of Ridley's jacket clenched in either hand.

"No tickling," he called back over the radio-intercom thing.

No, but pounding him senseless for doing this to her was definitely an option, if she dared let go.

Then she looked up and realized that her seat sat several inches higher than Ridley's. Except for the very top of his helmet, she had a clear view ahead and to all sides—with no windshield, door struts, side windows, or roof to protect her.

"This feels awfully ex-*posed!*" The last came out as a high squeak as Ridley stepped on the gas or whatever motorcycles did. "Yipes!" She held on for all she was worth, wrapping her arms around his waist.

"Ouch. Go easy on the ears, Erica. I can hear you just fine. And we're going about five miles an hour."

"That's like eight kilometers an hour. It sounds too fast!" But he was right, he was easing past the tourists just climbing out of the small bus from the train. No garbage truck this time, but it looked as if the bus driver had parked completely in his way on purpose, rather than where the truck driver had said he should.

The motorcycle was very smooth as they went through the dip in the road by the tiny café they'd had lunch in two days ago. Off to the left was a vast hillside of grapevines and to the right the little trail that led through the high side of town past the church. It was friendly, cozy. She'd been here little more than a week and it felt familiar. She knew the whole town. There were many unexplored trails, but she'd walked every bit of the main paths and cobbled streets.

In Boston and San Francisco it was impossible to know more than a few blocks well. Here there was a familiarity. She knew the shops and was starting to know the people. Giuseppe who would rather sit outside his shop and chat than be inside with his groceries. Claire who so loved having people in her shop that it was hard to pass by without being invited in for a cup of tea "while *i turisti* busy with the fingering my wares." Erica suspected that she was also still hoping to sell her the little hand-tooled leather purse she'd admired that first day. Marianne and her son Max definitely knew her at the gelato shop, and kept track of which flavors she'd tried—and always pretended to be offended when they discovered she'd already tasted a flavor at another gelato shop.

It wasn't the dense pack of cozy stores lining the streets that made Corniglia a town; it was the people who gave it richness and texture.

Finally clear of the town, Ridley sped up. The engine stayed quiet, taking on a contented thrum as it began working up the hill. It didn't vibrate or shake the bike; instead it offer a smooth ride as if she was floating.

At the first turn, Ridley spoke up. "Lean with me."

"Oh god." But she did, even though the pavement was right there, seemingly inches beyond their knees as the bike nearly laid on its side. She survived the turn and was able to pay more attention at the next. They actually didn't tip far at all, it only felt as if they were going to.

Somewhere up the hill, a turn looked eerily familiar. She twisted to look back at it. Seen from that direction, it was far *too* familiar. It's where her car had plunged into the *uliveto*—she'd looked it up. It did sound pretty and Italian. Way better than *grovochordinoria*.

Ridley started laughing.

"What?"

"I might have seen a tow truck here on the first day."

She freed a hand long enough to punch him lightly in the ribs.

He only laughed more.

What had been a tortuous, creeping descent for her was now an effortlessly smooth glide up the winding road. Olive trees swept by. A truck that would have scared her completely off the road barely caused Ridley to slow.

"Okay back there?"

"Uh, yes. It seems I am." She felt a little like a princess riding behind her knight-errant. Ridley definitely didn't fit the role of court fool—at least not very often. But to think of him as a shining knight was perhaps even more wrong. And more dangerous. He was hers…for now. For this insane moment of time. And when the knight left, it would be time for the princess to hang up her tiara and get back to life.

Not yet though.

He was right. Ridley *was* an expert on vacationing. She was along for the ride. She hadn't even asked how far they were going—and some foreign part of her was okay with that.

Or maybe not totally foreign.

She freed a hand to rest it briefly on her sea glass necklace where it lay beneath the leather of her jacket—her chic Italian leather jacket that they'd found in a little shop in Monterosso. New-girl Erica was okay with not knowing, so she fought back Good-girl Erica and didn't ask. She simply hung on to her lover and gave herself over to the ride.

Ridley had forgotten quite how far back along the coast the town of Bardino Nuovo lay. But the *autostrada* had let him open up the Chieftain's big engine and really cover some ground. The narrow highway slashed through olive groves and punched through tunnels—sometimes so close together that it seemed like flashing lights: blazing sunlight, dark tunnel, blazing sunlight, another tunnel. And beyond it all lay the shining Mediterranean.

He'd felt Erica ease into the ride quickly, but she spoke

little, answering his questions but little more. Unable to see her face and read her emotions there, he could only lean into the throttle and hope for the best. Portofino had passed by early on, somewhere on the coast far below the *autostrada* that ran high in the mountains. They soared past Rapallo and weaved their way through the dozen or so highways that fed the big port town of Genoa.

There'd been women in those towns, and normally he'd remember their names. But every time he tried to picture one of them, he recalled Erica instead. And not just as she arched over him in ecstasy or shuddered beneath him in release. But also as she laughed over gelato or her eyebrows knit as she concentrated on his hints about the flavor of a new wine.

It was the longest he'd been with anyone since he'd hit Europe. Which wasn't saying all that much. He'd stayed on the move. The new North Coast 500 route around Scotland had filled just three days. England and Wales had passed quickly as well. The Chieftain wasn't a race bike, but he'd run it over to the Isle of Man where speed limits didn't exist because they were deemed as some other country's idea of what was important. The stark, treeless expanses had been perfect for showing what the machine was really capable of. Once he had rented a couple hours on a racetrack with his grandfather's bike, but it wasn't the same. The open road had rolled by as effortlessly as the women.

But Bardino Nuovo he'd stumbled on by himself. And he knew it was something right up Erica's alley.

Off the *autostrada*, they climbed farther up into the hills along winding roads no bigger than the one into Corniglia. Less vertical than the Cinque Terre towns, but still dramatic by any standard outside Colorado. The big engine gave him the power, but the twists kept him in a low gear easing upward. Towns here weren't the busy tourist centers of the coast. They were small, sleepy hamlets of twenty or so houses.

The entrance to Bardino passed by a house covered in massive gears and lever arms rusting in the sun.

"It's like a crazy disconnected clockwork," Erica whispered over the radio.

He kept his mouth shut and slowed even more.

They climbed through an orchard that was practically a catalog of what grew here. Lemon, cherry, and plum for the fruit trees. Eucalyptus and olive standing tall. On the ground were grape, artichoke, and who knew what all. It was a town of one: one restaurant, one market, and, most importantly, one museum.

He rolled into the parking lot and shut the bike down. Large planters of nasturtium and petunia graced the boundaries of the small lot.

Erica didn't climb down. Instead she sat there for a long moment before whispering, "It's so quiet."

"Try taking off your helmet."

She climbed down and did, but she was right. Corniglia had layers of sound: chatting Italians, bustling tourists, the sea always crashing away somewhere in the background. Scooters and buses along the roads. Tourist and wheeled delivery carts bumping along the *carruggio.*

Bardino Nuovo had a soft breath of wind.

"It almost makes my ears hurt."

On cue, the town chimes rang out. Eleven strikes rang over the land and seemed to fill it and make it brighter.

"Oh, now it makes my heart hurt. That was beautiful." She rubbed her palm over her heart as if it really did.

"Then you're going to love this." He stepped to her and turned her around.

"Bergallo Museo dell'Orologio. What's it mean?"

"It's a clock museum. For something like a hundred years, most of the town clocks in Italy were built in that house at the edge of town. When the last clockmaker died about a decade back, he left it all to the town."

"The Corniglia chimes came from here?"

"I don't know. We can ask."

"No, don't." Erica grabbed onto his arm. "I don't want to know. We'll just pretend that they did. This is wonderful, Ridley."

And right there was what he'd been hoping for. The happy glow in Erica's eyes could have outshone the Italian sun as they entered the museum.

～

"I don't know what part I liked best," Erica knew she was bubbling ridiculously over the radio, but couldn't seem to stop.

"The cards," Ridley groaned. "I couldn't get over the cards."

The ground floor had been the start of a display of the evolution of Bergallo clock works. A primitive cast iron behemoth had dominated the floor. It was plain to see the device's crudeness. The next two were more refined.

A large display case including timepieces going back to the 1600s.

But the wall beside that had been covered in postcards. More were in large glass display cases. She'd expected images of the many clocks that must have come from here. Instead, there was a massive set of Papal collecting cards. Travel postcards, mostly from France and Italy—presumably sent by the clockmakers back to their families from places they'd done installations.

The museum curator was so excited to have visitors that she gave them a personalized tour...without having a single word of English. Their nonexistent Italian hadn't diminished her joy or the volume of information she tried to impart.

But the main portion of the postcard collection had been of Hollywood stars, especially Marilyn Monroe. Marilyn seemed to rule Italy, but no one could tell Erica why. She was on posters and t-shirts, playing cards and refrigerator magnets. And she was front and center in the Bergallo Museo dell'Orologio postcard collection. There were fifty or more of her alone.

They'd both had trouble sounding suitably impressed.

But it was a clock museum, and they'd finally moved on.

At each new clockwork that filled the three small floors of the museum, the curator had wound each mechanism, then reset the time so that it would run through its chimes—thankfully, small chimes rather than massive town ringers.

Her and Ridley's non-Italian had degenerated their host to pointing at every clockwork and crowing out, *"Tutto bene! Tutto bene!"* All good. They decided that she meant they were all operational. As they ascended the ramps, leaving chiming and ticking mechanisms whirring away behind them, the sound built and carried. And while the chimes ran down, the ticking continued.

Out of sync perhaps, but not out of time. There was a steadiness to that underlying beat.

"My favorite part was the ticking," and as odd as it sounded, it was true.

"Really? I thought it all got a little annoying by the time she had them all running. *Perché?*"

"Didn't you mean Perch? I don't know really."

She lay the cheek of her helmet on Ridley's back and watch one side of the world go by. Orchards, groves...*uliveto.*

To Good-girl Erica, it was the pace of her life. The ticking clock. Business on the move. The next task achieved ahead of the deadline. Always gaining time against the clock.

She liked that part of herself and didn't want to lose it. It helped her see the world as a good and orderly place.

But New-girl Erica liked it as well. It was one of the first times that the two of them had agreed.

She imagined each clock as the curator had led them to it. She would tap a mechanism and name a town. *"Stesso. Stesso."* Same. Same. This one in Genoa. That one in Rome. The next in France somewhere. One she'd unbelievably insisted, "Patagonia."

And as more and more of them came to life, Erica could feel the unexpected connections between the towns wrought on the ticking of their clocks. Over a hundred years, multiple generations of Bergallo clockworks built connections and tied the country together in unexpected ways. Each bell that rang. Each clock that ticked. Each mechanism that turned day in and day out created a layer of connectivity that she could feel in her own heart as if it too was a piece of Bergallo clockwork beating the rhythm of Italy.

She'd finally broken down and asked, "Corniglia? Bergallo?"

"Sì. Sì." Having so few words that seemed to work between them, the curator always said them twice.

"Yes," she told Ridley, and placed a kiss in the middle of his back—which turned out to be the inside of her own helmet, but it was the thought that counted. "I very much liked the ticking."

CHAPTER 9

But Bardino Nuovo hadn't cleared away the deeper silences behind Erica's eyes. Ridley saw shadows of it slipping in and slipping away over the next few days. He tried to coax it out a few times, but Erica didn't even appear to be aware of it. He was right, it had gone deep and he didn't have any experience in this kind of fishing.

One day, she simply came to a halt. She sat in a chair at that tiny table they'd first shared and simply stopped moving except for occasionally sipping the cup of tea that Hal had served her.

"You okay, Princess?" he had settled beside her.

"Sure. Just thought it might be fun to sit and watch the world go by rather than racing through it." And that was all she'd done. He'd have believed her, if not for her fingers idly rubbing the stones of her necklace.

That night, she'd come to his bed, curled up against him, and gone to sleep. Whatever it was, it had gone so deep that there hadn't even been any bad dreams—he'd been awake holding her all night and would have noticed.

Before she woke, he slipped out of bed and dressed. No sign of Bridget or Hal but he didn't have to go far. The woman who sold the purses across the street was just opening up. She was able to fill in some local history for him. And sell him what he needed. A friend of hers took care of the rest of it. He made it back before Erica woke up.

Had he ever been so happy to see a woman in his bed? In her sleep, she'd curled up around his pillow. The days in the Italian sun had pulled more of the dark reds out of her brown hair, and spattered more freckles across her nose. Her light skin had turned to the palest shade of honey. The covers had slid down enough to reveal most of one splendid breast— barely a handful, it was a handful he'd come to deeply appreciate. She had an athlete's body and was fast ruining him for any other kind.

He leaned down and whispered in her ear, "Rise and shine." Then he nipped it sharply with his teeth.

"Yikes!" Thankfully, he remembered how fast she woke up and managed to get his face clear before she bashed him with the top of her head as she sat up. The sheet slid down revealing that truly fine breasts came in pairs. "Oh. You're dressed."

"Yep!"

"Come back to bed," she collapsed back on the pillow and pulled the sheet back over her. "Make love to me. Get dressed some other day."

"Tempting, but no." Instead he yanked back the sheet, scooped her up, and carried her into the shower. He flipped on the water—which shot out an initial blast of freezing cold that had her yelping in distress. "Sorry," he slid the handle to the right position and left her to it.

He missed her departure while he was doing a couple of quick online searches, but whatever she did upstairs, she did it fast and efficiently.

"Is this okay?" White capris, a flowing top in swirls of soft gold and warm bronze that matched the tissue-thin scarf tied to the side about her throat—the ever-present sea glass necklace just dipping into view. Again the flat sandals revealed unpainted toes. Her hair was pulled back from her face in a clip that left her face (and ears) open to see.

"Damn, you do look good enough to take back to bed." Even better than usual. As if she was somehow shining with an inner secret.

"Missed your chance. Where are we going?"

"It's a surprise."

"Okay," and just that easily she trusted him. Not some bimbo's acceptance that whatever the rich boy wanted was fine. It was simply that she trusted him. He hadn't earned a lot of women's trust over the years and it still surprised him every time.

"Nothing big. Just a bit of a lark."

"Downplaying it already. Bad sign, Ridley. Must be a real stinker of an idea."

"Well, not that bad. But it's not like I discovered another fort or anything. Just a few old Italian women that I think I have a chance of taking on in a fair fight."

"If I hold their hands behind their backs."

"Hey! Now I know for a fact that my manliness was insulted that time."

She'd taken his hand as soon as they were out on the *carruggio*. They'd reached to the top of the long steps down to the train platform.

"Let me say this about your manliness." And she turned into his arms—right there at the very top of the steps, on full display to any ascending or descending—wrapped her own arms about his neck, and pulled him into a kiss with plenty of body contact spillover.

His arms came around her of their own accord, sweeping up her back. It took him a moment to notice what was missing…no bra strap. The colors of the blouse had dazzled him too much to notice, but the material was so thin that she might as well have been naked beneath his palms. He dipped his fingers inside her waistband. Nothing there either.

Erica had gone commando—sans underwear of any kind! Erica Barnett! He'd never have bet on that in a thousand years. But it fired his libido onto full high.

As the kiss heated, there were calls and teases from passersby. Ultimately…applause! It was Italy, he supposed, a land that had elevated love to an art form.

By the time they broke apart, both her ears and her cheeks were bright red. His may have been too. She hid her face against his shoulder until the applause died off.

She mumbled something against his shoulder.

"What was that?"

She just shook her head and stayed snuggled in until the crowd dispersed.

She should never have said it aloud. She never should have even thought it. But it had slipped out after that amazing kiss. Never in her life had she been kissed like that…and definitely not so publicly. Ridley had given her a great kiss, until he realized that she'd left her underwear behind—a choice she'd made only after several long minutes of internal debate in front of her mirror. Erica had done it to tease him for not coming back to bed.

But what that choice had changed after he discovered her subterfuge had made any prior kiss, *ever*, dim by comparison. The memory of *any* prior lover paled before that kiss. Except Ridley, of course. The thought of that kiss and his lovemaking coming together had melted a number of very careful locks in her brain. They were barricades she'd set up long ago, a word she never used because to her mother it was just a weapon to be wielded.

If it had been just the kiss and the lovemaking, the combination wouldn't have been enough. But adding in the considerate man who had joined in her explorations—even driving her half across Liguria because he thought she'd like the clock museum. That he listened when she had something to say was a shock. That he offered thoughtful replies in return was unheard of. He had forced her to lighten up each time she'd thought the world had gone heavy. His instinctual kindness—against all his carefully honed habits—had somehow set the final latch free.

Erica had never expected it to come true, had never believed it possible. But the words had stumbled out of her mouth as Ridley held her against the storm of emotion inside. There was no doubt at all. It hadn't been a question. It had been a deep, clear truth.

Until she managed to say the words again, they would always be there, resting safe upon his strong shoulder. And they'd always be true.

For the first time in her life, she'd said the words, "I love you."

In that moment, she wouldn't have believed anyone if they told her it would also be the last time.

~

He'd have preferred the water taxi, but it didn't stop at Corniglia. There was no harbor as such. No pier into the water. The train was how they'd started, so maybe it was appropriate if the train was how they continued.

At Manarola, he shooed her off the train, but when she turned for town, he hooked her hand about his elbow and led her the other way.

"This is how you conned me into walking with you that first day in Corniglia," she rippled her fingers inside the curve of his elbow. "Because it's 'what they do in Italy,' you said."

"It worked, didn't it? Besides, some Italians do."

"You're a con man, Ridley Claremont III."

"I'm all into good cons."

She offered him a haughty princess "Humph!" But she didn't remove her hand or look put out.

Unlike most of the Italian paths, the trail leading south out of Manarola was a slate-paved walkway never less than twenty feet wide and sometimes closer to fifty.

Along the cliff face, small restaurants were scattered. A few had tables out, but most were closed. He knew why, so instead turned to look the other way.

The wire railing was all that separated them from the sea. The Mediterranean splashed against the rocks close below. They moved to the railing and watched the spray shoot up and rain back down on the wet stone with each wave that came in.

When they started walking again, he asked her, "Do you know what this is?"

"The Via dell'Amore," her voice was a whisper no bigger than the waves.

"Right. The Path of Love. Turns out that these two towns were the closest, but also the last to be connected by a trail. For centuries, commerce moved by boat, but there was no easy way for the marriageable young to meet. Once they cut this trail, the youth of the two towns could meet and it became, literally, the Path of Love. I think that's kind of cool. Sure beats sneaking out into the high school parking lot."

Erica continued to walk beside him, though her steps slowed.

"There's this whole funny tradition here. Kinda sweet, I guess. Like that bridge over the Seine in Paris. A couple will come here, snap a padlock on the fence, and throw the key into the ocean. Hearts locked together and all that."

They'd reached the tall gate that blocked the trail. Another damn *chiuso* sign, but at least this time it was no surprise. There were hundreds and hundreds of locks snapped onto the fence of the gate.

"Trail washed out in some big rock slide a few years back, so it's closed until they can figure out how to fix it. Kids are fine, I suppose. Train still goes through. Probably less fun though."

Erica looked up at him and he could see that silence lying there. But he couldn't read her expression at all.

"Anyway, I thought it would be kinda fun. You and me." Then he pulled the lock out of his pocket and showed it to her. He'd bought it from the purse lady, who'd offered him an amazing smile. A local jeweler had carved both of their initials into it in great, loopy swirls.

Erica didn't react.

Instead she studied it lying there in his palm. Really studied it. The whole furrowed brow thing came into full play.

Then she looked up at him ever so slowly. "You said it was 'Nothing big. Just a bit of lark.'"

"Sure I did."

"And you meant that?"

"It's just a lock on a fence. What's the big deal?"

"What's the big deal? *What's the big deal?*" He'd seen a lot of emotions on Erica's face, but not this one.

It didn't mean he wasn't familiar with it. *Oh shit!*

"What's the big fucking deal, you asshole?" She screamed it at him—even fury couldn't make her ugly. "This is the Path of Love. This is a place I've dreamed about since I was a little girl. To stand here, with the One Man. To hell with all the rest of Cinque Terre. *This* is the spot that matters!"

"It's just a damn five-euro lock that—"

"It's not the lock that matters. It's the message." She clapped her hands so loudly together into a doubled fist than he half expected her to call down thunder and lightning from the heavens to cook his ass. "Two hearts. Locked together. Then you throw away the key. That makes it forever. It's the Via dell'Amore. The true path of love in the romantic center of the entire world."

"Okay, forget the lock."

"Forget the lock?" Erica stormed away from him up the walkway for a half dozen paces before turning and storming back.

She jabbed a finger in the center of his chest, sending him stumbling backward against the gate where all the locks rattled and clanked together like chains on a prisoner bound for Hell.

"Forget the lock? Don't you understand, Ridley? I'm in love with you. Knowing what you are didn't stop me. I fell in love with you anyway. Your kindness. Your compassion. The way I can hear in your voice how much you loved your mother. The way mine never let me love her. It spills out of you in an unstoppable wave and it swept me up."

She pounded the side of her fist against his shoulder, right where her face had been after this morning's kiss atop the stairs of Corniglia. Hit him again. Then twice more.

Tears streamed down her face. He'd never seen her cry.

"I would beat it away if I could. But the words are there, on your shoulder. And I can't."

And now he knew what she'd said this morning.

She ground down and looked sadder than he'd imagined possible.

"But that's my problem. You never promised me a thing. Your honor is intact. You have given me…such a gift." Her big eyes closed and she clasped her hands over her necklace.

He was half afraid she'd tear it away, but she didn't. Instead her voice was barely a whisper.

"Such a gift."

Then she turned on her heel and was gone.

Somehow between one eyeblink and the next she was simply gone. A figure away far down the walkway—walking, not running. But he didn't recognize her.

He knew Erica's walk when she was happy, sad, teasing, even playing at wantonly sexy.

He hadn't known her walk when she was mortally wounded.

At least he hadn't until now.

CHAPTER 10

*E*rica finally came back to her senses when she heard the sound of church bells. A different song, distant and far away. Notes were lost on the breeze and then brushed back in different places.

"That would be Sant'Antonio. Don't get to hear those bells often as the church lies in the next town beyond Monterosso." Bridget sat beside her on the tiny balcony of her top floor room.

A table roughly the size of a postage stamp bore a small pot of tea alongside cheese and crackers.

"I can get you some grappa or even whisky if you'd like, but I don't recommend it. It doesn't do piss all for a broken heart and hurts just wicked on the morrow."

Erica shook her head. "Tea's fine."

Bridget sat quietly beside her. Every ten minutes or so another set of church bells would offer up its own tune in its own time slot and Bridget would name the church or the town.

It reminded Erica of the clock museum. Of that ticking beat

of time that she'd so naively thought pulled everything together. It also pulled everything apart.

She'd known that about Ridley. She'd known it, but her heart had forgotten.

Climbing aboard that train this morning, some voice had whispered in her ear. When they'd exited at Manarola she'd almost spoken aloud. When he'd turned away from town to walk the Via dell'Amore, she'd known.

The two of them were always so perfectly in sync. And hadn't she just kissed him like a promise atop the stairs of Corniglia and hadn't her heart answered by offering up the words, even if she'd only managed to whisper them once.

How like him to play down the most important moment of all by claiming it was "no big deal."

Except it wasn't one.

That's what love was to Ridley: no big deal. A plaything.

If it hadn't been the Via dell'Amore, she could have shrugged it off as typically Ridley. A lock snapped on the bridge over the Seine? Sure, why not. They'd be locking these last two precious weeks onto the fence as a happy memory. And they'd have gone on. Another week. Another month. Who knew?

In the years to come, she would come to regret the lost moments. The longer time they should have had here together. But that had been lost into the sea.

"For now all you can do is hurt," Bridget whispered softly. "It's okay. It's what you're supposed to do." She rose to her feet, squeezed Erica's hand tightly as she placed a kiss atop her head.

She paused at the doorway off the terrace. "If he had come to me for the lock, I would have stopped him. I don't know if I would have been right, but I would have." And then she was gone.

It was when the bells of Corniglia rang the opening notes that the first sob unsnarled from around her heart and speared its way out of her chest like shards of glass.

~

"What am I drinking?"

"Wine."

"I can see that." Ridley squinted at it. It was a small glass. He looked over at his companion's. "Yours is bigger."

Then he looked up at his companion. "You're Conrad. Earl of something."

"Evenston, yes. I am sipping a rather pleasing Bordeaux. I find the Cinque Terre whites a little thin on my palate for any serious drinking. You, Mr. Claremont, are consuming grappa. Hence the smaller glass."

"Grappa." Ridley stared back at his glass.

"*Sì, grappa. Il mio grappa,*" a voice said from the other side of the table.

He knew the man's name. Had just a minute ago. A small man. Sixty, seventy, eighty, who could tell on an Italian? They tipped from aging to ageless rather than decrepit. Maybe it was all the wine they drank. If so, he should be all set here.

Ridley trusted the balance of his head to one propped elbow, took up his glass, toasted the two men, and knocked it back. It burned all the way down.

Emilio—that was his name, Emilio—matched him gesture for gesture.

They slammed their glasses back down on the bar together with a sharp thump. At the punch of the grappa, they both released a hard breath like a roaring steam engine, "Ahhh!"

Emilio topped them up again from a gallon-sized jug bound up in one of those Italian straw baskets. Ridley's head was back to needing two chin props to maintain its attachment to his neck. The next glass would have to wait awhile.

He looked around, as much as he dared without having his head fall off.

"Nice place."

Conrad, Earl of Somewhere translated for him.

"*Grazie,*" Emilio answered.

It was. Nicest restaurant in Corniglia. He'd asked around. Well, he'd asked Hal because it was easy and the guy looked like he knew things. Though why he wore such a sad looking tie was a mystery. Sad like gray rain that would never end. Like —Ridley didn't want to think about what.

"Just across the *carruggio,*" Hal had answered. "Best in town."

Ridley had made a reservation for tonight. He figured it was time for Erica to let him treat her to a nice dinner. Instead…today had happened. When he'd stopped in to cancel the reservation, Conrad had been dining there and invited him to join in.

"I remember this place." He remembered seeing it that first day when Erica found that cute little tooled leather purse that he should have bought for her.

Give her trinkets—that way you both understand what the relationship is.

But he hadn't. So now he didn't.

Then he'd looked in the next window and admired the wine collection and the restaurant's chalkboard menu. He'd been right; Erica would like this place. Old stone, cozy tables. Personal. Intimate…

Some part of his mind had that labeled as a danger zone to be avoided at all costs. So instead he focused on what was right in front of him.

"Good wine!"

"*Sì!*" Emilio agreed and they both slammed back another grappa.

Conrad raised his glass in a toast, but didn't drink.

"Don't know if I trust a man who doesn't drink on a drinking night."

"Is that what this is?"

"Sure not a thinking night." Nor apparently a thinking day. His head slipped off its singular support—he'd forgotten to replace his other chin-palm-elbow-table support after the latest round of grappa. His forehead thumped down on his forearm, all that kept him from denting the table with his thick skull.

"Perhaps you should consider Emilio's problems rather than your own," Conrad prompted.

"Emilio's problem is that his grappa might be excellent, but it hasn't killed me yet. C'mon, Emilio. Put me out of my misery."

Conrad translated.

Emilio shook his head and started to cork his jug.

Ridley made his best sad puppy dog look—the one that never worked on Erica, except it did because she always laughed. Damn but that woman had a laugh on her.

Emilio poured them both a half and then put the jug firmly on the table behind.

Ridley raised it in a toast to Emilio. "*Grazie* to a man who makes a fine grappa and a better meal." The meal he'd shared with Conrad had been excellent. An opener of calamari in a walnut sauce. Hand-rolled tagliatelle pasta with shrimp in a red pomodoro sauce for the main. Then a killer freda-something-or-other that had been half chocolate cake and half fudge.

He really should have brought Erica for that last. She'd have gone nuts for it. Why hadn't he? Oh, because he'd cut her heart out and thrown *that* into the ocean when he'd have been better off throwing himself in. Right.

Each course had been matched with a local wine. For dessert, the sweet Sciacchetrà had landed a high alcohol punch that had fit his mood perfectly. As the restaurant had emptied, he and Conrad had remained. Finally, the chef had brought his own form of moonshine to the table—fiery homemade grappa.

After Conrad translated, they all three drank to Emilio's mastery.

Emilio rattled out something, Conrad translating even as he spoke.

"The vineyards. My poor vineyards. You have seen them," Emilio waved a hand vaguely toward the outside world.

Ridley could only nod. He'd seen them. He knew the pain.

"All the young men leave: 1960s, 1970s, whatever. They go to the cities. Now the tourists come, but the young men don't return. We have big consortium now. A cooperative where we cooperate. And what does it get us? I'll tell you what it gets us. A lot of old men working the vines."

"Have to get the young men back." Made sense to him. Actually, despite the alcohol, it sounded as if it actually made sense.

"We tried. We offer free vines to anyone who maintains them for five years."

"Didn't work?"

Emilio gave one of those Italian shrugs that seemed to answer almost everything. This time it said "A little, not enough."

"Why not? Never mind." He knew. The hills were steep, the work would be hard. To fight that hard for the wines, you had to really love them.

He pushed to his feet and weaved over to a display niche that might have once been an arched window in the old stone wall. Photos peeked out from behind empty wine bottles. Emilio as a young man, stomping grapes in a vat.

"You still do that?"

Emilio shook his head. *"Macchina."* Machines, no need to translate that.

First prize at something called the Basilico Festival—Basil Festival.

An old menu card.

Then he focused on the wine bottles. Each of the ten was marked with a prize across a span of thirty years.

Emilio crashed a fist on the table.

Ridley turned to face him. Then had to reach out a hand to the stone wall as the room kept spinning without him.

"Primo. Primo. Primo." He emphasized each shout of "First Place" with a thump of his fist on the table.

Then he pointed to a niche farther down the wall. Again with the banging fist, *"Primo. Primo. Primo."*

"First Place. Sure didn't earn that today, did you, Ridley?" he asked the wine bottles. Then he focused on the rusted pruning and harvesting tools that were tacked to one of the wooden beams. "Just be glad that Erica couldn't get her hands on one of those this morning."

He weaved his way back to the table, managed to land mostly in his chair, then leaned forward to thump his head against the table. It hit once and stayed there.

Emilio asked something.

"He wants to see this lock of yours. The one you had his cousin work on this morning. Based on certain, ah, observed events—such as you being alone for the first time in two weeks —he's supposing that you still have it upon your person."

"His cousin?" Figured. Couldn't get away with shit in a small town. Together every night for two weeks? Didn't sound like any Ridley Claremont he knew. Even wild flings needed a night out at a sports bar or racing motorcycles or something.

He tugged the lock out of his pocket on only his third attempt and dumped it on the table.

"Should have thrown the damn thing in the ocean."

"The sea," Conrad said carefully. "The Mediterranean is a sea, not an ocean."

"Sea. *Sì.*" At the moment, that struck his wine-soaked brain as kind of funny. "S-e-a. S-i." But no one else was laughing. Maybe it wasn't a funny kind of moment. "Whatever."

Only silence answered him. He sat up and saw the two men leaning forward like tipping Towers of Pisa to look at it. He waited to see if Emilio would tip right over, but apparently old Italian men were made of sterner stuff than that. So he leaned in as well and made them the three leaning towers of Corniglia.

"*Bel lavoro,*" Emilio noted.

"He states that it is nice work."

Ridley looked down at it. It was a good lock. A stout piece of brass with a thick shackle that could really take the pressure if needed. The kind of lock that felt good in your hand. Not some wimpy symbolic thing, like the ones he'd seen on the gate. He'd chosen a lock meant to really lock things—making the symbolism even more heinous, if that was possible.

Their initials RC and EB had been engraved in elaborate capitals with curlicue flourishes. Instead of a plus sign, the cousin had used a far more elaborate and decorative ampersand. Not two things to be added together but rather two things that belonged together. It was nice, but...

"Can't say as she liked it much."

Both men turned to him. Conrad managed to straighten, but Emilio continued to lean into a strong wind.

"Hey, don't look at me like that. I thought it was kinda sweet."

Emilio said something but Conrad didn't translate.

"What'd he say?"

Conrad just shook his head.

"What?"

"You may not wish to know."

There were a whole lot of things he didn't wish to know.

"Hit me with it anyway."

"He said it is the kind of lock you make promises with."

"Oh shit. Why did you tell me that?" But it was. Except Ridley hadn't seen that. Not even when Erica had yelled it at him had he gotten it through his thick skull.

He'd seen a pretty bauble for a sweet moment. It was the next scene in the movie. Girl swoons for guy, gets her happy-ever-after for a day, end credits roll. He'd taken enough women to chick flicks to know the scene. Every Bond film, too, as if he needed more proof.

End-credit sex. Then in the next movie, Bond was single once more and the girl was never mentioned again. James only broke the rule once and married her—which had earned Diana Rigg a bullet to the brain instead of end-credit sex.

That's how it worked.

Except not for a woman like Erica.

He offered her a promise...except she'd *known* it was a lie.

He hadn't been just dumb, but cruel on top of it.

Shit.

"*Tu!*" Suddenly Emilio aimed his finger at Ridley's chest.

Ridley jumped like he'd been shot. Lord knew he deserved to be.

He couldn't follow the next part, but Conrad translated for him. "You will come work the vines with me."

"*Sì!*" He needed to do something. And it had to be something without a heart he could break.

"*Domani!*"

"Tomorrow? *Sì.*" If he could get out of bed, which experience told him was gonna be a tough one.

Emilio named a time.

Ridley was wrong, not tough. Brutal.

"*Sì,*" he barely managed a whisper. No less than he deserved. Didn't they just have some medieval Italian dungeon they could cast him into instead? Bound to be one or two still hidden away in a town this old. Perhaps at the base of some ancient tower…

He glanced out the window. Over there, in the dark tower above the *Il Cane* café…

Prepare to meet your doom, Mr. Bond.

Too late, he already had.

Ridley looked back at the two men.

"Either of you have a couch I can borrow?"

CHAPTER 11

In the mirror, Erica saw that Good-girl Erica was back. She wore a plain blouse, jeans, and sandals.

"No," she told her reflection. "I've changed." She methodically stripped off jeans and blouse and slipped them back into the small armoire. Glaring down at her cotton underwear and bra, she had to think hard.

What part of that was her? Was she a woman who went without? Or was she a woman who went without because men liked it? It had certainly heated Ridley's kiss to a fiery heat, a lethally fiery heat. It had consumed her heart and…

Down that path lay more tears and she'd cried enough of those last night. She could feel more, deep in her chest, but they felt as if they were going to stay there for now.

Instead, her chest was wrapped in a plain white cotton bra and she had a decision to make: her or not her?

Her, she decided, and pulled out a blouse the color of the Mediterranean Sea just before the morning sun broke over the high hills. Slacks followed.

And then she stared into the armoire again and considered.

Her pack lay at the bottom in a flaccid heap. How little it would take to stuff it full and walk out the door. She understood the Italian trains now and could be in another town, another city, even the airport by midday. Or another country by this afternoon.

She remembered her first day of college when the American Society 101 professor—the first required course in the economics and business track—had started reading out the statistics of their class. "Fifty students are now sitting in this room. Within twenty years, eighty percent of you will have married, fifty-three percent of those will have divorced, two-thirds of those despite having children. Four of you will be dead..." And he'd gone on and on. Some students had been horrified, but she'd seen it as the underlying basis of life. She wasn't a statistic, but a society could be reduced to numbers.

When he'd finished, and the nervous giggles of some of the students had subsided under his bushy-eyebrowed glared, he'd said one more thing.

"You cannot escape these statistics. They are your generation's future. It may not mean that they are yours individually." Then he'd delved into how the statistics had been generated.

But Erica had already understood, could see the underlying truth.

And now, standing in front of her closet, she could see that society might expect *her* to be the one to run away. The woman's role: to retreat. Yet Cinque Terre had been her dream, not Ridley's.

He'd nearly usurped it. Not through malice the way Dwayne would have, but with his sense of charm and adventure.

Well, it had worked. He'd changed her. But into what? She

wasn't going to find that out any better in Boston or Prague than in Corniglia.

She closed her armoire, leaving her empty pack as little more than a prop for her few pairs of shoes.

One more decision.

The sea glass necklace.

It wasn't a question once she'd thought of it. The necklace was New-girl Erica. Even if she didn't know who that was yet, a pretty necklace of sea glass was a part of it. She deserved to wear it.

That was a new thought: *she deserved.*

What else did she deserve? The woman in the mirror wearing the pretty necklace didn't know, but maybe it was time to find out.

Her newfound determination nearly failed her as she came down the treacherous staircase. Around the very next bend was Ridley's door. She half hoped and half feared that he would show up with flowers and an apology. But he hadn't.

A deep breath, then she rounded the landing.

No Ridley.

Down two more flights.

The monster motorcycle was still in its spot. She wasn't going to think if that was a good thing or bad. He was the one just passing through. And now she'd be just some memory along with the actresses, masseuses, and models of his past. But he was still here.

She chickened out enough to peek through the window rather than walking in the front of the café. Hal was tending the few patrons, his long graying ponytail a clear identifier even though he was on the far side of the room at the moment.

Close by the window, Bridget sat at a table with her laptop open before her.

She spotted Erica and waved her in. She might have mouthed, "All clear."

Erica hoped so. It took only two more deep breaths of courage before she found enough nerve to peer around the corner.

Hal delivered a cappuccino to a German couple seated at one of the outside tables. They'd be obvious from the walking poles and stout daypacks if not from their speech. He turned to her.

Much to her surprise, he walked up and simply wrapped her into a big bear hug.

She let herself sink into it for a moment and feel comforted. His tie was a smiling cartoon grizzly bear.

"I thought you Brits weren't big huggers."

"For the best ones, I make exceptions." Then he patted her on the back once more before shooing her into the café. "Hot cocoa coming up."

And that's when she realized that she'd never ordered it that first time, but somehow Hal had already known that she preferred it to coffee, especially in the mornings.

Inside (still no Ridley), Bridget patted the place beside her at the table.

Snoop lay in his dog bed between them.

"You've certainly got it tough, haven't you?" Erica greeted him with a belly rub that earned her a moan of happiness. After all, what did Snoop know of broken hearts?

"You are looking better, luv," Bridget narrowed her eyes at her. "Is your pack empty or full?"

Erica couldn't help but laugh. "Empty, but it took me a while to decide that."

"Good girl," Bridget patted her hand. Then she slapped her laptop closed. "And thank you for saving me from this."

"What is it?"

"You remember Conrad?"

She nodded. They'd passed him a few times in Corniglia—even stopping to chat a time or two. When she'd found the nerve to ask, he'd assured her that the car was all taken care of.

"I maintain his accounts. Not the day-to-day money, but his business interests are…" she heaved a big sigh that showed off her generous chest. Just the kind Ridley liked on his wom—

Now she was going to have to stop thinking about Ridley. Curiously, Ridley had purged her of constant thoughts of Dwayne, though she remained unsure if that was progress or just a step sideways.

"…becoming a significant challenge." Bridget slapped the laptop in disgust.

"Why?" She wasn't going to ask "Perch" because Ridley wouldn't be here to get the joke.

Bridget eyed her.

"I'm smart about business. Maybe I can help." It was the one thing she was *sure* of about herself and it seemed as good a place to start as any. Smart about men was clearly absent from her resume.

Ridley hung on for dear life and prayed that his death was not near to hand. Or perhaps with how his head felt, he should pray for it to come get him sooner rather than later.

Emilio sat at the controls of one of the tiny monorail cars Ridley had spotted but never given much thought to. The steeply terraced vineyards were laced with steel rails no bigger than his forearm; each held aloft by a pair of crossed steel posts every twenty feet or so. He'd even inspected one of the little conveyances that hung over the rail. Pulled by little more than a lawnmower engine driving small cogged gears, it was designed to drag several trailers a couple feet wide and six feet long. It was an elegant, if rickety-looking method of getting supplies up to the terraces, and grapes back down at harvest time.

He'd never thought about it moving the people.

But Emilio had clambered aboard and waved Ridley to sit in the tiny car behind him. The too-short couch, the blinding sun, and the throbbing headache weren't sufficient abuse. Now he was teetering over the brink as the tiny monorail churned along the thin band of steel. To his left was the sea, to his right, the vertical walls of grapevines towering about them. He tried to turn back and see Corniglia, suddenly the too-short couch looked pretty good, but his hangover said that turning his head that far wasn't an option.

First, it swooped down as they plunged through a ravine. He leaned back until he head was nearly touching the car behind him. Then they were climbing once more, up onto the other side, practically forcing his head to his knees.

"James Bond never had to put up with this shit." But the tiny lawnmower engine drowned out his words and he simply hung on.

The trail that he and Erica had walked from Vernazza to Corniglia that day sliced by somewhere above them. He turned to look back at the town—an ill-advised motion as Emilio slammed through a gut-wrenching turn.

From here, Corniglia was postcard perfect, sitting proudly high atop an Italian cliff. An image he'd shattered for Erica.

He was such a shit! "Bring it on, Emilio." This punishment was the least he deserved.

Instead, Emilio stopped the little monorail. They were parked on a terrace high up the steep wall. From the town to here, the terraces had been well-tended. The rock walls standing firm, the vines pruned and healthy. The fruit bunches little more than tiny green globes the size of the tip of his pinky—just what they should be this time of year.

Emilio climbed down in the last of these.

The very next terrace was a demonstration in disarray.

A whole section of the wall lay as a pile of stone rubble in the back of Emilio's last good terrace. Some dirt had escaped, but not much. Emilio waved a hand back and forth over the lower terrace to show that the dirt was still there, but couldn't be moved back up a level until the rock wall was repaired. Beyond it stood the vines.

They were much worse off than the ones outside Vernazza. They needed a harsh pruning now, then another when they were dormant in the winter. Even with that, next year would be unlikely to be a banner year.

But Emilio had grabbed a gnarled hand around the stout base of one of the vines.

"*Bene! Bene!*" Then he made a fist as if to say the vine was still strong. He thumped his fist against his chest over his heart to emphasize his point.

"*Sì*," Ridley acknowledged.

Then Emilio began pulling down the stone wall.

Emilio was right. Ridley sighed.

Bibi had wanted gardens at the Claremont Manor. Ones that were fitting for the Tuscan style of the grand mansion. She hadn't been much for lifting rock, but he'd spent a whole summer helping the stone masons build dry-laid walls to bring Bibi's gardens to life. It had made her happy and it had made him strong in ways that the girls appreciated. A win-win situation.

Ridley knew they had to tear down the wall until they reached a stable base layer, and then begin the rebuilding.

He groaned as he lifted the first rock and tossed it aside. Drinking night paybacks were hell.

He felt a little better when he noticed Emilio was also wincing with each stone he lifted and sorted by size into the growing piles.

~

"Enough," Bridget shoved the laptop closed, actually nipping the tips of Erica's fingers.

"But—"

"You didn't come here to work, luv."

"Actually, I don't know why I came here." And Erica knew it was true as soon as she said it. "I thought I did, but I don't."

"For now, it is enough that you're here. So go out and *be* here."

"But—" They'd barely scratched the surface of the Italian accounts and it was clear that Conrad held many interests in other countries. "The organization needs—"

"—fixing. Yes, I understood that even though you put it so incredibly tactfully. It's a right royal, bloody disaster, it is. Not be fixed in a day though, will it? An hour here and there will get us there. What's your hourly rate?"

Erica could only blink at her. "I've never worked freelance before. I don't think I want money…" Then she winced as she thought of her bank account. It wasn't appreciating the start of her third week vacationing in a foreign country. She was fine, but…

"Well, until you figure it out, you have free room and board here."

"I couldn't!" To stay in Italy for free?

"Trust me. If you can fix *that*," Bridget snarled at the laptop. "I will be the one making the good deal, not you. Now go. Play." And she ended the discussion by tucking the laptop under her arm and walking away.

Clearly dismissed, Erica stood once again at the threshold between café and *carruggio.*

"Which way?" she could hear Ridley asking. "There's adventure along every path."

And he'd proven that for two. But what was it for one?

Struck by the idea, she trotted up the stairs, changed into her sneakers, and slathered on some sunscreen. She'd had to check the mirror rather than with Ridley to make sure she hadn't missed rubbing in any, but she'd gotten it.

Downstairs, through the dip at the base of town, there was the head of a long ravine to the sea. It was a steep path down the cliff, between the towering banks of vineyards. At the base had been a surprise—like a gem, the heart of Corniglia. Down there, she and Ridley had discovered a rough landing little more than boat-wide. Fifty feet up the cliff stood a crane and a small platform, crowded tightly with the five small fishing boats used by the locals. Corniglia did have a harbor. Or perhaps it had been more of an escape by sea.

In the other direction, the road led out of town, and she turned for it. A hundred meters along, she spotted the trail leading north to Vernazza.

She and Ridley had walked that trail toward Corniglia. She would now walk it backward toward Vernazza—sort of unwind her experience with Ridley and see what she thought of it her own self.

The first step almost dropped her to her knees.

They had walked here...*together.* They had stopped to share a kiss and admire the view. They'd been—

She leaned her back against the hard stone wall.

Erica had been able to lose herself for a few hours in Bridget's accounting mess, and it was a mess. Not a disaster, but her system had clearly grown organically until it was beyond cumbersome. It would take hours, days perhaps to get a handle on it, never mind straighten it out. *That* she understood.

The knife in her gut, the one that had just stolen all her air, she didn't understand at all. But it was no less real.

No, that was wrong. It wasn't real. It wasn't physical pain, though it was trying to cripple her. She checked her gut, actually peeking down the front of her blouse and earning her an askance look from a trooping couple who scurried away quickly. No knife protruded. No blood streamed.

It might feel real, but it was all in her head. Or her heart.

Pushing off the wall, she forced herself to move. To walk past the ghosts of Ridley and herself moving along hand in hand. The trail plunged briefly between rock wall above and thick, rich green vines below. When it emerged, it was once more the cliffside trail above the sea. The salt mixed with the chlorophyll. The tiny globes of the grapes were too young to have a scent, yet she could smell their hope on the breeze. It mixed with olive, eucalyptus, and the occasional batch of wildflowers.

A seep trickled out of the cliff face above her. A small stone bridge arched over the tiny trickle—almost comic in its tininess. And on the other side, at a spot wide enough to form a narrow grassy strip, a solid cloud of daisies spread for five steps along the trail. Thousands of them turned their smiling faces aloft and buoyed her steps for a long way after.

This time, rather than being a goal beckoning on the horizon, Corniglia was a memory, only visible over her shoulder.

Alone, the trail looked new and fresh. Without the electric awareness of their first kiss—across a policeman's baton of all things—sizzling through her every step, she was able to see more of the trail itself. The labor that had gone into it. So unlike the Via dell'Amore, which had been built by railroad workers in the 1920s to make punching the train tunnel easier. That, and a load of pain she was still going to ignore, lay buried under a 2012 landslide that had closed the trail.

This and the other cliff-edge trails between the towns were built for mules to carry olives and grapes centuries ago. Another set of trails lay farther up the slope, but she'd explore those another day. At the moment, she was thrilled to be able to walk at all.

Vernazza pulled at her, making each step easier. Maybe she should have gone there instead.

Then she never would have met Ridley Claremont III and had her heart tromped on so thoroughly.

But she'd probably still be thinking about Dwayne and have that ball of anger wrapped in her gut.

Now all she could feel was pity. Not for him. Instead for the woman who had thought a man like Dwayne was offering so much. Erica of Old.

Old Erica. Better than Good-girl Erica. As she and her underwear had discovered this morning, there were parts of Good-girl Erica that New-girl Erica wanted to keep. From now on, she'd stay focused on New Erica and find out who *she* was, instead of being some man's version of herself.

Whatever else Ridley had done, just by being himself, he had opened doors that could never be closed again. Doors she had now walked through and had no interest in revisiting ever again.

Then she staggered and nearly sprained her ankle.

Her instincts reached out to grab Ridley's arm, but he wasn't there.

She found her balance again…

CHAPTER 12

It had taken three days to rebuild the wall. Another to heave the dirt back over the wall one shovelful at a time, every now and then climbing up the foot-wide set of stairs he'd rebuilt into the wall to tamp it down.

Then they'd gone after the vines with hand clippers.

There had been a long debate with many words on either side (that neither understood) and far more gestures. He wanted to cut them to some semblance of shape, maybe doing a green drop as well to winnow it down to a dozen grape clusters per vine. Emilio argued for a graduated cut across multiple years. ("Years" had taken him a while to get as Emilio kept gesticulated at the sky showing the sun higher and lower then higher again. Then he'd finally understood *anno* as the root of "annual" but they'd moved on by then.)

Eventually Emilio had done one of those "whatever" Italian shrugs and stomped away to go work on the other vines in the lower terraces.

Now that it was quiet, Ridley could start.

But he hesitated.

The old man knew the soil and the vines, but through a mindset that ranged back over centuries. Father had acquired old fields before—none as neglected as these, but old. They'd both gone in and cut hard. It hurt the first season, but the payoff in the second and third season had been very strong. Emilio's method would ease into place by the third year. Maybe the fourth. Being brutal now, Ridley'd get a solid yield in the second year.

Ridley traced the arc of the sun across the sky—Emilio had been very concerned with that. Then he knelt down to look beneath the heavy canopy of leaves and inspect the positioning of the vines themselves. Whoever had planted them originally had been smart, choosing his angles wisely to maximize exposure, even at the cost of more labor. Not the most efficient set, but the *best*.

He liked that. He liked that a lot.

He moved to the most sunward plant, checked the imaginary arc of the sun once more, and began cutting.

By the end of the day, they were trimmed to his satisfaction. He'd had to find a saw to get through some of the long-untended branchings, but he'd gotten it done.

Emilio returned late in the afternoon.

He spent a long time inspecting the plants. He walked up and down the short rows. Sometimes he made *tsking* sounds, other times he shrugged as if asking the vine a question but uncertain of its answer.

Ridley sat at the far end of the terrace. His back against the sun-warmed stone, he watched the sea. Weather was brewing out there somewhere. High, thin mares' tails clouds down to the south.

"Storm's already been here," he told the sky. "And it's blown her out to sea."

He'd seen Erica occasionally. If it was morning, she'd be

hunched over a laptop or playing with Snoop by the bar. In the evening they'd passed along the *carruggio* in opposite directions, trading careful nods—careful for his part anyway, she'd seemed courteous…but not really willing to talk.

Once, he'd stopped for lunch and sat upon the wall with a flask of wine and a baguette thick with smeared soft cheese and generous cold cuts. He could just make her out as she came down the distant B&B stairs. She paused near his bike and did some leg stretches. Then bounced on her toes a few times and stepped out into a quick jog. He'd caught tantalizing glimpses before she'd disappeared along the road leading out of town.

A runner. How had he not known that about her? He imagined that trim body in tight Lycra and groaned.

"Che cosa?"

Though he understood Emilio's question, not a chance would he be trying to explain what he was thinking. He'd lost any hope there but good.

Once he'd passed her on the narrow stairs, so close he could smell her hair.

"Hi," she'd said softly.

She'd given him a moment before continuing past, but he'd been beyond speech.

Unable to face the memories, he watched Emilio as he finished his inspection and returned along the long terrace.

"Ridley."

That startled him to his feet. Until now, he'd mostly been some form of *"Eh!"* No more than a generic call.

Emilio clasped his hand and held it hard. He might be old, but he had a grip of iron. He shook Ridley's hand between both of his.

"Bene! Molto bene!" He continued and though Ridley didn't follow the words, he could follow the gestures. He tapped

Ridley's chest, then put a finger to his own eye. Then he held up three fingers.

"I see three things. Got it. What three things do I see?"

"*Uno,*" Emilio knelt down far enough to pat the soil.

"*Due,*" he held up two fingers, then pointed toward the sun.

"*Tre,*" three fingers, then he brushed a hand over the nearest vine.

"*Bene! Molto bene!*" He patted his hands downward as if indicating the entire terrace.

It *did* look like a vineyard now. The pain he'd caused the vines was there to see, but he could also see that while this year's harvest might be marginal. With luck and rain, next year's set would be strong.

Emilio took his arm and led him to the front center of the terrace. Then he turned him so that they were both looking up the hill rather than down at the sea.

"*Uno,*" he patted his hands toward the terrace again. Then he raised his hands, and patted them higher, clearly indicating the next terrace. It was in no better shape than the one he'd just finished.

"*Due,*" Emilio pointed.

"Yeah. Yeah. I got the message. Another terrace." And looking up he could see the one beyond that and the next. When he'd first seen the hillside, he'd only seen the overgrowth. But now he could see the ancient, neglected terraces ranging up the slope and off to either side as thick rolls in the form of the overgrowth. Each terrace ten or twenty feet deep and fifty to a hundred long. There were dozens, no, hundreds of terraces hiding beneath the leaves of thousands of vines.

"*Merda!*"

"*Sì! Merda! Merda santa!*" Emilio agreed happily.

Holy shit indeed.

Erica had given up on any simple approach. It wasn't a matter of building a few macros or making some tweaks to Bridget's system.

It was so bad that she had to start a spreadsheet of spreadsheets. And these were all top-level numbers—the feeds from various accountant's packages. Experience had taught her that at this level, every system was custom. Commercial packages just couldn't create the kind of views needed. She'd interned for the president of a national insurance company in Boston, and the reports that came to him were all distilled down to a few spreadsheets—a few, very custom spreadsheets —that had given him a manager's view of the company.

That's what was supposed to be happening here, but nothing was talking to anything.

And then she'd started to look at the scope of Conrad's holdings and tried not to be awed by how much the polite old man in the olive grove was worth. Or that she could theorize he was worth, it was hard to tell with the mayhem here.

In her spreadsheet of spreadsheets, she began categorizing the holdings. Two major and a dozen minor properties in England, clearly set up by three distinct accountants with very distinct styles—none of which she liked.

Italy—the olive grove and a vast area of grapes were but one tiny sliver of his holdings. They'd all been tracked using the same method…scanned longhand notes clipped together in an electronic binder.

He had interests in a major cruise line; Vancouver Island, Canada; Africa; and as far away as New Zealand. French holdings included Mediterranean fishing and a castle tucked away deep in the heart of the country.

Some had data going back only a few years, but a Scottish

island went back centuries—records that had been laboriously keyed and heavily annotated from some clan's ledger. Germany. Austria…

"What's this one?" Erica asked Bridget as she walked up. She consistently arrived with an uncanny sense of timing that was so good Erica had been tempted to ask if it was witchcraft. Bridget dropped into the chair next to her and handed over half a grapefruit already sectioned in the rind and sugared.

She glanced at the screen. "Oh. You should ignore that one."

Erica squinted her eyes at Bridget.

"What are you on about?" Bridget poked up a section of bright pink fruit.

"Out of all this mess, that's the one that's done right. The only one, I think. But there's no label on which property it's associated with."

"Really?" Bridget popped forward to peer at the screen more closely. "Well, blow me down and call me a Welshman."

"Welshwoman."

Bridget saluted her acknowledgement of the correction with a spoon before digging into her own grapefruit half. "That one is me and Hal's B&B here."

"If we standardize everything to that, would it make your life easier?"

That made Bridget stop. "You can actually do that?"

Erica shrugged, "It will take a bit. But I've got a handle on most if it."

"I had no idea you were that good."

"What, you just thought you were being kind to a poor American by giving her an excuse to not pay for her room and board?"

Bridget might be English, but she had the Italian shrug down—neither admitting nor denying anything.

Hal came by and dropped off a Pellegrino—the orange

flavor she'd grown particularly partial to. His tie—which was becoming a hobby for Erica, she never wanted to miss a day's tie—was all grapevines. They all seemed relevant somehow, but that one passed her by.

"What have you found?"

"That your system has deep-seated schizophrenia, but I may be able to cure it."

Hal's belly laugh surprised her.

She hadn't really meant to be funny. But then Ridley had often laughed at her non-jokes as well.

"No, it does. It was pasted together in so many different layers and methodologies that it really is—"

Hal rested a hand on her shoulder. "Never try to explain a good joke. It takes half the fun out of it."

Ridley had always just smiled when she did that, letting her try to explain why she'd said what she said. It had often earned her a second laugh, but it also earned her a nod because he saw *why* she'd said what she'd said.

Forcing her thoughts away from him, she plunged deeper into the data and another hour or more slipped painlessly by. Painless was good at the moment and counted as a victory.

She looked up to see Max, the gelato shop owner standing across the table from her with his fists on his hips.

"*Buongiorno*, Max."

"*Buongiorno. Buongiorno* you say to me. Not even friendly *ciao. Buongiorno!*" he turned to the room and gestured to several of the locals. "Like I am city person standing here."

Erica didn't know what to say. Now that she thought about it, she did hear *ciao* far more often among the locals.

"I ask: Max, where she hiding?" Max was clearly upset about something. "I now—"

"Be nice, Max," Bridget cut him off as she delivered a plate of steaming pasta to a nearby table. "She's going to fix my accounting system for me."

"Ah! *Bene!* That is good. Bridget, when she work on little computer, we all stay very much away."

There were several nods of agreement around the room. Then he glared at Erica again.

"But it still no explain why you stop coming to see me and eat my gelato. *Eh?*" He was back to the two fists on his hips.

Erica almost hung her head to let her hair slide forward. She hadn't had gelato since that day on the Via dell'Amore because she didn't want to be reminded of her and Ridley's new-flavor-every-day game. She started to hang her head, but it didn't feel right anymore. New Erica wouldn't do that—at least not as often as the old one.

So instead, she looked up at Max and made him wait a moment. It had the unintended result of making the other patrons take interest and go quiet as well.

Oh well.

"I'm sorry, Max. I'm a very bad girl. I have been seeing another gelato vendor."

He slapped his hand to his heart and looked mortally wounded as translations rippled around the room and laughter erupted. Knowing how to work a crowd, he held the pose like an operatic hero until the noise died once more.

"Tell me, I no too late. Wait! Wait!" He reached for a small container he must have set on the counter when he came in. It was a small paper cup with a gelato of the palest yellow, and had a small plastic spoon stuck in it.

"For me?" She didn't have to pretend the surprise. He'd actually come to find her and entice her back to his shop. It was awfully sweet. As if one customer more or less really mattered. No, as if *she* really mattered.

"*Sì,*" he held out the cup and then stood there, leaning

forward and looking more worried than some supplicant wondering if he was to be beheaded at the Queen's whim.

Everyone was watching her, but she knew most of them. Claire from the leather shop in for her teatime treat. Cedric, the carpenter who had come to Corniglia on school holiday forty years before and never gone back to Wales. Vanessa the baker, who was one of the most beautiful women Erica had ever seen. She was the perfect Italian that every woman wanted to be: long dark hair, lovely smile, and perfect dark-honey complexion on a baker-strong body. Bridget had whispered that she was actually several years older than Erica —which was hard to believe—and that many of the men had tried courting her with little success over the three years since her arrival in Corniglia. There were rumors of a sworn pact with a lost love, a broken heart, an offer of marriage by a king —none of which the thoroughly pleasant Vanessa had confirmed or denied.

Erica *knew* these people. She'd always been a behind-the-scenes business gal and she'd liked it that way. But now she knew more people here than she did after a decade in Boston. At least it seemed that way.

So, if it was to be an Italian-style show, she discovered that she was willing to play it that way. Definitely New Erica all the way.

She took the cup reluctantly, as if it was a snake that might bite her. After inspecting it carefully, she leaned forward and sniffed it carefully, earning her a small laugh.

"It is Corniglia specialty," Max wasn't able to restrain himself. "Only here," he jabbed a finger toward the ground.

That earned him several ahs of acknowledgement, but she still didn't know.

Taking the tiniest spoonful she could, she eyed and sniffed it again for show.

"Miele di Corniglia." She didn't know that word.

She took the taste. The cold creamery. The smooth texture. Then the flavor slowly bloomed to life. But she'd taken too small a bite and couldn't identify it before it slipped away.

Erica took a bigger scoop—careful not to be too forceful and break the tiny spoon, a real beginner's mistake.

Cold. Smooth. Then the flavor unfolded like a spring morning until it overwhelmed her other senses and her eyes slid closed. Honey. Warm, lush honey, swirled deep in the cold gelato. It made her sigh with happiness.

But the continued silence told her that the drama wasn't over yet.

She reopened her eyes and saw that everyone was waiting for her reaction.

Old Erica was predictable.

New Erica ran the hills of Italy, worked on complex reporting systems, and had taken a handsome playboy for a lover. That she'd fallen in love with him and was having a hard time falling *out* of love with him was a different problem.

But New Erica lived *here.* Even if only for this moment, she had come to life in Corniglia.

So, rather than paying some sincere compliment, she set the little cup down and rose to stand in front of Max.

"I'm yours!" she cried out. "I will never stray again!" And she threw herself at him.

He crushed her into a big hug and spun her once around so that her feet cleared the floor. The room echoed with applause.

He made a show of kissing her on both cheeks even as he held her aloft.

"Ahh, if you not love another man so much, *mia amore,*" he whispered before giving her a final squeeze and setting her back on her feet. He kept her pulled close against his side as if they really were sweethearts, waving and bowing to the applause of his friends. Their friends. Her friends.

Erica had to blink hard to keep the tears back.

She wasn't sure if it was for the sake of finally having friends.

Or for the man she still loved despite himself.

Ridley stood in the shadowed doorway of Emilio's restaurant and gazed over at *Il Cane* as another roar of applause and laughter rolled out into the evening light.

He barely recognized the woman at the center of it all. Her hair was back, her face showing. She was the center of attention, yet she didn't retreat or hide. Instead she glowed with a radiant smile somehow even brighter than that first time he'd seen her.

And she was laughing.

Laughing as if she was on the verge of tears.

He double checked. She wore the necklace. It was definitely Erica, just some form of her that he'd never imagined. It bothered him that he couldn't quite read the emotion on her face. It was so clear, but he didn't know what it was.

Emilio tapped him on the shoulder and gave a slight tug to head him into the restaurant. He closed the door.

"*Chiuso,*" he declared.

Ridley knew that one. The door was closed. The physical one here. The metaphoric one there. But he could only stare at the aged wood in front of him. This one he could open with a simple gesture. The other one...

He closed his eyes against the brutal pain. His palms were blistered and every muscle ached from the week he'd spent repairing that one terrace. But it was good. God he wished Bibi could have lived to see it. She'd have loved it.

And he wished Erica could see it. Even if he wasn't there. Even if she didn't know he'd done it. He just wanted her to see that perfect bit of vineyard brought back from the edge and given a new lease on life.

"*Hey!*" Emilio called to him. "*Ristorante chiuso.*"

"Perch?" But Emilio just looked at him strangely. Of course he wouldn't get the joke. "*Perché?*"

Emilio began listing off names and pointing as if they were sitting around a long table. Conrad's was the only one he recognized. Then Emilio yanked out a cell phone, dialed, and shouted into the phone, "*Ciao, Bartolo,*" and that was the last Ridley understood. He made hand signs for Ridley to rearrange the tables into a single long table down the middle, then disappeared into the tiny kitchen in the back while dialing someone else.

By the time Ridley had the tables rearranged, shuffling several chocks under different table legs to keep them stable on the old stone floor, the front door swung open.

Someone he didn't know came in, carrying two bottles of wine. Unable to understand anything past the first word, he responded in kind.

"*Ciao!* Pleased to meet you. I'm Ridley."

"Tomas," the man tapped his own chest. He was just another version of Emilio. A little more round, a little less weather-beaten, but ageless and with a welcoming smile.

Soon he was reduced to, "*Ciao!*" Chest tap. "Ridley," as he struggled to catalogue each new arrival's name. Each brought at least one bottle of wine that was added to the collection lined along the center of the table. Almost all whites, almost all young. But there were some older dusty bottles—the type saved for special occasions. He wondered what the occasion was. It couldn't just be his clearing one measly little wine terrace of the vast array fallen into neglect.

"What are you guys doing here?" he asked the pair of reds that had somehow slipped into the crowd. Old, French reds.

"Either basking in the warmth of their brethren or huddled in fear for their very corks," Conrad remarked from his elbow. "I always like to bring a few reds from my own winery to keep the conversations interesting."

"Oh, thank god. Someone who speaks English," he shook Conrad's hand. "I'm so out of my depth here. Can you at least tell me who these guys are?"

Some were standing and chatting as if they hadn't seen each other in years, or maybe it was as if they were just picking up a conversation from earlier in the day. Either way, the small stone restaurant was echoing with rapid Italian. A few went back to help Emilio, which was good—Ridley had been feeling guilty about not going to assist, but he could barely cook pasta.

"These *guys* as you call them," Conrad looked around the room. "Are the vintners of Cinque Terre. It looks as if all of them were able to join us."

"So quickly?"

"Oh, Emilio put out the word this morning that he'd be cooking for them tonight. He does this on occasion, or one of the other chefs. There are three of them here who should have Michelin stars, in my humble opinion, except they prefer to be more rustic than would be required."

Michelin star? And he'd been thinking of offering to help? He felt less guilty now for staying out of the fray back in the tiny kitchen.

But as he watched them, he began to see that these were definitely men of the craft of winemaking. There were certain gestures that were universal: the cutting of a bunch, the twist of a bottle, the sighting through a refractometer for assessing sugar content. Even though he couldn't follow any of the conversations among the dozen men in the restaurant, he could soon tell who was discussing the vine, who the processing, and who the flavor.

He'd talked his way into a couple of wineries in France. But it was always just him and the vintner. These men might command fewer bottles among all of them than an average French or American winery, but they were all together in this one room and he could hear their shared passion.

For the first time since that awful morning along the Via dell'Amore, he felt like laughing. And he felt like crying because Erica wasn't here to share the moment with him.

And that's when he finally understood the expression she'd been wearing at the center of the crowd in *Il Cane*. Filled with joy, yet impossibly sad in the same moment.

Which meant…

A shout sounded from the back of the room and the three chefs who'd been shouting Italian in the kitchen loudly enough to be heard over the other conversation—it sounded like a brawl—began sending out the first of a whole string of platters. They looked amazing as they were passed hand-to-hand and set on the table.

"Do you think these dishes even have names?" He made sure to grab a seat next to Conrad.

"I would conjecture that they would all have the same name: Chef's Special."

The closest platter had a sea of spaghetti. It smelled of garlic and olive oil and mounded on top were mussels, crayfish almost the size of a Maine lobster, and shrimp with the heads still on. Next to it was a platter of artichoke hearts and olives in some sort of marinade. The next platter to hit the table was a massive pan-fried fish. Farther down the table, tortellini were slathered in pesto and more seafood beyond that. Loaves of focaccia were shoved into unlikely empty spaces. There was enough food for an army.

Wine was poured down the table. This was done with care. Little more than a shot glass-worth until everybody had some.

One of the vintner's spoke up.

Conrad leaned closer as he translated. "He is particularly proud of this one. It is called Cheo Percìo. Watch for notes of star fruit, pineapple, and under-ripe yellow apple. In addition to the Bosco and Vermentino grapes, Bartolo has also used fifteen percent of the less common Piccabun grape."

There was a long silence as everyone observed, sniffed, tasted. For perhaps the first time since grade school, Ridley was the amateur in a wine tasting room. He'd rarely worked the one at the vineyard because he had little patience with the pretenders up from San Francisco who thought they knew a Claremont Reserve from a jug Gallo, but didn't. Most of these men had been tasting these wines and these grapes for decades longer than Ridley had been alive. There was only one other his age and two between them and Emilio.

The finish of the wine was particularly striking. "This is just begging for something salty, like an anchovy antipasto."

Emilio pounded his fist on the table, then jabbed a finger in Ridley's direction. *"Acciughe!"* Then he grabbed the plate nearest him and tipped it up for everyone to see.

"Misto di acciughe delle Cinque Terre."

"What's that?"

"He calls it Mixed Anchovies of the Five Earths of Cinque Terre. They are prepared five different ways, one for each town. A traditional dish that is considered an exceptional match for this wine. You have taken the first step to proving your palate to all these good men, Mr. Claremont."

The others were chattering happily about his success.

Emilio began speaking once more as the dish was served round and the eating began.

"Emilio is regaling the party with tales of your first terrace."

"I was just helping out Emilio."

Conrad's look said he was definitely missing something.

He was. A mere slip of a woman with a smile that could light up an entire café.

~

Old Erica would have wondered about an onset of psychosis. Perhaps not seriously, but she definitely would have toyed with the thought.

New Erica simply sat atop her tower and fought against the storms of giggles when they attacked. She was alone with the sunset and it was too late for the church bells. They had rung while she was still in the impromptu party in the café. Her and Max's little scene over gelato had been merely the spark-off point.

Hal made espressos and served beer. Bridget had churned out pizza in surprising varieties: pesto cream sauce with chicken and artichoke, a spicy red sauce with tiny shrimp, as well as more recognizable varieties. Giuseppe provided a hard salami that put New York pepperoni to shame, which Bridget also dressed with wild mushrooms. There was even a truffle pizza, cut into thin slices to ease the overwhelming richness.

At the end of the meal, Max had hurried back to his shop and returned with a tub of the Miele di Corniglia gelato. A few tourists slipped in and were welcome, but it was a locals' celebration built upon the thinnest of excuses.

Again the giggles overtook her on her lone little terrace in the sky, as the Mediterranean rippled beneath the rising moon.

And again the overwhelming sadness that Ridley was not there. Even if he wasn't beside her, he'd have loved the event.

Old Erica would have him be there as a shield. And to take cues from as to best behavior.

Without that reference point, she'd had to...be herself.

That thought had her jolting upright in her chair.

She *had* just been herself. And it had been fine. Ridley had helped crack the mold she thought she belonged in, but she was the one who had stepped out of it. What version of Erica had kissed Max square on the mouth after that second serving of the Honey of Corniglia gelato, eliciting everyone's cheers? Though she could tell they read nothing into it. And had her whispering for his ears alone, "It *is* too bad how much I love that other man." Which had earned her a knowing smile and a kiss on the forehead like she was a good girl.

She *herself* loved Ridley Claremont III. There wasn't any point in avoiding that thought. Oh, in the past she'd have tried, but he'd been so good for her.

And, she'd spoken those words aloud again—without dying. At the beginning of the week, she'd known to do so would be fatal. But somewhere along the way she'd grown more certain. Stronger.

They might never be together again, but as they both seemed to be remaining in town for now, it was time they stopped avoiding one another. She wouldn't let him pass her by in silence another time. He might not be able to deal with it, but she could.

Or she'd figure out how to.

The meal seemed to have flowed for hours.

Conversation was raucous and impossible to follow, except

when a fresh wine was opened. Then silence would descend. Everyone would swill a little water in their glass to cleanse it, and whichever vintner had brought the bottle would describe what he'd done and what he'd been trying to achieve as it was passed around.

True silence would descend as they were tasted. It had taken a subtle elbow in the ribs from Conrad to make Ridley realize that no one would speak until he had.

Testing the newbie. No more than he'd have done had their situations been reversed.

The nods from around the table when he did speak seemed to say, "Not so bad for a beginner."

By the end of the night there was a substantial line of dead soldiers along the middle of the table—and a lot of drunk vintners around the sides—but Ridley had just received an amazing education in the wines of Cinque Terre.

"Why didn't I know about any of these? There are some exceptional wines here…if you don't count those two reds that god alone knows who brought."

Conrad smiled tolerantly at the tease. The two reds had been exquisite, partly because of their contrast to the fresh young whites of Cinque Terre and partly because they were simply fantastic wines that had paired perfectly with the *cinghale* (which much grunting and fingers curved near the mouth told him was wild boar even before Conrad could translate) and Italian lasagna soup (which sounded awful but tasted marvelous).

"You are unaware of these wines, Mr. Claremont, because the locals and tourists who come to Cinque Terre consume all that is produced. Most of these wines are produced in quantities of less than two hundred cases a year. This one," he tapped the final wine of the evening (a sweet and punchy Sciacchetrà that had been served with narrow slices of strong cheese), "is one of only a few hundred *bottles* per year. The entire region only produces sixteen thousand cases."

Ridley could only whistle in surprise. Sonoma alone produced roughly two thousand times that at over thirty million cases per year. Add in another twenty million for Napa... Even the elite Claremont winery—which had focused on quality (and higher price) versus volume—produced ten times what all of Cinque Terre bottled.

The men in this room really were an entire wine industry unto themselves: grown, processed, bottled, and consumed locally.

Ridley rocked his chair back, then thought better of it when the old wood groaned in protest.

They were a part of something authentic here. Had he ever really been that?

He had, in a way. He, Bibi, Father, and Marissa—Claremont Family Wines' long-time chief vintner. He had gone to UC Davis because it had been Marissa's alma mater about the time he'd entered kindergarten. Just five years younger than his mother, she'd entered through an internship in the fields and been the obvious person to take over by the time Pearson retired. A tall, dramatically beautiful Latina, he'd had a boyhood crush on her apparently from the first day of her arrival.

The four of them had come together over the nurturing of the Claremont wines. The day Father had died and taken Bibi to the grave with him, it had ended. He'd been thrown... No, he'd *let* himself be thrown off the reservation and had been peripatetic ever since.

His parents had died, ironically, on a Valentine's weekend vacation along the coast. Bibi's idea probably. Her "crazy" ideas were clearly something that Father enjoyed so much about her. He'd always pretend resistance, but cave in with a big smile.

Father didn't smile much when she wasn't around, but when they'd all been together in the winery, Ridley had been included in that warmth.

Almost four months now he'd merely been unanchored.

He *hadn't* been rootless despite thinking of himself that way.

Surprised the shit out of him.

Or maybe it didn't. Throughout his teen years—when he wasn't at the winery—he'd portrayed a fine imitation of rootlessness. Fast motorcycles, big parties, loose women. Yet there was that small core, those moments when they'd all been together.

And here it was again.

He looked around the room. Tomas and Bartolo were off at a side table. Chins resting on crossed forearms, they might be having a staring contest, contemplating their next wine, or have slipped into drunken slumber. A trio were working their way down the long line of empties. They were picking up each bottle, making a show of debating about it, but also tipping it up to see if there were any dregs to dribble into their glasses.

Emilio heaved himself up from his chair with a heavy grunt and two fists propped on the table. The small Italian made an impressive display by *not* staggering as he circled around the table and dropped into a chair across from Ridley and Conrad.

"*Bene?*"

"*Molto bene!*" Ridley agreed. Then turned to Conrad, "Please tell him that such fine food and wine in the company of such good men is a real gift. *Grazie!*"

Emilio nodded heavily. It was hard to tell if he was nodding drunk or preparing serious thoughts. There was a bright humor in his dark brown eyes that made Ridley suspect the latter.

"*Uno,*" he made the two handed sign he'd used to indicate

the finished terrace of vines. *"Due,"* and then he moved his hands in multiple pats to indicate all the untended terraces that lay above. Next he pointed at Ridley's chest and spoke to Conrad at some length.

"Ah," Conrad barely glanced at Ridley before answering him back.

Ridley really needed to start learning Italian in a more serious way. In the vineyard he'd gotten by on hand signs and manly grunts, but this was getting awkward. Soon the discussion expanded to include the others who huddled about them—except for Tomas and Bartolo, who apparently were still too deep in their silent consultation to notice anything.

Those still conscious eyed him speculatively as the conversation continued.

"Sì?" Emilio finally asked the group.

They all nodded in reply, those who'd been inspecting the dregs of each bottle having a somewhat harder time with the simple motion.

Then Emilio made a waving motion from Conrad to Ridley. Conrad made a show of turning to face him and collecting his thoughts. Though he'd drunk no less than any of them, Conrad's erect posture showed no sign of wavering except in an overly rapid blinking of his eyes after he swiveled his head. Every other motion remained distinct and deliberate.

"The combined vintners of Cinque Terre wish to make you a proposal."

"Fire away. As long as they don't want to marry me, we're fine." Now why had he said that? Because marriage was the one word that always made him clear out of any relationship. But tonight he could easily picture...but that was ridiculous. He restricted himself to a nod for Conrad to continue.

Conrad's small smile implied that he had understood the half thought, which had better be impossible. The man was just drunk, even if he was the only one left not slurring his words. Breeding paid off. Which left him where? The mongrel son of a fourth-generation melting-pot immigrant turned wine multimillionaire and a runaway street girl turned actress.

"Their proposal is both simple and complex."

"Figured out that much on my own."

"Indeed. You are aware that they created a program under which any vintner willing to tend the vines for a minimum of five years will receive ownership of them."

"Sure."

"But they are also aware of your heritage and that you could buy a whole hillside perhaps out of petty cash."

He shrugged. Close enough to true.

"But they also see in you a man who loves the vines and knows the wine."

"Yep. No denying that." Even if it had taken Emilio bludgeoning his body for a full week in the vineyard for him to remember it.

"So, in addition to offering you immediate ownership of any terraces you recover, they offer their services as mentors to teach you the vagaries of working the grapes of Cinque Terre. The old methods and the new. They are offering you the chance to join this simple brotherhood."

That did rock Ridley back in his chair. A moment too late he realized he'd overbalanced. He missed a grab for the table and crashed over backwards into Tomas' lap. Even that didn't rouse the man from his well-soused contemplations.

He got himself squared back away and looked around the table. They were all watching him closely, except for Leon, who appeared to be watching the table his forehead was now resting on.

"Do *not* accept this offer idly," Conrad warned.

"Yeah, even I got that." And it hurt that not only had

Conrad seen fit to warn him, but worse that he'd been right to do so.

Had he ever really committed to anything?

He could hear Erica's question, "You *never* had a job?"

Nope. Never committed to a thing in your life, Ridley.

It was a hell of an offer. Someone willing to take a chance on him. He flexed his hands. The work had felt good. He'd never minded hard work when it came his way. But it was Father's winery or his brothers' business or…

However, a chance to build his own wines. Not a Claremont label, but a Ridley one. For some idiot reason he saw the two sets of graceful initials carved on that dumbass lock.

Conrad was right. It wasn't a simple answer.

"Thank them for me, as sincerely as—Screw that!"

Ridley looked at each of the men in turn, looking last at Emilio. Emilio who had taken him into the vines and reminded him of his passion for them.

"*Grazie! Grazie mille!* I… *Io…*" he tapped his temple to show that he needed to think. "But…" he clasped his hands over his heart. "*Grazie!*"

There was so much handshaking that followed that he had to ask Conrad, "They did understand that I haven't said yes, right?"

"They understand, Mr. Claremont. And at the risk of sounding even more pompous than usual, I'm proud to know you, Ridley." And Conrad shook his hand very sincerely.

The room slowly emptied. Bartolo, Tomas, and Leon staggered out the door weaving against some internal hurricane.

Conrad was gone, so he tried to ask Emilio if they were okay getting home. He could barely drive these roads sober in the daylight, he couldn't imagine doing it blind drunk in the middle of the night.

But Emilio had pointed *up* the *carruggio,* away from the street where vehicles were allowed. In companionable silence, they put the restaurant back together. Emilio showed him how to run the commercial dishwasher crammed in the tiny kitchen. They soon had it put to rights and parted ways out on the stone cobbles in the heart of Corniglia.

Once Emilio was gone, Ridley tried to wrap his thoughts around the magnanimity of the offer. And the enormity of it.

He needed someone to talk to. Father or Bibi. Someone to talk with about it. Someone who knew him.

No one here, he gazed up and down the street.

Then he looked up at the moon. It was just slipping by the tower of the B&B, appearing to highlight the top floor. Slipping past…and into the thickening clouds that presaged rain. He was too drunk to mind the cliché—rather finding the irony to be really goddamn irritating.

The person he really wanted to ask was up there in her princess' bower.

Not a chance could he do that.

Was there?

CHAPTER 13

The cold rain had moved in overnight. Erica missed her morning run because she was a total wimp about freezing to death. Besides, she'd had an idea last night.

The B&B's reporting structure was good, but it was too simple. She knew what an executive reporting system had to encompass. The problem was to create it so that it would meet the client's needs and yet not be so difficult to tweak that a programmer had to be hired each time an asset was added or removed.

Once she saw the structure, it was trivial to set up. It was the conversion that was going to be the real challenge. She'd have to map and build a custom routine for each old-form asset, but she should be able to move all of the historic data as well as the current bottom line. That was essential for meaningful trend analysis.

She was several hours into it when she became aware of a customer hovering in the middle of the restaurant, uncertain what to do. Glancing around, neither Bridget nor Hal were in view. It was the quiet lull of midmorning and she was the only other person here. Just her and the sleeping Snoop.

Erica turned to offer her help—and was staring straight into Ridley's eyes.

"Hi," he offered a questioning smile.

She tried to speak but neither Old nor New Erica were being of any help.

His smile faded as she continued to stare at him. He looked so good. She could see beyond him that the rain had tapered off, but his long hair was soaked as if he'd been out in it all morning. The slicker was plastered to his broad shoulders. His knuckles were marked with small scabs, one looking particularly fresh. Talk about a man with his manliness intact. He was utterly breathtaking. And apparently speechtaking.

"Sorry," he whispered and turned for the door.

He walked away like a man defeated. Like—

"No! Wait!" She'd practically screamed it out.

Snoop woke with a quick bark, gazed around blearily, then settled back into the depths of his morning nap.

Ridley froze but didn't turn.

"I—" What was she supposed to say to that unturning back? "You startled me is all."

Still he hesitated.

"I didn't know you were still speaking to me."

At that he finally turned. "You're the one who isn't *supposed* to be speaking to me. Not if you had any common sense."

"I know. But I think I've had too *much* common sense in my life. I'm trying to get over it." And now that she was starting, it felt good. Surprisingly good.

Ridley kicked a boot at the floor, like a little boy. Which made her smile. He looked like a little boy who knew he'd been very bad.

She gave him the space to gather his thoughts. At least she'd think of it like that because she had no idea what to say.

"I suppose that saying I'm sorry is pretty damn unimaginative."

"It's a place to start."

"How do you say it in Italian?"

"*Mi dispiace* means I'm sorry."

He quirked a small smile at her. "Looked that one up ahead of time, did you?"

"I looked it up for myself. You told me yourself how you perceived women and relationships. And I was okay with that. I'm sorry for going past that. I looked it up for me." But she couldn't seem to form the words. Now that the moment was here, she couldn't be sorry for anything except the ending.

Ridley edged over and waved one of those big hands at a chair on the other side of the table.

She nodded that it was okay.

He pulled it well back before sitting, then leaned forward and rested his forearms on his knees to study his clasped hands. He looked up at her, but only for a moment before looking back down.

"*Mi dispiace,* too. I *am* sorry."

How was he supposed to look into her beautiful brown eyes when he apologized?

And how was he supposed to make sense of Erica trying to apologize to him?

"Were you just going to say that to confuse the crap out of me?" Ridley watched the water slowly pooling on the floor around him. "Because if that was your plan, it's working."

He glanced up enough to see her shake her head.

"Well, it's working anyway."

And she giggled.

He looked up in surprise at the completely unexpected response.

"What?"

"I like you, Ridley."

"You love me." And why did he find it necessary to throw that in her face? Or was it in his?

"I do," and she didn't even blink. "But I like you too."

"Why?"

"Don't you mean Perch?"

All he could do was shrug. It was too much. Too personal.

Maybe she felt the same because her face went quiet and her voice soft.

"I just do. You're a nice man, no matter what you think of yourself."

"Yeah, right. At least one of us knows better."

"Yes, I do."

Ridley sat back in the chair, because leaning in he could imagine that he felt her warmth. He almost asked how she could be so nice, but then he remembered. It was because Erica Barnett really was nice, right down to her very core.

He could ask anything of her and she'd probably do it. Not because she liked him or loved him, but because she was just that nice. Bartolo, who she'd probably never met, could stop her on the street to ask a favor—and Erica wouldn't shrug him off.

"Could I ask you to do something…" It had all made sense last night as he lay awake staring at the ceiling of his third-story room so close beneath hers. Now it sounded imposing.

She was already nodding, but he held up a hand to stop her.

"I don't want you to do it because you like me or love me or because you're so damn nice."

"Unlike you," she teased back, but was dead on the money.

"Unlike me."

She shrugged. "It's difficult to say what my motivation would be then."

"Huh," he thought about that one a bit. "How about professional interest?"

That earned him the arch of a single eyebrow.

"I have a stupid idea. Or maybe the beginning of a stupid idea. And I don't have anyone to..." Christ, wasn't he a sad sack. Rich playboy with no friends in the world. There were plenty, but they were all at least as shallow as he was. He hated to admit it, but most were actually even worse than that.

"Oh, Ridley." And he could hear it in her voice.

"Not that either. For crap's sake, don't pity me. I'd just like..." so many things "...your opinion."

She made a show of saving whatever she'd been working on and closing the computer. Clearly offering to give him her full attention. Damn her kindness for making him feel so small. He hadn't even asked what she was doing and now he was yanking her away from it.

"What's that?"

"Bridget manages all of Conrad's holdings—which is saying something. Her system is on the verge of a nervous collapse so I'm fixing it for her."

"How are you at business plans?"

"Center of the wheelhouse."

He nodded. There it was, that sharp brain of hers finally showing itself. Yeah, he'd wager Conrad was a mover and shaker. Ridley had certainly recognized the label on those two bottles of red last night that Conrad said were from his estate.

"Is that what you need? A business plan?"

"I don't know. I don't think so. Maybe. Honestly, I haven't got a clue. I understand the vines. I know wine. The business and marketing mess? Never paid two minutes' attention to all that crap."

Again the arched eyebrow, but he saw the smile behind it as well.

Right, real smooth. "That, uh…"

"—crap—" she supplied.

"…*stuff* you do."

"Which is crap under the old 'my stuff, your junk' rule. I get it."

Since her smile was still there, Ridley opted for keeping his mouth shut. He'd never really thought of it that way, but he'd certainly lived it that way. "You fall for me, that's your problem, babe." What a dick. It would be better if he didn't know a hundred more just like him—far too many of whom he'd called friends. Thankfully, most of the ones he knew were still back in Sonoma working the tourist bars and clubs.

"So, what *junk* do you need help with?"

"Uh, it would be easier to show you, if you don't mind going for a ride."

The light in her eyes slammed down.

"No. No. Not on my bike." Then he couldn't help smiling. "Though you might prefer that by the time we're done."

Erica peered into the abyss and decided that she should have opted for the motorcycle, even if it meant wrapping her arms around Ridley.

The morning sun was bright on the grape leaves atop stout vines as the tiny monorail seemed to waver between dumping her to the right into a thicket of them. Or to the left to tumble endlessly downward until her broken and battered body was consumed by Poseidon or Neptune after it splashed into the

Mediterranean. Perhaps the Greek and Roman gods would fight a mad battle over her earthly remains. If they did, she rather hoped that the Norse Valkyrie would swoop down and carry her off to the hall of heroes instead.

But the noisy little engine chugged away taking them over vine and valley until Ridley finally ground it to a stop.

He reached out to help her down, thought better of it, reached again.

While he wallowed in his indecision, she hopped down onto the top of the rock wall he'd parked above.

Vines spread in every direction, both up and down the hill and off to every side. When she turned around, she was faced by another wall of vines on the opposite side of the ravine. And perched atop it was the town of Corniglia.

"It looks sweet from here."

"It does."

What was going to happen when she finished Bridget's project? She didn't want to sabotage it, but she suddenly wished that it would take far longer than it was going to.

"What I wanted you to see is over here."

"Oh right." She followed him as he ducked between the vines, climbed a tiny stairway notched into a rock wall.

Then he stepped aside and stopped.

She looked around. More vines. "What am I supposed to be seeing?"

"That'll teach me," Ridley muttered softly. "A week ago, this terrace looked like that," and he pointed at the snarled mass of vines above the next rock wall. Except the rock wall was a snarl as well—whole sections of it were tumbled down and the vines were sagging into where the dirt had slumped away. To the left and right, the terrace stretched long across the hillside. The terrace they were on was neat as a pin. The steps had been firm and solid beneath her feet.

"Why do these vines look rougher than the ones down below?"

"Because they haven't been pruned in over a decade, maybe decades. Perhaps I was a little harsh when I did it, but I think it's best no matter what Emilio says."

"Who's Emilio?"

"A vintner. He owns those lower vines. You'd like him. He'd like you," Ridley sounded a little surprised as he said the last.

"Maybe I should have fallen for him."

"I like you too." And he did. A lot.

There was one of those silences that he'd forgotten about. Silences around women were never comfortable. But Erica was often simply quiet. It was a new experience.

"You did all this?"

"Emilio got me started. But, yeah, this was me."

"Why?"

And now he was such a sap that he missed the "Perch?" joke.

"It was a way to not think about…"

"Me."

"About how stupid I was about… Yeah, you. Anyway…" And he told her about the hillside, showed her how to see the nearly endless section of overgrown terraces. Then he told her about the offer they'd made him over last night's dinner.

"I've been standing out here all morning…"

"Getting soaking wet."

"I guess. Staring at this damn hillside, and I don't even know how to think about it."

"Is it something you want to do? Become a Cinque Terre vintner?"

"Maybe?"

~

And there was her problem.

Erica turned her back so that he couldn't see her face and sat on the newly redone wall.

She'd fallen in love with a man who didn't know what he wanted. All things considered, she didn't exactly earn stellar points in that area either. America or Italy? Consultant or employee? Princess in her tower or lunatic in her lofty dungeon? By the time her hair reached the ground, would she be as mad as Rapunzel?

Maybe if she helped Ridley, she could somehow help herself.

He sat down on the wall not too far from her, but thankfully far enough. No one ever said that Ridley hadn't had practice in judging the state of mind of women. At least ones who weren't busy falling in love with him.

"Okay. Let's break it down. This," she waved toward the vines, "is obviously something you are good at and care about."

"Check."

"And the wines."

"The whole process."

"Business is a part of that process too."

"Right. Sorry."

"Stop apologizing."

"Sorry."

"Rid-ley!" But when she looked over at him he was smiling.

"Hello, Gudgeon."

"Go to hell, Claremont." But she could feel her own smile. "Other things you're good at? Besides picking up loose women."

"You were less loose than any I picked up before," then he whistled in disgust. "That sure could have come out way better."

"Court fool." It earned her a snort if not a laugh. "What else?"

"I'm a fair motorcycle mechanic, but nothing to write home about. If I had a home."

That got her attention. It took a while, sitting there in the Italian gray, with the sky and the sea almost the same color of slate, but Ridley began talking about his mom and father.

"Why Father?"

"My evil stepbrothers called him Dad. Besides, I thought it was his name. Bibi was one of those moms who always referred to him as 'Your father.' It kind of stuck."

The more he told her, the more she could see the shape of the man. And the real problem was that the more she learned, the *more* she felt for him rather than less. He was so close to being such a good man if he could only get out of his own way.

"Your mom sounds amazing."

"The best. The very best."

"Mama's boy."

"No argument."

And what was her heart supposed to do with that?

"Why me?"

"What are you asking?"

And suddenly she wasn't sure. Why had he been attracted to her? Because it was clearly more than she was just the next woman available, even if he couldn't see that.

But she chose the safer question.

"Why did you come to me about this? That couldn't have been easy."

"It was damned hard. But I needed someone who knew me enough to tell me if this idea was stupid or not. And you know me. Even if it's better than you should."

Erica wondered who she had left to go to if she had a question like this. Not a whole lot of names came to mind.

Even Becky wouldn't be helpful—she was thoroughly convinced that Erica had lost her mind in choosing to come to Italy. Muggings and rapes were only the beginning of her litany of fears. Earthquakes, terrorists, and the re-eruption of Mt. Etna burying Erica in a modern Pompeii had been only a start. Becky had probably never been farther from Boston than Cape Cod in her whole life.

"Okay, Ridley. Snap quiz. Ready?"

"I guess."

"Yes or no answer. You're thinking about abandoning the family winery with all of its good memories and ongoing bad blood because you can't shed your brothers any more than they can get rid of you. In exchange, you're looking at creating a winery—through backbreaking work and against massive odds—here in Cinque Terre that is completely yours. As mentors, you will have the best vintners the area has to offer. And you get to live out your days in Corniglia."

"Yes."

"That wasn't the question."

"Okay, wise-ass Princess Gudgeon, what's the question?"

"Not yet," Erica ignored the tease because she could see the shape of it. Both on the hillside behind her and in her mind. "This isn't a problem you can just throw money at to solve. You have to make it into a going concern. You can float the company some startup capital, but it has to eventually support itself. Even turn a profit."

"I guess so. Sure."

"Now comes the question. You ready?"

"Uh-huh."

"Now, I'm serious on this next part, Ridley." She turned to face him and felt the jolt of how close he was.

He was staring right at her, hanging on her every word. A hundred percent of Ridley Claremont's attention was a lot of attention as both she and her body well knew, and it was difficult to breathe beneath the impact of it.

"This isn't an 'I guess' or a 'maybe' kind of answer. Only yes or no is allowed. One word max. It's not a commitment, just an answer. So whichever comes into your mind first. Okay?"

He saluted her like a military general.

"Okay, Ridley. Here we go. Can you think of anything else you'd rather be doing?"

He blinked at her in surprise as the humor slipped off his face.

And there he was: Ridley the man.

No games going on. No defenses set on stun. No charm set on overkill. Just Ridley. He looked up at the gray sky and down at the vines below.

She tried not to watch him as he stood and turned to face the work he'd done and the work he had yet to do. But she couldn't help herself. It was so right for him. So perfect. It was easy to imagine him standing there after the hillside had been transformed and gray was touching his temples. He was so handsome now, he'd be devastating as he aged. It wasn't hard picturing a son or daughter beside him either, perhaps both.

She rubbed the base of her thumb up and down her sternum. The image made her heart ache.

～

Ridley could see the vines. Not overgrown, choked out with weeds and one another, but transformed, bearing grapes. Once he understood the soil, he could amend it, planting, then turning under mustard or mint, rosemary or oregano. Subtle flavors to be picked up by the vines.

It wasn't a challenge of a season, a year, or even a decade. It was a lifetime challenge. He'd been seeing it as a set of concrete tasks. Ten terraces to clear for an acre. A hundred for a ten-acre yield. He'd be lucky to get a ton an acre in the first year, but he might get as high as eight or ten within five years.

No, it would be Father's method: best yield, not greatest yield.

Fifty terraces, five acres, five to six tons to the acre, thirty tons of grapes… That would produce just over a hundred and fifty cases or eighteen hundred bottles. Also room to grow more, up the abandoned terraces. Maybe a hundred terraces with time.

He could do that. Five years, maybe ten, but he could do that.

The choices later on of which vines, what grapes. Maybe an acre on another slope, perhaps near one of the other towns to extend the terroir to work with. Then…

That would all wait for another day.

"Can you figure out what it would take?"

There was such a long silence that he turned to look down at Erica. Before he could see her face, she spun away to look at the horizon.

"I can probably put together a first-order estimate and an initial plan." Her voice was suddenly as cool as the day and he saw her shiver.

"Oh, crap. You're freezing. Come on, I'll take you back."

She glanced at him only once, as he stopped at the end of the monorail closest to the town. It wasn't long enough to read her expression.

"I take it that the answer is: No, you can't think of anything better?" She asked him softly.

"Nope. Can't. Not even a little."

Erica nodded, confirming that he'd made the right decision before she hurried away toward a hot shower.

That simple nod meant more than anything.

~

One mortal wound wasn't enough. She just had to double down.

"Not even a little," Ridley had said. All her idiot images of the family standing around him. Not putting herself in the picture, but aware that someone had to observe the scene for it to be seen. And for a brief instant in her imagination, she was that outside observer.

Erica didn't go back to work on Bridget's management system, or start on Ridley's business plan. She went upstairs, locked the door, threw the latch, and shoved a chair in front of it for good measure. Shedding her shoes and jacket, she crawled under the covers fully dressed.

The idiot dreamer. The Gudgeon Princess. Boy oh boy, had Ridley nailed that one.

What part of her was so broken that she needed a man in order to feel whole?

For the moment that the image had shown brightly, she'd been swept up in the joy of it. Ridley's heart had been so clear on his face as he surveyed the vines. His vision of the dream so clear that she'd been able to see it herself.

What dreams had she ever had of her own?

Work hard.

In Corniglia she'd found a glimmer of light. Work hard was still an aspect of it, but so was having a life. Her affair with Ridley (that's what she'd call it). Her growing friendships in the community. Her slow discovery of New Erica.

And now back to this: fetal position under the covers, wishing the world would just go away.

Too weary to cry, what was left to do? Who was there to blame?

Stephen? Her father image. A perpetually exhausted and

worried man left with two and a half daughters when all he wanted was a beer in front of a football game before he crashed into bed.

Mother? Erica could hardly remember what she looked like. Her main memory of her was her mother's suitcase in the front hallway while her own was still under her bed. For a week, she'd slept under the bed hugging it, but it hadn't brought her mother back, not even once.

On her own. She understood that. But she'd kept trying to plug men into the picture so that she'd be complete.

Dwayne—a married man *and* her boss. She was so much smarter than that, yet she'd gone there.

Ridley—the bad boy who had even told her that's exactly what he was. But she couldn't regret Ridley, not even when she tried.

Why was that?

She threw back the covers and looked around the room. The rain was back, hard and heavy, beating against her terrace door. But inside, her room was safe and warm. There were a dozen signs of Ridley here. Not only the items they'd found together. There were also purchases she'd made because he'd made her feel prettier and more special than she'd thought she was. And those purchases hadn't been for him, they'd been for her. A celebration of who she was finally turning out to be.

About freaking time, Erica.

Why was that a bad thing? Perch?

She laughed alone in the empty room, but could detect no edge of hysteria. Not much anyway.

Never in her life had she told a man that she loved him. That was the lock on her heart that Ridley had somehow unwound like one of those town clocks until it rang true again.

What if...

There was a glimmer of hope somewhere. And it certainly

wasn't coming from the storm outside, so it must be coming from her.

What if rather than being somehow incomplete without a man—time to face it, without Ridley—what if he was the man she deserved?

"Ha!" Wouldn't that thought surprise the daylights out of him.

It should surprise her. But it didn't. He was the best man she'd ever known. And with the dream of a vineyard, he'd looked as if he'd finally come completely into his own.

She shoved out of bed and paced around the tiny space. From rain-splattered terrace doors to the entry, then the bedroom and back.

"Think, Erica. Think. It's what you do." She'd always been the big-picture gal in business, able to see how all the various pieces must fit together to make a unified process. What about her life? And Ridley's?

For a long, painful week, she'd given up on them. But that was wrong.

"Just plain *wrong!*"

She *loved* his dream. And not only for how it had transformed him standing there. It was an exciting idea to create a business from nothing—something she'd never tried. His words had painted it so clearly in her mind's eye that she could see the pieces unfolding even now. There was a huge amount of work to do, but she already knew where to start. What a gift the vintners had given him. She'd start with interviewing each of those fifteen men who had volunteered to help. She'd learn until she understood.

But one thing she understood right now!

If Ridley was the right man for her, she was the right woman for him. He'd never have stopped moving long enough to discover the dream without her. And it was her help he'd need to clarify his thinking.

It was *her* he needed.

It was just a matter of helping him figure that out.

Ridley meant to go check on Erica at lunchtime. But at the unexpected renewal of the downpour, he ducked into the entry to Emilio's restaurant. It was only open for dinner, but the door was unlocked when he tried it.

Inside, Emilio was just making himself a lunch of pasta with pomodoro red sauce and thick slices of fresh-baked ciabatta. He threw an extra handful of pasta into the water and in minutes they were sitting at one of the tables.

Business and food might be the standard practice in America, but here they were separate. So, as well as they could, they talked of other things—even with ridiculous simplicity.

"Corniglia. Living. Good. Quiet." Emilio had offered.

"Weather like today?"

"Winter. Yes. Summer?" and an Italian shrug saying sometimes.

Most of the meal passed in companionable silence.

Afterward, over a glass of cool white, which finished with the Cinque Terre trademark salt and mineral, Emilio asked the question with raised eyebrows.

Ridley tapped his temple that he was still thinking. Then he gave a thumb's up, swinging it to a thumb's down, before turning it to a little above level. Maybe more than a little, like forty-five degrees up.

Riding high on Erica's approval, he was tempted to give it a full thumb's up. He could afford to run it out of pocket for his entire lifetime, but Erica had been right. It had to pay for itself. And that was an exciting challenge. Not just an Italian winery, but a successful one. He had no idea how to do that, but she'd tell him.

"Erica," he pointed toward the café, tapped his temple for thinking, then pretended to be making calculations on paper.

"*Sì. Per Conrad.*" And Emilio wiggled his fingers as if working a keyboard.

"*Sì,*" Ridley agreed.

Emilio was eyeing him closely.

"What?"

"Erica?" Then he pointed at Ridley and then his own eyes, the same way he'd told Ridley to look at the vines.

"*Sì,*" Ridley kissed his finger tips and tossed the kiss in the air in what he thought was an appropriately Italian gesture. "*Bella.*" Very damn pretty.

Emilio reached over and thumped him hard in the center of the chest.

"Ow! What?"

Emilio looked pissed. Again he pointed at Ridley, then his own eyes, then emphatically across the street toward the café. "*Importante!*"

"Crap!" She *was* important. Really important. Her approval this morning had meant so much. As if she believed in him. He wasn't even sure that Bibi had done that. She'd loved him, no question there, but she'd seen the choices he was making and he could see the disappointment there sometimes. She hid it well, but he'd seen it.

Erica believed in him at a level he'd never believed in anything. Not even the idea of the winery. He'd been able to see the pieces clicking together in her head, what it would take to do: resources, money, time.

But it was really the way she'd asked the question, "Can you think of anything else you'd rather be doing?"

Somehow she'd even taken into account that he was a creature of emotion, not calculation. He leapt before he thought.

He barely noticed as Emilio cleared the table.

All he could think about was the woman across the street.

"Yes, Emilio," he told his friend, even though he wasn't there. "I see her clear as day. Maybe for the first time."

He rose to his feet and tucked the chairs back into place. Maybe he should go find her and talk about something other than his vineyards. He wasn't sure what, but there had to be something.

Emilio tossed his slicker at him.

Because he hadn't been paying attention, Ridley caught the wet mass square in the face. He shrugged it on, not sure if it made him drier or wetter.

Then Emilio led him out the door, past the café, and to one of the tiny trucks that serviced so much of these villages.

Resigned, he clambered aboard. He'd find Erica later, maybe after he'd figured out what the hell to say to her.

They drove up the hill, then turned toward the *chiuso* sign that had sent him here. Maybe he should have the thing bronzed, or burn incense in front of it, or whatever one did for such things. Most of a month ago, it had turned him toward Corniglia.

What a difference a month made.

Before they reached the sign, Emilio turned onto a narrow track that led farther up hill. After another climb through the trees, they reached a small town. It had a run-down church and a few dozen houses. It also had an old barn in good repair that Emilio parked close beside.

He led Ridley inside into a wonderland. It was modern and ancient combined.

"*Macchina!*" Emilio patted a crushing machine. A line of

fermentation tanks followed. But the next step was a line of oak barrels for clarification. Emilio went down the line of barrels naming grapes, mixtures, and popping off the bung to dip for sugar content. Smaller barrels for more aging. A bottling machine and finally racks and racks of bottles aging in the tipped-down position to keep the cork wet. At the third rack, Emilio began giving the bottles the standard half turn and Ridley helped.

The size of the operation was ludicrously small in his experience. However, based on the number of bottles produced here, it was probably plenty. A small, efficient winery.

He asked why the last aging was in oak rather than steel. Energetic whites were often finished in steel.

Emilio tapped his own chest and then the oak. He tapped Ridley's chest and shrugged "maybe you."

Ridley nodded. It was something to consider.

Then Emilio led him out into the rain and tromped along as if it was summer sunshine rather than a chill deluge that kept slipping down the back of his neck.

At the other end of the tiny town was a small barn. Emilio led him inside through a broken door half off its hinges. There had once been cow or horse stalls, but those too had fallen into disrepair.

Emilio pointed at the ceiling and Ridley realized that no water was coming in. It was a good space. He paced it off. Yes. It was possible. Tight but possible.

He turned to get Erica's reaction…

But of course she wasn't here.

CHAPTER 14

She'd passed Ridley on the stairway the next day. "I'll start today, but it will take time."

He'd accepted that without question, then told her about the old barn on the hill.

"I'll think about that. First I have to finish what I'm doing for Bridget."

He'd looked disappointed, but then gone about his business. Thankfully, he'd returned to the vines and the next terrace. When she realized that his vines were visible from her little top-floor terrace, she'd bought a small pair of binoculars.

"Not voyeuristic," she assured herself as she looked at him working for longer than she should have. "I'm not being voyeuristic. It's just that as long as he's out there, I can be working here."

Bridget still got her mornings, but her afternoons were for Ridley.

She started with Emilio. Numbers transcended language and she soon had a gauge for the amount of work the terraces would require. The hug he gave her afterwards was far more than normal, even among Italians. Though he was barely taller than she was, he held her close for a long moment, patting her gently on the back.

"*Bene, Erica. Molto bene.*" Not pretty, but rather good. Very good.

He'd left her feeling sniffly for reasons she couldn't quite identify.

He sent her to Leon for the harvest and Tomas for the processing. Bartolo gave her to understand what a vintner went through to make a palatable wine into an exceptional wine.

At marketing, she hit a wall. Cinque Terre wines were in restaurants and shops. They sold nothing outside the region. They didn't need to promote the wines, they simply sold. She backtracked one by one all the way to Emilio, but each merely shrugged.

On one of her runs up through the hills, she found the little barn that Emilio had showed to Ridley. It would *work*, but was that enough? Ridley needed it to excel.

She researched Claremont Family Wines' history. She knew nothing about wine, but the prices that Claremont commanded per bottle was stratospherically out of her price range. A basic bottle was forty dollars and the reserves started at over a hundred. She poked through a few other wineries' websites. The split became obvious very quickly: drinking wines (some better, some worse), and premium wines (some exceptional and a rare few up in Claremont's category).

Erica *did* know Ridley. Perhaps better than he did.

Just to confirm it, she researched his motorcycle. The Indian Chieftain Classic wasn't merely an exceptional machine, it was one of their best. Various websites also noted that it was one of *the* motorcycles for the real connoisseur. They weren't just selling the bike, but also the history and tradition. This wasn't some monster Harley declaring "I have the soul of a biker!" Nor was it some speed demon. This was a real rider's machine.

Ridley all over.

She factored in lower crop yield, better processing equipment, and a marketing campaign. Even with an infusion of startup capital, two limiting factors rapidly became clear.

One, Ridley could either take the lead on the vines or the processing. But there was only one of him and he couldn't possibly do both.

Two, he needed a business and marketing manager badly.

That made her smile.

She signed up for an on-line course in marketing and started the first session that night.

Another week had gone by, another terrace done. He'd worked right through a pair of rainy days, but had been glad of the sun for the day-long task of pruning the vines on the second terrace. He could have fifty terraces inside a year if he did nothing else.

While his first year's harvest was going to be crap, he still had to set up the processing line to be ready for the fall. That would be hours of thinking about the wines and then the processes. He needed to repeat the tour of Emilio's line with each of the other vintners and then think about the wines they created to understand how the grapes behaved before even starting on designing his own.

He sat on the newly finished rock wall of his second terrace and dangled his feet out over his first. He drained a bottle of water as he watched the sun head into the Med; the light giving the vines a warm orange glow of new hope at their rediscovered freedom from the tangle. A roll of his shoulders told him just how lax he'd become. Another week, maybe two and he wouldn't feel the aches so much.

Still no word from Erica. Every time he saw her, she was head down over Bridget's laptop. More than one evening he'd sat out at a table on the *carruggio* (though not their first one), and eavesdropped. Any of the locals who came in always made a point of greeting her and asking how it was going. She always answered them cheerfully. She missed more than her fair share of teases, but that was Erica. Straightforward and pleasant to a fault...and a total gudgeon. He liked that about her.

As a matter of fact, he couldn't think of anything much to *not* like about her.

That too was outside his experience. Women always had shortcomings. The main one was that they wanted a slice of him or his wealth. He knew he was "a catch" by Napa/Sonoma standards. And a lot of women came aboard with grappling hooks at the fore.

They all assumed that, of course, he'd pay the way. And get them into the best parties. And buy them insanely expensive little gifts.

Erica hadn't even let him buy her a goddamn leather purse.

It wasn't pride either. It was...what?

Damned if he knew.

One thing he did know though. He needed some serious help.

He had moved ahead with tackling the vines, confident that Erica would figure out how to make it all work. He'd thought about hiring a laborer to help him. He still might for the rock work. But he wasn't going to trust the pruning to anyone else. That trapped him out here.

Then he had an idea and yanked out his cell phone.

"Marissa, my favorite vintner on the planet." He shouted out when Claremont Winery's chief vintner answered her phone. "You must run away with me."

"Ridley, my favorite vagabond. Where are you?" It was so good to hear her voice, to hear her laugh that big open laugh of hers. The lush tones of her Mexican heritage were like a piece of his childhood.

"How do you feel about Italian men? Or perhaps an English Count? He's a sweet old chap."

"Eh," she made a shrugging sound. "You sweeping down the Italian ladies?"

He opened his mouth to assure her he absolutely was, but nothing came out.

Marissa made a thoughtful humming sound. "So, why are you calling?"

"I need a reason?"

"Months of silence, then a call out of the blue from Italy. Must be a reason."

"I knew there was a reason I always liked you." She was as straightforward as Erica. Well, not quite, Marissa was a teasing Latina as well, but she was all business when it came to wine.

"You always liked me because I am *soo* beautiful."

"It's true. It's so true. You were the older woman I always longed for."

"Don't say it that way, I was all of twenty when I first came to Claremont. Of course you were five. It is so impossible that you are motorcycling your way around Italy. You're too young!" And they laughed together. From the Italian sunset to the Californian noon. It was a good sound.

"So, if you're ambivalent about Italian men, how do you feel about Italian wines?"

The sudden silence said that he had her full attention as he knew he would.

"I'm sitting here in Corniglia, Cinque Terre, in the heart of Liguria. I'm sitting and watching the sun set into the Mediterranean from my new vineyard."

She gasped. It made him laugh. It was hard to surprise Marissa. "You bought a winery?"

"More like building it from scratch. But the vines are old and very good. The wines here are young and fresh."

"Like you?"

"Worse."

"That's hard to believe."

And it would have been before he met Erica. But she made him feel less youthful, more like a grown-up. More like… himself. Like a man that Bibi would be proud of. It was a strange sensation, but it fit. Like the new winery fit.

"How much area do you have under cultivation?"

Ridley glanced over his shoulder at the just finished second terrace. "About two-tenths of an acre."

"Two-tenths…?" Marissa managed to sputter out.

"Uh-huh."

"Your new winery is going to produce twelve cases of wine?"

"Only if I'm lucky. The vines need a lot of help."

Marissa waited. "So why the call?" Again that forthrightness.

"I'm good at the wines, but you're better."

"Why thank you so very much."

"How would you like to get away from my evil half brothers, come here, work for almost nothing, but have control of our new wines? The terroir is interesting here: a lot of citrus and a lot of salt. I have some ideas, but the vineyard will need major work to bring it to bear. I need someone with your touch in the winery itself."

There was a long silence. She was one of the most highly

paid vintners in either Napa or Sonoma—Father had made sure of that so that she'd stay.

"Complete control?"

"In consultation with me, but yes. Same criteria: top quality, not quantity."

"You can not have much quantity with two-tenths of an acre."

He ignore the jibe. "And, if things go well, there just might be a business partner. But she's the business side and doesn't know the wines."

"She?"

Ridley kept his mouth shut. Had his tone given away something of what he was feeling?

What he was feeling? Like if Erica wasn't a part of all this, there wasn't going to be any point to it at all.

Another of Marissa's thoughtful hums sounded over the line from America.

"A woman who was finally able to strike you speechless. Not even your mother or I could do that. This is a woman I *must* meet."

Ridley opened his mouth, but still couldn't think of what to say. He wasn't asking her to come and approve of Erica. He'd called about the wines.

"I have a vacation in a few weeks. I was going to go up to Oregon and try some of their new wines, but Italy… I could be talked into coming to see what you are up to and meet this woman."

"Tickets are on me. But it's the wine I want the opinion on."

"Free tickets to Italy. Deal. As to the wine versus the woman…" This time the hum was thoughtful and told him he wasn't going to avoid that either.

He'd better warn Erica that he wasn't flying Marissa out to pass approval on her, no matter what Marissa thought.

"You know, Ridley, you never asked me what I thought about Italian women."

"Italian *women?*"

"Um-hmm!" She made it a very happy and rather lascivious sound for a woman fifteen years his senior. At that he had to actually pull the phone away to look at it and make sure that it had Marissa's name on the connect screen.

"How didn't I know that about you?"

"Well, you were so in love with me as a little boy, I didn't want to disappoint you. Now you are in love with someone else, so it no longer matters. Yes, Italy sounds so *very* nice. Two-tenths of an acre!" She ended the call on a laugh.

"I'm not…" But the line was dead.

Was that what was wrong with him? Had Ridley Claremont fallen in love and not even noticed?

James Bond never knew, except that once.

How was he supposed to know?

"There are two ways to run a conversion like this."

Bridget was leaning close to watch over her shoulder. They weren't alone in the café. It was evening and the place was busy. Bridget had left Hal and a woman who came in to help at night to take care of the place. Erica was surprised at the number of locals, and more than a few were listening in with interest.

"Two ways," Bridget nodded, then looked up in surprise. "What two ways?"

"Like a Band-Aid. Ease it bit by bit, or yank if off."

"Both are terrible," Bridget's shudder earned her a few laughs.

"Easing your data over means either moving one category

at a time or moving all of the ending totals. First you have to make sure that you are entering the correct new information into the old or new system as you do the migration. And second, and this is a bitch, you have to hand enter all of the history. The advantage is that it's careful and methodical."

"What's the yanking method?"

"Write a conversion routine that addresses every single thing. Run it. Then check that the old and new systems report everything exactly the same. To the penny to be sure. And even then, you have to double-check."

"Which choice are we doing?"

"Press that key." Erica pointed and Bridget pressed it after only the briefest sideways glance at her.

"Now what?"

Erica pointed. The data scrub and convert was a task bar running across the bottom of the screen. As it rolled along, the master spreadsheet started populating line by line.

"Each line represents a subsheet of historical data—including the Scottish castle right back into the 1500s."

Bridget's eyes kept getting wider as more and more lines dropped into the master sheet. "I was managing all that?"

"Essentially by hand. I don't know how you did it."

Bridget shook her head. "Neither do I, luv. Neither do I."

The status bar hit a hundred percent.

Erica split the screen. "And now the double check."

She ran her test routine comparing the old data with the new. The numbers flashed by in pairs. The entire restaurant had gone silent. All eyes were on her and she did her best to ignore that and focus on the job.

"I standardized to British pounds," explaining gave her less excuse to think while the final test ran. "That was by far the largest sector of Conrad's holdings. But I'll show you how to change the standard if you want to run dollars or euros. Or even yen, for that matter."

It reached the end with a soft ping that sent a gasp through the room.

She wasn't the only one holding her breath.

Her desire to have this work was so overwhelming that she had to force herself to slow down and compare the old and new system totals digit by digit, just to be sure they matched. While the total was staggering, it tallied to the penny.

"That," Erica pointed on a sigh of relief, "is the ripping off the Band-Aid method."

"It's done?" Bridget looked at her aghast.

"*È finito!*"

Bridget actually shrieked with joy and threw her arms around Erica as applause broke out around the room.

Large-scale data conversions were a total bear and there was still hours of training Bridget on the new system, but the end of a hard cutover after weeks of hard work was always a good feeling. She'd been running test conversions for three days on sample sets, and debugging dozens of problems. But this run was *clean*. It was actually the third repetition on this exact data set and all three had checked out identically.

The applause continued. Whistles. Cheers. Snoop barking at the sudden noise.

Bridget was probably the only person in the room who could come near to understanding what she'd just done. But still, they all knew something grand had been achieved and her Italian friends were simply glad of any reason to celebrate.

It made her feel better about who she was and what she could do on her own than she had in a long, long time. This moment had been completely hers.

She hugged Bridget back and didn't even bother trying to stop the tears.

Ridley stood out on the *carruggio*. The crowd was far too thick to get into *Il Cane.*

But he didn't need to go in to understand.

Whatever Erica had been working on these long weeks, she'd done. And by the scale of Bridget's reaction, it had been something fairly spectacular. Which didn't surprise him at all.

The only thing left about Erica that surprised him was that she loved him. That one still had him scratching his head.

"The lady has truly done something," Conrad said from close by his elbow.

"She's amazing. Converting all you accounts to a single standard. I'd wager that was a hell of a task."

Conrad nodded solemnly. "It was. But that is not the achievement to which I was referring."

"Oh, what then?"

"Look at the woman."

And Ridley did. Beautiful, smart, unintentionally funny, sweet to the core. But she was also the master, or perhaps mistress, of the moment. The fairy-tale princess was gone. In her place, looking both the same and completely different than the woman he'd met a month ago, sat the Queen. Not from some fairy tale or long royal line. And yet she was.

He'd spent a lifetime imagining himself with Bond girls. "Claremont. Ridley Claremont," said in that original Sean Connery voice. Hell, he was the child of a Bond girl, so it made sense.

Back in the vineyard he'd wondered why Erica hadn't let him buy that silly purse. Perhaps now he understood. Not pride, but rather because she knew that she could do for herself whatever she needed. The princess might not have known that she knew that, but the Queen absolutely did.

Oddly, looking at Erica, he could see the cracks in Bibi's facade. His mother had always been happy, always seeking the joy of every moment. But looking at Erica, he knew that there had been a very hidden layer that Bibi was careful to never show, not even to him. Her constant search for joy had been almost manic in its intensity, perhaps based on the fear that her wonderful new reality would shatter at any moment despite living it for more than half her life.

Erica's joy was rooted in something far more centered, as if it came right out of who she was.

"She *is* amazing." But Conrad was no longer at his elbow and Ridley was left to watch from outside in the dark.

$\mathcal{E}$rica was a hundred times more nervous about meeting Ridley alone than running that conversion in front of an entire crowd. She'd checked everything a dozen times and was down to the point where she'd revised a comma into a semicolon, and back, about ten times before she managed to stop herself.

She sat out at *their* table on the *carruggio* for the first time since they'd stopped sleeping together. She was shivering there before sunrise because she hadn't been able to wait any longer. She watched his big motorcycle slowly emerge from the line of shadow as if it too was waiting.

Ridley couldn't ride away on it. He simply couldn't. There was too much here to just leave.

And her hands shook with the hope that he thought the same thing.

Erica was still there, with her second cup of hot chocolate at the much more rational hour that Ridley descended.

He stopped abruptly when he saw her.

She'd moved the other chair in and out, trying to turn it

invitingly, before she got ahold of herself and tucked it back under the table just as it had been that night.

With a silent nod, he asked permission.

With an equally silent nod, she granted it.

"Is that it?" He pointed to the slim notebook she'd assembled and now clutched like a lifeline.

"Sì."

"First word you ever said to me."

"Sì," it had been and the memory made her smile. Her one-word defense against the bad boy who'd ridden his motorcycle out of the sunset and into her life.

"And that absolutely killer smile that blows me away every time."

And her heart stumbled.

Erica forced herself to take a calming breath. She had to get through this. There had to be a way to know. She wouldn't survive if this was a one-way relationship. She just wouldn't.

"Can I see it?"

Her heart? How could he not? Oh, the business plan. Right, just focus on the business plan.

"I have a couple of questions first."

"Fire away," he took a sip of her cocoa without asking. Such a simple gesture, she wouldn't read any deeper meaning into it. She really wouldn't. Not about sharing. Not about—

"What's your estimated yield per acre?"

That had him blinking in surprise. Then a bark of laughter.

"What?"

"Just remind me to never underestimate you again. Not that I do, but that is a key question to any vintner, but you already figured that out. Low. Five, maybe six tons."

"Quality over quantity? Like Claremont? Like your motorcycle?"

"Don't know what my bike has to do with it, but yes. I'll

take quality every time." She wasn't going to read anything into the look he aimed her way.

"Really exceptional? It will have to be if you want to take on the likes of Bartolo and Leon."

"Top dollar and worth it."

"There's one more question."

"Okay."

"You know that you can't run both the vineyard and the winery yourself, right?"

He nodded. "The best vintner in all of Sonoma is flying out in two weeks. She'll be a hard sell, but I think she'll do it."

"But…" Erica looked down at the still closed business plan. Then back up at him. "How did you know I could…" She could only tap the plan with the her finger.

"I might be stupid, Erica, but I'm not dumb. Or something like that. I knew you'd figure out how to make it all work."

"You knew…"

"Don't need to see the damn numbers. You say it'll work, I'll believe you."

"I—" She looked down at the plan. It wasn't right. She glared up at Ridley. "No business owner accepts a plan in the blind unless he's an idiot."

He held up an admonishing finger. "Might be stupid, but I'm not dumb. Remember? Take it up with my business manager."

"Your—" But the blow was too deep. He was flying in a vintner *and* a business manager. No room for little Erica in his life. No room for her ideas. No—

"Erica," a voice said from far away. "Erica Barnett!"

Suddenly a hard hand clamped over both of hers.

"Breathe, goddamn it!"

She couldn't. It hurt too much. Going down for the third time. *So long, it's been good to know ye.* The line from the old

Dustbowl song flitted through the pain, complete with Woody Guthrie's melodic guitar.

"Erica!"

Then something happened.

Something she could focus on. It jolted her system hard enough to bring her back to consciousness before she died on the spot.

Ridley was kissing her.

Kissing *her.*

Too hard. But it felt so good that she didn't want him to stop.

It ended too soon. Too abruptly.

Her head didn't stop spinning for several long seconds.

"Perch?" She barely managed to whisper.

He roared with laughter, but he didn't let go of her hand. That was good. It gave her something to focus on.

"You mean aside from averting your panic attack?"

"Is that what happened?" That didn't sound like her. It had felt far worse than that sounded. At least until the kissing part of it.

"Aside from that," Ridley's voice was a soft tease. "I wanted to. And don't say perch again."

She opened her mouth, but couldn't think of what else to ask.

"Erica," Ridley's voice became dead serious. "I'd be a goddamn idiot to have anyone other than you as my business manager. You loved this place, this town, even before I did. You were born to be here. The people welcomed you into their hearts. Just one of the many gifts you have."

"You want me to—" She patted her hand on the business plan as words again failed her.

"Damn straight."

She looked down at it in wonder.

"Well?"

"There are things in here we need to talk about. For example, that barn will never do. You need to be right here in town. A dedicated shop, just for your wines—a destination winery. There are a couple of good buildings here that are vacant. Cellar tours. Tasting room. Gift shop. Only the very best. All local. Maybe get Claire to run it. I have a couple drafts of a logo, but I'm not happy with any of them yet. And—"

Ridley stopped her with another kiss across the small table. This one was longer, less forceful. It lingered and teased.

It also left her breathless when he finally sat back looking far too smug for his own good.

"I'll take that as a yes about the job," he spoke into her stunned silence. "Now I have a question for you. Different topic."

"It was a yes." To run a business. To build it from the ground up the way she wanted. She could see it. She could do it. She knew she could.

"How did you know?"

"How did I know what?" Then she looked at his eyes and saw the worry in them and she understood the question. "How did I know I loved you?"

Ridley didn't look away. Not all the way away. But she could feel the caution coming over him.

"Saying I just knew isn't going to help you, is it?" But where he felt fear, she felt such a surge of hope that she almost lost her breath again.

He shook his head. "In the length of one lousy phone call, Marissa said she just had to meet the woman who'd finally made me fall in love with her. But how do *I* know?"

Erica had *just known*. It had come from so deep that there had been no questioning it.

Giving him the old line of "If you don't know the answer,

the answer is no," was both not helpful and far too scary to contemplate.

Ridley wanted her to run his business. That was huge.

But now he was asking *her* to tell *him* whether or not he loved her?

The laugh bubbled out of her.

Ridley looked hurt, but it took her some time to stop it and apologize.

"You do understand how ludicrous it is to ask me that?"

He grimaced, but didn't relent.

"Okay," she swallowed down a final giggle. "I know how *I* knew. But you're asking how do *you* know?"

He nodded.

Erica wanted to look at the sky, the fields, even his motorcycle, hoping to find some inspiration. But she couldn't look away from Ridley's eyes. His lovely eyes.

"I guess it's the same question as before."

"What do you mean?"

"It sounds a little strange for *me* to be asking this, so for a moment pretend I'm just your friend and not the woman who loves you and *so* wants to bias the answer you give."

"Oh, I get that now. Sorry. Okay. Right, I'm asking my best pal Erica and not the stunning Queen."

"Queen Gudgeon."

"Didn't say that." And he hadn't. Again, it gave her hope.

"Okay…Pal," she tried to drop her voice like a guy friend and earned a bark of laughter. "This here Erica lady, she ain't no princess or a queen. She's just a woman with a head for business." *And a body and a heart that can't be with anyone else but you.* "Can you imagine wanting to be with someone other than her? Ever?"

"Huh," Ridley grunted. He dropped back in his chair. Now it was his turn to inspect the sky and the town and every damn where else other than looking at her. How did a guy get to do that, but she couldn't? Something genetic that didn't seem fair.

But then he looked right at her. He slouched in the chair and stuck his legs partway out into the *carruggio*, doing his first night of arrival bad-boy act perfectly.

"You know, Erica old pal…"

"What?"

He just smiled at her.

"Rid-ley!"

"Remember, dumb but not stupid."

"Or the other way around," she snarled at him.

"Or the other way around. Either way, I'm not dumb enough that I think I can ever meet anyone I want to spend my life with even half as much as you. Maybe not even a tenth…old pal."

It took her a second to unscramble that the most important words of her life were being spoken by a man slouched in a chair and teasing her.

Then he jumped to his feet and knelt in front of her.

"As for Erica Barnett," his voice was suddenly soft as he took her hands. "If you marry me, I'll do my damnedest to make you happy every single day of our lives."

All of her words were gone. Or perhaps all the ones that mattered had been spoken.

Queen Erica, descended from her tower, answered her Prince Ridley with the softest kiss, and a gentle spill of tears.

The wedding had been a grand affair in the middle of the *carruggio,* spilling a long way up and down the street.

Emilio and Leon had cooked. Bridget and Hal had filled in the edges of the feast. And Max had provided the gelato for dessert.

They'd also put a serious dent in the town's wine production for the year.

Ridley hadn't noticed Marissa slipping out of the crowd early, arm-in-arm with Vanessa the lovely baker, but Erica did. She saw them go and decided that they made a fantastically striking couple.

There was so much to be done that a long weekend cruising on Ridley's big motorcycle was all the honeymoon they'd wanted. He'd taken her north, past Genoa, to the old towns of Dolceacqua and Apricale. Monet and others since had loved the light there, many paintings had been inspired by that soft light on the river. They'd walked hand-in-hand through the extensive *carruggios,* older and far more twisted than

Corniglia's or the others in Cinque Terre. They'd eaten the gelato, watched the swallows soar above the river at dusk, and made love.

But all it had really done was prove that they were coming home as they rolled down the steep winding road into Corniglia. Though the honeymoon had been short, it still seemed too long to be away.

Ridley rolled up to the back of the café and let the thudding of the bike fade away.

"Good to be home," Erica whispered.

"Good to have a home to come back to," Ridley agreed.

Erica rounded the corner of the building and stumbled to a stop so abruptly that Ridley almost toppled her over when he plowed into her from behind.

She peered in, but something was wrong. Everything was wrong.

"Are you seeing this?" Ridley whispered.

"I don't know." Erica actually pinched herself, but nothing changed.

The four tiny tables along the edge of the *carruggio* were now two larger rectangular tables with a bench along the café's front wall and chairs lined up facing inward.

From inside came the roar of a soccer game in full swing. Two big televisions were showing a World Cup game and the tables were packed. Max and Cedric were there. Tomas waved from a back corner where he sat across from Bartolo.

She glanced back out the door, but Emilio's restaurant was right where it should be. Claire's shop was next door.

"Why would they remodel?" Ridley asked.

She could only crush his hand in hers for strength as they stepped over the threshold together.

Erica stopped him a few steps into the café.

"I don't think they remodeled, Ridley."

"What do you mean?"

The counter was now a bar. The menu was changed to more typical tourist fare: spaghetti with meatballs, and pizza.

And no ceramic dog sat atop the counter or real one beside it.

Erica pointed at the top of the menu board. "Not *Il Cane. Il Gatto.* The cat."

Before Ridley could say anything, a young Italian woman came up to them and asked in passable English, "You are being Erica and Ripley?"

"Ridley."

"*Scusi.* I have *lettera* for you. *Un momento.*" She crossed to the bar and shouted over the soccer game to a man, who definitely wasn't Hal and didn't wear a tie, in a rapid string of Italian. She proudly bore back a letter. "I thinked it was you from how you described." Then she hurried off.

Erica opened it slowly and was simply glad that it didn't go off in her hand like a bomb.

A key slid out of the folded letter and dropped into her palm. She handed it to Ridley, then began reading the letter aloud.

My dearest Erica and Ridley,

"Must be Conrad," Ridley looked over her shoulder.

She flipped it over. It was. She turned it back and kept reading though each word seemed to catch in her throat.

I am called off to another locale. I shall greatly miss my friends of Corniglia.

Remember, if you ever truly need something, you have but to ask. Someone will hear you and be glad to provide.

Though I doubt I shall return, if I should, it will be a privilege to purchase a bottle of your wine. I know it will not disappoint as it is not in either of you to fail—neither the wines nor one another.

I have taken the small liberty of gifting you as a wedding present what I believe shall be an ideal location for your new shop and winery just two doors past Emilio's restaurant. It has some lovely rooms above, sufficient for you and your future family. The bells of the towns sound particularly lovely from the top floor.

Erica had to lean against Ridley for just a moment for strength. The tightness of his grip said that he felt the same. That one element—the proper winery and storefront—had eluded them but there was no doubting that if Conrad had chosen it, it would be perfect.

I also took the liberty of shifting your effects there. Among Ridley's I found a rather curiously engraved lock. I have used this to secure the door of your new business.

"That's why I couldn't figure out the logo," Erica said in surprise.

"You forgot to put yourself in the picture," Ridley held her close and made her feel so safe because he knew even that about her.

She kissed his cheek. "It's *better* than it being on the Via dell'Amore."

His smile agreed and was all for her.

Erica sighed happily, and turned to read the back of the one-sheet letter.

It has been an honor and a privilege. And I pass on Bridget's heartfelt thanks for your kind assistance in managing my affairs.

"They're gone too," Ridley whispered on a rough tone.

Ciao,

Conrad

"Do you think they know?" Erica asked, nodding toward the people in the room. They acted as if the bar had always been here and the café had never existed.

"I'd rather not ask and find out." Then he glanced up at the ceiling. "Though I guess I wouldn't be too surprised if we find that our old rooms are no longer there. Look." He pointed out the window.

Erica turned in time to see a bright pink Ferrari as its engine purred to life. It was parked with its back to them. The top was down. The high seat backs mostly hid the occupants. But the driver had long brunette hair that flowed over her shoulders and the passenger was tall.

Then, just as the car rolled off into the night, she could swear that she saw Snoop's head stick up between the seats to look back at them.

They held each other's hands tightly as they went over to join Marissa and Vanessa at a small table. Hugs were offered and congratulations repeated.

But the talk of the night was about the soccer game on the television, their honeymoon, and the wine. Not the strangely altered café.

Erica pulled Ridley down to her and kissed him. She let herself get momentarily lost in the head-spinning power and the perfectly centering wonder of his kiss.

Then she held him close as he whispered in her ear.

"It makes perfect sense. The princess came down from her tower and married the court fool—"

"Who turned out to be a prince in disguise."

"—and the tower melted away because it was no longer needed."

"We're home," she whispered in her husband's ear.

"We're home," he assured her with all his heart.

And she was. She would miss Bridget. She'd miss Hal's ties and scratching Snoop's head. But life still rippled through the heart of Corniglia, the center of the "Five Earths."

Here she and Ridley would have a business and the finest wine. Here she would have friends and family. And they'd have children.

Here she would have her very own prince and there would be love for as long as they both should live.

(*Don't miss the adventure of Love Abroad B&B #1 "Heart of the Cotswolds: England" or the complete series of Eagle Cove set in small town Oregon. Turn the page for an excerpt.*)

RETURN TO EAGLE COVE (EXCERPT)

IF YOU ENJOY THE LOVE ABOARD SERIES,
YOU'LL LOVE A TRIP TO EAGLE COVE

RETURN TO EAGLE COVE (EXCERPT)

(FRIDAY MORNING)

"Almost home, sweetie."

"Oh joy," Jessica Baxter tried to clamp down on her sarcasm. It was a bad habit that worked fine in her social set back in Chicago, but sounded more petty with each mile they drove toward the Oregon Coast. She slumped down in the passenger seat of her mom's baby-blue Toyota hybrid. It still had that new car smell. As much as she'd dreamed of owning a hot sports car some day, she knew that she was enough her mother's daughter that this was probably the exact sort of eminently sensible car she would buy when her VW Beetle finally gave up the ghost.

Just like her mom.

Maybe she'd get it in red to be at least a *little* different.

Jessica sighed again, keeping it to herself so that she wasn't being overly offensive. Her mother was one of the many reasons that she'd gone as far away as possible for college and did her best to rarely return—she didn't want to turn into her mother and it was too easy to imagine doing so if she'd stayed in the small town of Eagle Cove, Oregon.

They were like twins separated by twenty-two years. The two of them had been able to trade clothes since Jessica hit puberty and had shot up to match her mother's slender five-foot-ten. Other than a very brief mistake of dying her hair black as part of a tenth-grade dare, which had turned her fair complexion past goth and into bloodless vampire, they were both light blond.

The one part of twin-dom that she couldn't seem to pull off even though she wanted to was Mom's casual-chic. Monica Baxter was always dressed one step above the world around her; not fancy, just really well put together. The closest Jessica ever managed was Bohemian-chic which wasn't really the same thing, but she'd learned to make it her own. Of course, Bohemian was easier on the budget and often available in consignment stores which had only reinforced her chosen style.

Jessica did her best to not regress as they drove up into the Coast Range that separated the beach towns from the rest of Oregon…and failed miserably at that as well. She felt as if she was rapidly descending back toward being a pouty, pre-pubescent twelve from her present urban and worldly thirty-two.

Why did crossing the Oregon state line always take twenty years off her intelligence?

Maybe it was only Coast County. Because of the landscape the Oregon Coast felt incredibly far from anywhere. The Coast Range topped out at a mere four thousand feet high, but only a half dozen passes made it through the three hundred mile range of rugged hills that separated the beaches from the broad farming and industrial realm of the Willamette Valley. The interior of the state might as well be in a whole other country for how little it had in common with where she'd grown up.

"It's so strange being back here," Jessica rolled down the

window and sniffed at the air. The scents were so rich and varied that they tickled. Bright with pine. Musty with undergrowth. Damp. A first hint of the sea.

"Well, it has been four years, honey. That's bound to make it seem a bit odd. But I'm so glad that you came."

"Me too, Mom." Better. She managed to say it as if she meant it, however unlikely that might be. Chicago fit her like a…but it didn't. The city was…something she was not going to give a single thought to for the next eight days. If she didn't fit there and she didn't want to fit in Eagle Cove, Oregon, then where did she belong?

Jessica breathed in deeply this time, trying to clear her thoughts with the fresh air of the Coast Range and nearly choked herself on how green everything smelled. The harsh slap of the mountains was almost an affront. The two-lane road dove and twisted along narrow corridors sliced through towering spruce and Douglas fir trees. The babies were sixty feet high along the shoulder as the car twisted up toward the pass; the mother trees behind them were much, much bigger.

And it wasn't just the trees that were lush. As they wound deeper into the Coast Range, each branch became covered with mosses and lichens. It soothed her eyes, so used to towering concrete and glass, with a living tapestry of greens, golds, and silvers. Beneath the trees grew an impenetrable tangle of salal and scrub alder. Old barns on the roadside didn't have shingle roofs, they had moss ones; some of them were covered inches thick. Many RVs, left unattended in front yards for too long, had a sheen of green growth on their north side.

"I really want to hate this," the Coast Range had three times the rainfall of Chicago, often surpassing a hundred inches a year. She expected to feel the weight of all that biomass crashing down on her shoulders, but instead she noticed the start of a disconcerting lightness as if coming home was a good thing. Jessica did *not* like that encroachment of pending appreciation, perhaps even enjoyment, upon her *true* feelings. "But it smells so good. Like sunshine and new growth."

Her mother's laugh was amused as they twisted along the two-lane road slowly climbing up a narrow valley.

"I didn't mean to say that out loud."

"But you said it anyway."

"Not helping, Mom."

Thankfully her mother's laugh said that she had understood Jessica's response as a tease. Which it mostly was, partly.

Jessica didn't *want* to like coming back to the coast. She didn't have small-town dreams. That was the main reason she'd left Eagle Cove. She had big city dreams...which weren't exactly coming together for her despite her efforts over the last fourteen years. But scurrying home wasn't going to fix those. And the selection of men in such a tiny town was, to put it kindly, pitiful. Puffin High—

Why they hadn't called it Eagle High in Eagle Cove was a subject of heated debate by every single class.

Puffin High's problem was that she knew every male her age all too well. The only reason the town had its own high school was that it was too far away from everywhere else for busing to make sense. Her senior class had just thirty-four students. Grades seven through twelve numbered under two hundred. And she knew far too much about every single one of them.

Even more obnoxiously invasive on her sense of right and wrong, instead of dumping rain, it was a perfect day. The sun sparkled down revealing a thousand shades of green in the living walls that lined the road. The air coming through the open window was thick with pine sap and the gentle tang of rotting undergrowth. There was so much oxygen in the air that it made her feel a little giddy.

Yes, a perfect day, if she'd been alone…and still in Chicago.

"I could have rented a car and saved you the drive, Mom." Actually, her budget had been thrilled when her mother had offered to come and fetch her. Also, once in Eagle Cove there wasn't a lot of use for a car, except when the rain poured down. The whole town was only a few miles long and she could walk most places she'd want to go. As if there were any old haunts that she'd care to revisit. She'd made good her escape to Northwestern University's School of Journalism at eighteen but every now and then the town still sucked her back.

"Nonsense, honey. I'm always glad to drive up and get you. Besides, I needed a few things for the wedding."

"How many is this?" As if she didn't know. It took much of her journalistic skill to keep "that judgmental tone" out of her voice. Something her early teachers had dinged her on until she'd learned to eradicate it. But since she was regressing as they neared the coast, it was trying to make a comeback.

"Number four."

"Why, Mom?"

"Because I love the man." Her mother actually glanced away from the road to offer her a scowl. "I'd have thought that was obvious."

"It is. But you've divorced him three times."

"Because *your* father can drive a woman crazy without even trying." They giggled together because that was an absolute truth about Ralph Baxter.

"I meant, why marry him again? You're both legal age, your daughter lives in Chicago," and wouldn't complain if she lived on another planet entirely. "Just shack up together. Then you can lock the door whenever Daddy becomes too much like himself."

Ralph Baxter was always getting caught up in monster projects. Without a word of warning he would suddenly rip out the entire kitchen, once on the morning before a dinner party, because he'd thought of a better way to design it. Or he'd start building a new boat from scratch in the middle of the driveway, rather than in the generous side yard, which blocked parking near the house for months.

"Oh, honey. I'm too old fashioned a girl to 'just shack up'."

Which was almost believable, even in the twenty-first century. To hear Aunt Gina—who despite her name was as not-Italian as a pastrami sandwich—tell it, Monica Lamont had chosen Ralph Baxter as her sweet sixteen love. She'd never even shopped around. How 1950s was that for a woman who hadn't even been born then?

Jessica had shopped plenty, or at least window-shopped. She'd found only a few men worth the cost of trying on for size. Definitely not a one worth taking home to keep. She might look like her mom, all blond, tall, and waiflike—which she kind of hated though the men seemed to like it—but inside she wanted to be like Aunt Gina.

Luigina Lamont looked nothing like her twin sister...or Grandpop...or much like Grandma for that matter. She was a statuesque redhead, in every voluptuous sense of the word and completely lived up to her name: Luigina meant "Famous Warrior." Her merry laugh slapped up against you at the most unexpected moments and constantly poked at your ticklish spot until you were curled up on the couch begging her to stop. Unlike Mom and her serial marriages to the same man, Gina brought home plenty yet had only tried to keep one.

That "unholy disaster" (as the family tales described it) had produced Natalya Daphne Lamont—Jessica's three-hour-older (and Natalya never let her forget it) first cousin and best friend. Just like Gina, Natalya didn't look like either her mom or Gina's brief husband. Maybe that was hereditary on that side of the family to balance out how much Jessica resembled her own mom and their shared grandma. Jessica had a sudden flash of her own future daughter looking just like her…and felt the world spin just a little at thinking about children at all.

"If I hadn't seen her come out between my legs myself," Aunt Gina would announce loudly, "I'd have thought I adopted the kid. Maybe I signed up to be a surrogate then forgot all about it."

Mom blushed every time Aunt Gina let that one loose in public, without understanding that if she didn't, Aunt Gina would have stopped long ago.

"Such an exotic offspring deserves an exotic name. Natalya for the Russian Bond girl in *GoldenEye* and Daphne for du Maurier the romance writer, *not* the nymph who had to turn into a tree to escape that lusty jerk Apollo." The fact that *GoldenEye* hadn't come out until Natalya had already been in grade school hadn't changed Aunt Gina's story one bit.

Maybe Jessica's own child would be lucky and take after Cousin Natalya who was slender like Jessica, but had all of the curves Jessica had prayed for throughout her teenage years but never been granted. Natya was also dusky skinned like a permanent tan and leggy like some French model. Jessica's and her mom's fairy light hair and Aunt Gina's mass of red curls had been transformed to a smooth cascade of dark chestnut on her cousin. Yet she and Jessica felt like twins from different mothers: one light, one dark, but much the same on the inside.

Jessica smiled at the sign as they cleared Maxine Pass: eight-hundred and three feet according to the sign. The "three" always made her laugh. It was like Becky, her other best friend from Eagle Cove, firmly insisting that she as five-four "and a quarter" as if it made a difference.

Maxine Pass was technically Maxwell Pass. Or it had been until the day that Aunt Gina had declared it just wasn't right for all of the passes to have male names merely because men were the ones who drew the maps back in the 1800s.

For her sixteenth birthday Jessica hadn't received her first kiss—already happened a year before—or gotten laid—two more years until that event. Instead, she'd been recruited for a "Mission!" At two in the morning on their shared birthday, Aunt Gina drove her and Natalya up to repaint the Maxwell Pass highway sign to Maxine. It had become a tradition that every time the highway department changed it back to Maxwell, the three of them would have a two a.m. gals' outing and change the sign once again. The highway department had given up years ago. A few of the more recent road maps had even changed the name.

"Girl Power!" they'd shout after each time they finished repainting the sign, usually about three a.m. Then they'd break out the thermos of hot chocolate and drink it from a shared cup while they admired their handiwork by moonlight.

One time Martin, the town cop, had shown up while they were doing it. Jessica and Natalya had ducked, but Gina hadn't slowed down a single brush stroke.

"Thought it would be you," Martin had observed through his open car window, obviously talking to Gina.

"Out of your jurisdiction, Marty," had been Aunt Gina's awesomely calm reply. She had always been Jessica's hero, but that totally clinched it. The town limits had been left far behind.

He'd joined them for the hot chocolate and had a good laugh at the "Girl Power!" chant.

Today Jessica just waved hello to the sign as they crested the pass and began their descent.

"Didn't you ever bust out, Mom?" Jessica tried to imagine her doing so, but couldn't quite conjure it up in her mind.

"Bust out? You mean cheat on your father? Never!"

"But what about between times, when you were divorced? That wouldn't be cheating."

Monica Lamont's lips thinned as she tightened her jaw and finally shook her head in a sharp little snap. "I was only living in the other end of the house."

"What about with Dad? You and Dad could just...you know?" The thought of her parents having sex was uncomfortable enough that she couldn't quite say it aloud.

"Ralph says that if I feel so strongly about things that I have to divorce him, then I shouldn't be expecting any special concessions while we are divorced."

Jessica felt she had to side with Dad on that one. He'd become used to his wife's antics, but that meant he didn't get any either in the interims. No wandering for him—it had always been clear that Ralph Baxter was absolutely crazy about Monica Lamont. Jessica felt kind of sorry for him.

"Wait. You mean you haven't had sex in two years?" This latest was their longest divorce yet.

Again that little snap that made Jessica's neck ache in sympathy. Mom moved to the right as the road added a climbing lane to reach the six-hundred and thirty-four foot (not quite so much bragging) Rogue Pass. That name at least made perfect sense by Oregon standards...because it wasn't anywhere near either of the two separate Rogue Rivers in Oregon. A half dozen cars roared past. Mom always drove exactly at the speed limit instead of the nearly mandatory ten over that prevailed throughout the state.

"So you're waiting for the wedding night?"

This time her mom's nod was a little sad.

"I'm sure tomorrow will be a great night, Mom."

At that she smiled brilliantly. "If the past three are anything to judge by, yes, it will be. It's just too bad we had to delay it."

"Delay it? Wait! What?" Jessica bolted upright in the car seat and almost throttled herself with her seatbelt. The wedding was supposed to be *tomorrow*. She'd secretly planned on staying just one day past the wedding, and then catching the Airporter Express that wandered through the small coastal towns once a day. She'd already warned Natalya to expect her in Portland for the rest of the week until her flight back to the Windy City.

"Well, we were meeting with Judge Slater about the ceremony. As he performed the first three weddings…"

Jessica resisted pointing out that he'd done all three divorces as well. Maybe her Oregon civility was coming back. Yeah, like a toothache.

"…and he had all of the old records in a file; even had the new marriage license pre-filled out, the dear man. However, it turns out that the first time we were married was on July fourteenth, not July seventh as I had remembered. You know how your father loves the cycle of things. So we moved the wedding to next weekend to coincide properly with the original. I knew you already had your plane tickets, so I didn't see any point in telling you."

Didn't see any point? She'd have moved heaven and earth to — Actually, her mother was right because she'd purchased the cheapest non-refundable, non-changeable tickets she could find.

A week! She was going to be trapped in Eagle Cove from Friday morning until Sunday morning nine days later? Oh, that was so bad.

"I can't believe that we celebrated it wrong for all of those years," her mother continued, completely oblivious to the panic she'd just created. "The seventh was the date that had always stuck in my head for our anniversaries."

Mom's dropping voice spoke volumes. She'd always been terrible at keeping a secret.

"So why *did* the seventh stick in your head?" Jessica kept it as casual as she could, rather than rubbing it in that her mom always gave up whatever she was trying to hide. It must be the journalist in her coming out: ask the question and then wait patiently for a reply. Not pushing was another change between them. Jessica didn't feel as if she was mellowing with age, but perhaps she was. Being disillusioned at thirty-two was no more newsworthy than it had been at twelve or twenty-two; but a woman shouldn't mellow until…well, maybe a hundred-and-two.

On the back side of Rogue Pass, Mom concentrated on the winding descent. Jessica waved at a massive Roosevelt elk who grazed in a small clearing beside the road. Coming back to Eagle Cove might be only one step better than a nightmare, but it was a very scenic one. The road was soon joined by a stream rushing in a deep ravine on Jessica's side of the road; the problem was that they were both racing in the wrong direction—toward, not away from, her childhood home. The stream tumbled along almost as fast as they did down toward Eagle River which would eventually define the end of town where it opened into a broad bay before it reached the sea.

No one quite knew why the bay had been named a cove, but it showed that way on even the oldest maps. It gave the town an off-kilter personality to Jessica's mind, as if it was always seeking to find its true identity. No bridge crossed the Eagle to the wilderness area on the other bank. To reach that required either a boat or an hour drive back up to Highway 101, across the river, and then a long crawl back to the Coast over marginal logging roads.

"C'mon, Mom, give." Since not pushing at her mother had failed, Jessica went with regressing and shifted to the wheedling tone she'd perfected as a child. She might hate herself in the morning for slipping back into it, but it always worked. Sure enough, her mom gave in right on cue.

"July seventh was the one time we cheated. We didn't actually wait for our first wedding night," the blush on her mother's fair skin was almost bright enough to lighten the dark corridor between the towering trees. "Your father made it amazing. But that's also the day I became pregnant, though I didn't know it until after the wedding. All those years I was celebrating the wrong date. That's why we never fool around unless we're married."

"Sounds like you were celebrating *exactly* the right date, Mom." She tried to pin down the exact date of her own first time, but it hadn't been all that memorable. Good, but "earth-shattering" was just another one of those 1950s' myths that didn't happen in the twenty-first century. Except, apparently, for her own mother. How unfair was that.

"Maybe," her mom admitted, "but we're going to get married on the fourteenth anyway."

"So, I'm illegitimate?" Not that it bothered her, but she couldn't resist needling her mother about it. Maybe she hadn't matured all that much.

"Yes dear, but only by one week. I swear I didn't know." This time Jessica heard that her mom's confession was a sigh at Jessica's question rather than sounding contrite. Maybe it was time Jessica grew up a bit—even when in Eagle Cove.

"Does Aunt Gina know about all this?"

"No one does, except your father and now you. You only arrived three days early, which was actually four days late. No one gave it any thought."

Excellent! Forget being mature. Aunt Gina would love the

extra dirt for teasing her sister and Jessica couldn't wait to be the one to tickle her aunt's funny bone.

~

It had been another long morning of assisting the Judge—always with a capital J. Monday through Friday, six a.m. to ten, Greg Slater helped his father. At first it had been something that Greg did to help out, but he'd come to like the simple routines and structure to his mornings.

"Ready?" he called back to the kitchen as he did every day. There was no real need to ask. The big old clock hung high on the wall said it was exactly six a.m. and the Judge was a very punctual man.

But Greg looked for the solemn nod before moving out into the diner and flicking on the fluorescents, "The Puffin Diner" sign, and the porch lights. There wasn't much need for the last, sunrise was twenty minutes ago, but the sun itself wouldn't clear the Coast Range ridge until at least six-thirty. For now, Beach Way, the town's main street, was mostly cool shadows and darkened buildings.

The bell mounted on the back of the door rang almost right away as Cal Mason Jr. came in. Greg had already set a mug of coffee on the counter for him. Cal ran the Blackbird Bakery and was hours into his day. Five days a week he was as punctual as the Judge. Cal Sr. wouldn't be in for a few hours yet.

"Your standard, Cal?"

"Double," though Greg knew that was a joke. Cal was one of the few men in town big enough that he could have eaten two of the Judge's generous portions. Six-two and as powerful as a bulldozer; his hands dwarfed the coffee mug.

Because Cal sat at the six-stool wooden counter, the Judge

was less than five feet away through the broad service window that connected the dining room with the kitchen, but he waited for Greg to fill out the order slip and clip it to the spinner.

It was Greg's own fault. The diner's service had been a bone of contention, or rather "lengthy negotiation" just as most things were with the Judge.

"They can pick up their own plates at the window. Coffee pot is right there behind the counter where anyone who wants a refill can get their own."

Greg had won that round by subterfuge. He'd numbered the tables and then only put the numbers on the order slips, making it impossible for the Judge to boom out with "Veronica, your order is up." Customers had slowly adapted to not having to leave their tables for every little thing.

At least Greg thought he'd won, until a full three weeks later his father had winked at him while sliding across a short stack with bacon and hash browns for Karen Thompson, "Like I don't know who orders what on a Thursday."

Now the Judge wouldn't cook a thing without a proper ticket. Well, he'd cook it, but he wouldn't serve it no matter how busy or harried Greg was.

Cal's plate came up less than thirty seconds after Greg hung the ticket just as it did every morning: western omelet, hash browns, farm sausage, and English muffin. The last was about the only kind of bread that Cal didn't bake.

"Gotta have something that I can order out for and enjoy without baking it myself."

Greg moved the plate across to the counter and refilled Cal's half-drained mug of coffee.

There wasn't much call for a judge in a town the size of Eagle Cove. Semi-retired for the last five years, he no longer spent three days a week in Newport to sit on the bench as he had throughout Greg's childhood. Instead he'd set up a small courtroom in town. He mainly handled family matters like marriages and estates, and fines for drunk and disorderly tourists who soon learned that Judge Slater was a fierce protector of the town. There was only the occasional speeding ticket—no matter how hard Martin the cop tried to catch someone. The town was perched against the Pacific Ocean at the dead end of a winding two-lane that had left the coastal highway a dozen miles back; it had enough "Sharp Curves Ahead" signs to quell even the most lead-footed of souls.

So, "for something to keep me busy," the Judge held office hours only in the afternoons because his weekday mornings were all spent working as a short-order cook. And ever since Greg's return to Eagle Cove three years ago, he'd been his father's front-of-house man: waiter, cashier, and busboy.

The Puffin Diner had been a near derelict before his dad had bought and reopened it. It was a classic small town place built to serve the early morning fishermen, especially those returning from a long night's work on the offshore shoals; it was little changed over the last ninety years.

The clapboard building stood high enough on a heavy stone foundation that even the Christmas storm flood of 1964 had crested two steps below the front entry. It was one of the only structures on the town's main street that didn't have a street-level entry. All of the other businesses that had existed then had high-water lines drawn halfway or more up their walls. The Grouse Hardware store, the lowest spot in town close beside the docks, had a small wooden plaque of a fish screwed in just above the main door lintel. It was bright yellow with "Dec 22, 1964" painted on it in tropical blue—it was generally considered to be a little boastful, but old man Jaspar refused to tone down the color scheme that he'd painted on that fish in his youth.

The interior of the diner was so retro that it would have been ironic-modern if it wasn't quite so authentic. The steel-edged tables of blue Formica were scuffed nearly colorless by the thousands of plates and silverware settings that had been slid across their surfaces over the years. The chairs' red leather was sun-faded and the old chrome had pitted with rust from the salt air, making them uncomfortable to the touch without quite being painful. The linoleum floor had been replaced... back in the 1980s when mauve and hunter green had been trendy colors. The six round stools bolted to the floor at the counter squealed every time someone spun on or off them. The kitchen was authentic right down to the large service window, the steel spinner rack for order slips dangling in one corner, and the big grill and burners in the back. The scents of eggs, hash browns, and frying bacon filled the main street each morning enticing all passersby to come and find comfort food.

Ralph Baxter and Manny McCall came in and took their usual spot by the corner window. They'd have tourists out fishing off their boats within the hour and were both after black coffee and tall stacks.

At first Greg had resented serving the Judge's fare—it was as invariable as his father. Scrambles, omelets, pancakes—no waffles because the iron had broken the same day Mom had died and he couldn't seem to fix it and wouldn't let Greg try. The pancakes were big and fluffy. The very crispy hash browns were not an option; they were on every single plate, even with the pancakes. Farm fresh sausage or bacon was the other staple on every plate—not that it was a choice. Everyone received whichever Carl Parker had delivered the day before along with the eggs.

All of Greg's efforts to vary the oatmeal recipe, served with bacon or sausage and hash browns of course, had been in vain. The Judge served only rolled oats—not steel cut—with sliced, not diced, dried apricots and diced, not sliced, fresh apple. Whether brown sugar or maple syrup was used to sweeten it was wholly up to the customer; local honey was also available.

Omelets were the Judge's real specialty and by six-thirty there were already a dozen slips up for them. Omelets were the only dish where variations were allowed. He offered them with cheese, mushrooms, or smoked salmon fillings. Never all three of course, because there were limits to what was proper.

The Puffin Diner mostly served coffee. Greg's sole triumph at adjusting the menu had been when he managed to switch from Dad's "fresh ground" granules purchased in large plastic tubs to fresh-ground French roast. Tea or hot chocolate were the only other options, but asking for marshmallows with the latter was frowned upon unless you were a kid—the whipped cream came out of a spray can.

They'd fought royally over the Judge's inflexibility, but of course fighting over things was a tradition in the Slater household. Not that voices were ever raised, because that would never do. The few times Greg had tried that tactic he'd been ruled "Out of Order" and banished from the dinner table: the sole forum for Slater "discussions." With Ma gone to cancer three years before—Greg's original reason for returning to Eagle Cove—he didn't have the heart to "force" the Judge into driving him from the table after that first time. When he'd been remanded to the kitchen two weeks after Mom's funeral, he'd made the mistake of glancing back as he'd moved off to finish his meal. His father had looked old, sad, and impossibly alone.

Greg hadn't been able to face living in the big old house out on the beach, so he'd moved into the guest house. Once he finally understood that no number of cogent debates were going to sway the Judge, Greg had let the menu go. It had been unchanged in either content or price in the last decade—other than the wavy black line of magic marker through the "Waffles (with blueberries when in season)."

Greg had been on the verge of leaving town when the Judge sat him down at the big house's dining room table. Ma Slater had been in the ground for a month. Greg knew he didn't really have anywhere to go, he'd learned all he was going to from the banquet chef at the Sorrento Hotel in Seattle and there weren't any top positions open for an untested executive chef wanting to make his mark. He didn't have the capital to make his own splash, not in the insanely competitive restaurant markets in the big cities. But he'd find something.

"Been watching you, son. Been tasting your food," the Judge had tapped a fork on his dinner plate. Greg had roasted a pair of fresh-caught trout in hazelnut butter with a dressing of spring greens and homemade basil vinegar. Though Greg had cooked half the meals since Ma's funeral—"fair is fair" the Judge had declared—it was the first time his father had spoken of it.

"Uh-huh," Greg had gone for a neutral acknowledgement. He knew the Judge hated such prevarications, but Greg didn't know where this was heading and went for caution.

"This is good. Real good."

Greg hadn't been able to offer even a neutral grunt over his surprise at the Judge's remark.

"Still needs some work, though."

Before Greg could snap at him about what did a man who scrambled eggs and ruled on law know about fine cuisine, the Judge continued.

"You need more seasoning," and he aimed a fork at Greg's chest, "and I'm not talking about salt. Your technique is the best I've ever seen, but I don't taste anything special. There's nothing here that isn't in any other fine restaurant. You need time to find your own voice, not some other chef's."

"My own voice?" But he didn't need to ask, he'd heard it a thousand times growing up.

The Judge looked down at the trout, one of the only times he'd ever said anything without looking at whoever he was addressing straight in the eye, "Your mother taught me that."

Ma had been a painter, a good one. Her seascapes had sold in galleries up and down the coast. Tillamook, Newport, Gold Beach, they all snapped up as much as she could produce and was willing to let go of—Grosbeak Gallery in town had always gotten first pick though. She'd often talked about finding your voice in your art so that it didn't look like everyone else's.

"So, here is the deal I'm offering you."

Greg knew that it wouldn't be open to negotiation; no one negotiated one of Judge Slater's "deals."

"The diner is mine on weekdays from six to ten every morning. I'd like you to stay as my assistant because you're good at it. That pays rent here at the house, a small salary, and we split the tips. What you do with the diner for the rest of the time, that's up to you."

And for three years, Greg had stayed in Eagle Cove and searched for his own voice. In the first year, he'd never cooked for anyone but himself and his father—who never again spoke about the food itself. Then one night Greg had invited a couple of buddies from high school who were still in town to the diner, as a test audience. Word got out about how good it was and folks had started asking when he'd do it again.

He'd eventually started "Irregular Friday Dinners at The Puffin." He only opened when he had a new meal to test. It was all *prix fixe,* fixed price—a twenty in the jar—and a set menu. After two years of those he felt almost ready to take his cooking out into the world; maybe spend a while as a pop-up restaurant—there and gone—rather than a full launch. He'd been saving his half of every morning tip and every cent for when he went back to the cities. At first he'd simply been trying to be better by the time he left Eagle Cove, but he'd become obsessed with finding and perfecting his "chef's voice." He wanted it to be so clear that it was undeniable. When he went back to Seattle, no one would label him the protégé of Charlene at Maximilien's or Angelo at The Tuscan Hearth. He'd be his own—

The old brass bell screwed into the top of the diner's front door rang like a small ship was coming into port. Morning service peaked as usual around eight and had now tapered off to just a few lingering diners.

Greg glanced at the big-face clock above the cash register—9:57—and suppressed a groan. Judge's rule was that if you were in the door by ten, you could take as long as you wanted. If it was ten sharp plus a second, you were turned away—"Fair is fair." Maybe they'd be quick; he'd had an idea for a savory roulade that he wanted to try out.

Greg turned back and had to blink, then blink again. The morning sunlight shone through the front window and silhouetted two dazzling blondes, their hair practically set afire by the sunlight streaming in from behind them.

Then his eyes adapted as they moved farther into the room.

Mrs. Baxter who was soon to be Mrs. Baxter once again.

And a woman he hadn't seen since the day she'd left for college, but he'd know anywhere.

Jessica matched his own five-ten and her hair, instead of being the waist-long waterfall he'd remembered, now floated about her shoulders in choppy wisps that framed a face of high cheekbones, full lips, and eyes that sparkled with mischief.

Halfway across the old linoleum floor, she stopped and looked at him.

"Greggie's gaping, Mom."

And he couldn't do a thing about it.

ABOUT THE AUTHOR

M.L. Buchman started the first of over 50 novels and as many short stories while flying from South Korea to ride across the Australian Outback. All part of a solo around-the-world bicycle trip (a mid-life crisis on wheels) that ultimately launched his writing career.

In addition to science fiction, he also writes thrillers, fantasy, and military romantic suspense books. His titles have been named Barnes & Noble and NPR "Top 5 of the year" and 3-time Booklist "Top 10 of the Year." In among his career as a corporate project manager he has: rebuilt and single-handed a fifty-foot sailboat, both flown and jumped out of airplanes, and designed and built two houses.

He is now making his living as a full-time writer on the Oregon Coast with his beloved wife and is constantly amazed at what you can do with a degree in Geophysics. You may keep up with his writing and receive exclusive content by subscribing to his newsletter at www.mlbuchman.com.

Other works by M. L. Buchman:

The Night Stalkers

Main Flight
The Night Is Mine
I Own the Dawn
Wait Until Dark
Take Over at Midnight
Light Up the Night
Bring On the Dusk
By Break of Day

White House Holiday
Daniel's Christmas
Frank's Independence Day
Peter's Christmas
Zachary's Christmas
Roy's Independence Day
Damien's Christmas

and the Navy
Christmas at Steel Beach
Christmas at Peleliu Cove

5E
Target of the Heart
Target Lock on Love
Target of Mine

Firehawks

Main Flight
Pure Heat
Full Blaze
Hot Point
Flash of Fire
Wild Fire

Smokejumpers
Wildfire at Dawn
Wildfire at Larch Creek
Wildfire on the Skagit

Delta Force
Target Engaged
Heart Strike
Wild Justice

White House Protection Force
Off the Leash
On Your Mark
In the Weeds

Where Dreams
Where Dreams are Born
Where Dreams Reside
Where Dreams Are of Christmas
Where Dreams Unfold
Where Dreams Are Written

Eagle Cove
Return to Eagle Cove
Recipe for Eagle Cove
Longing for Eagle Cove
Keepsake for Eagle Cove

Henderson's Ranch
Nathan's Big Sky
Big Sky, Loyal Heart

Love Abroad
Heart of the Cotswolds: England
Path of Love: Cinque Terre, Italy

Dead Chef Thrillers
Swap Out!
One Chef!
Two Chef!

Deities Anonymous
Cookbook from Hell: Reheated
Saviors 101

SF/F Titles
The Nara Reaction
Monk's Maze
the Me and Elsie Chronicles

Strategies for Success (NF)
Managing Your Inner Artist/Writer
Estate Planning for Authors